Lost in Sunshine attracts Northerners looking for a warm breeze and a peaceful place to call home. It's a village of tiny houses located down south perched next to a lake.

Part I: Benny Swan, an early retiree explosives expert, and his cat Esther sell their worldly possessions and buy a small adobe house. Esther possesses doubts but Benny is bent on finding the love of his life in a village he imagines to be perfect. Unbeknownst to him, his former colleague Elena stalks him along the way and begins to make her presence known by blowing up landmarks in Chief Earl Hubbard's jurisdiction. This new development throws a wrench in Benny's dreams and causes Earl's ire to lean toward his redneck side of dangerous.

Part II: Gloria Dobbins and her mystical, dancing cockatoo Pete hit the road shortly after Benny and Esther settle in their new adobe nest. Gloria, a contemporary philosopher and renowned academic, is asked to take a sabbatical and put her opinions in a book. The Dean of her department gets wind she's combining Professor Aaron James's book *Assholes a theory* with the Eastern philosophy of Oneness and pressing her students to determine whether or not the assholes in our society can be redeemed by introducing them to the concept of loving all beings.

The story adds another level of surrealism when Pete befriends a baby ball python suffering from a crisis of faith and low self-esteem brought about by Esther who is considered a goddess by the resident chihuahua Manuel. Maisie, the mountaineer manager and animal communicator, acts as the glue that binds together this beautiful village of befuddled, well-meaning eccentrics searching for a place where their natural way of being has enough value to change the world for the better.

Other Titles

Fools & Naked People
An Obscure Writer
Rooming House Blues
The Book of Husbands
The Zen of Yuki
A Woman and Her Dog
Solitary Pussytoes
Pretty Weeds
A Chocolate Comedy
Women on Love

Film Scripts

Talkin' to the Mirror
Speakeasy women talkin' mostly 'bout men
Boxing Yesterday and Today: the combat sport
Autism: A Behavioral Approach

Lost in Sunshine

A Novel By

Bonnie Jae Dane

Cover Design ~ Nathan Evans

Lost in Sunshine
A novel
Bonnie Jae Dane

Copyright © 2021

Published in the United States by Good Tern Press, Boston, MA.

This is a work of fiction. Names, characters, places, and incidents either are the work of the author's imagination or are used fictiously. Any resemblance to actual persons living or dead, events or locales is entirely coincidental.

Cover design by Nathan Evans, Boston, MA.

ISBN: 9798486860232

Part 1
Benny Swan & Esther

ONE

Benny Swan decided to buy a tiny house similar to the one pictured in the latest issue of *Better Homes & Gardens*. He tended to be detailed and spent the better part of a month searching the internet for a peaceful setting of tiny houses. He was a shy man possibly suffering from Asperger's or some other popular but subtle form of autism assigned to people who didn't quite fit comfortably into their surroundings. His job as an explosives expert never suited him. He thought when he passed the civil service exam years back, he would be given a comfy desk-job in a quiet corner of a government building.

Unfortunately, his exam results showed a striking aptitude for mathematics combined with a visual acuity of ninety-nine percent, adding his mind's tenacity for precision, not to mention his penchant for detail, which taken together would most likely assure ninety-five percent accuracy on all assigned targets. He would be invaluable for blowing up buildings and blasting the sides off mountains to clear a path for federal highways. However, he drew the line when asked to re-enlist and annihilate the enemy du jour.

General Howser unexpectedly appeared one day on a job site and begged Benny to return to his post. Benny smiled tenderly at the old soldier. The General mistook his smile for a smirk and threatened him with a turn in the brig. Again, Benny smiled and reminded the General he had been honorably discharged twenty-five years earlier and was about to retire permanently from government service. Two soldiers escorted the old general off the grounds minutes before a nearby building imploded as neat as you please. It was Benny's last job. He sighed with relief and imagined himself living quietly in the sunshine surrounded by lovely trees set alongside a lake.

Sometimes, he even imagined a woman living in the tiny house with him. Despite never having lived with anyone except his cat Esther and her predecessors, Benny still dreamed of enjoying the companionship of a tender-hearted woman. He gave enormous thought to desirable attributes that would be compatible with his own. His fantasy wives possessed a sense of humor and a warm heart. He assumed such a combination would also come with lovely hair and a broad smile that would make him feel welcome when he stepped across the threshold of his new home.

Benny currently lived in his parents' Victorian hand-me-down house and for one reason or another never felt quite comfortable there. Perhaps, his mother's presence still lingered and haunted him with her rose sachet lifestyle or maybe he had given up feeling like any woman's dream come true and had resigned himself to living out his days in the emptiness of the family home. Contrary to Benny's image of himself, his chiseled face and silky grey hair prompted many women to look in his direction, but due to his shyness, he never noticed them or thought they were looking at the man standing next to him. His self-esteem was shot to pieces along with his nerves, and besides, he often thought who would want to risk being married to a man who handled dynamite for a living? It had occurred to Benny no wife could bear the possibility of having an amputee for a husband. His mind ran rampant over these thoughts, so through the years he decided it would be more considerate to wait until his retirement with the hope all body parts remained in their appropriate places. It never occurred to Benny women fell in love with the whole package no matter what the wrapping. However, two days after retirement, he began to worry his imaginary wife might be allergic to cat hair, causing a new set of mental problems to occur.

Esther being a Maine Coon cat rather than a fussy Persian made her the perfect man's companion animal. She required little upkeep, other than a daily brushing, clean litter box, and designer cat food that would tax the food bill of your average Appalachian family. However, in Benny's world nothing was too good for Esther. He hoped his imaginary wife would appreciate all of Esther's qualities including the enjoyment she received on their evening walks through the neighborhood. Yes, Esther learned to tolerate a harness at age ten weeks and was often seen tethered to Benny's belt while he moved about the yard tending to his flowers. Eventually, she began jogging along next to him but on occasion would threaten to chase a squirrel up a tree, hiss a couple of times, and then easily fall back into the rhythm of their walk.

Now, though, he envisioned a lovely woman walking next to him, holding hands and talking about their respective day. Being retired, he wondered what he would talk about. The brilliance of Esther, perhaps. It never occurred to Benny most women don't want to hear about a man's cat. Possibly their dog, but a man doting over a cat might be too much to bear for even the most patient woman, especially when noticing Esther slept in a small canopy bed next to the large one Benny had inherited along with the family house. The word eccentric would best describe Benny's inter-feline family, but he felt confident only love mattered. Not even Esther's occasional hairball could disrupt the harmony he envisioned in his future tiny-house life.

Emptying the Victorian seemed the first order of business. Benny considered an estate agent but then discarded that idea when remembering all of his mother's relatives showing up at her extravagant reunions in their backyard. Benny's shy nature had caused him to hide in the attic and watch his cousins' antics through a sailor's spyglass from the round window neatly placed under the eaves of the third floor. He tried not to feel superior to the raggedy lot calling themselves his extended family, but their crudities and natural ability to demolish everything in sight made his heart sigh. Even the backyard shed had nearly been destroyed when stumbling across his father's ax. Later, he had repaired the damage before his mother saw the sad little building where she had once spent many hours of happiness. She adored her sisters and overlooked their children's criminal behavior but the loss of her potting shed might put an unpleasant end to her annual reunions. Benny had briefly wondered if this was a bad thing.

Memories aside, he decided to call all the relatives and ask if they wanted any of his mother's furnishings before he sold the house. Excitement ran high and soon he set a date for the following Saturday. He reminded them to bring their trucks for some of the more cumbersome pieces. The idea of seeing the adult versions of his cousins filled him with dread, so he thought it best to hire a team of professionals under the guise of helping them pack. Naturally, Benny moved Esther's bed and other possessions along with his own to a nearby Candlewood Suites while making the transition.

Esther objected at first to the cramped quarters until noticing the large picture window looked onto a wooded area filled with birds and a few squirrels and one overly friendly chipmunk who sat on the other side of the window gleefully tormenting her by eating small mounds of seeds and berries within easy reach for Esther if only there weren't a screen between them. Eventually, the screen hung in shreds costing Benny the price of a replacement.

The more Benny considered his plan, the more he realized the importance of putting in an appearance. He should at least introduce himself to the team of professionals. He also felt it only ethical to warn them of his cousins' propensity for destruction. Although, he confessed he had not seen them in years possibly making all of his worrying an unnecessary emotion. Three burly men gathered around Benny and wiped the sweat off their arm tattoos and readjusted their ballcaps all the while shaking their heads in agreement. "And what do you do for a living, Mr. Swan?" One of them asked.

Benny cleared his throat and mumbled, "Retired explosives expert."

"Well, ya don't say. I gotta brother lost his foot when foolin' with a stick o' dynamite. Had in mind to blow up our neighbor's outhouse but dropped the thing down his boot after lighting a short fuse. Dumber than a rock we called him." The men laughed and assured Benny not to worry that everything would go off without a hitch and for some reason Benny felt confident it would. He paid up front and gave them a hefty tip for their trouble. He also gave them his phone number and said he would be nearby in case anything unexpected happened. Nothing did. Even the flower gardens remained intact.

The next day, Benny and Esther inspected the empty house slightly dismayed at its worn out interior and sagging wallpaper. He decided to call a realtor but had no idea how to choose a reputable one who had enough taste to make suggestions on perking up his parents' house. He scrolled through the entire metropolitan area before lighting upon a woman posing with her cat, a small orange feline with a pretty face and green eyes that shone with happiness. He concluded, if a person's cat companion appeared bathed in the blissful light of pure joy than its owner must be similar in nature. Of course, Benny's interactions with women, as mentioned, was limited, so his criteria for measuring their character might be slightly deficient. Some animals after all were just born happy.

Beth Hanson appeared on his doorstep the following day with clipboard in hand and several brochures suggesting cross country moving services. Benny made little eye contact but instead stared down at Esther as though expecting her to pick up the slack in the conversation. However, Esther occupied herself sniffing the orange cat smell on the woman's clothes, including a spot of drool on her navy loafers. Once satisfied, Esther walked into the kitchen for a drink of water.

Benny's shoulders drooped and his arms hung in a loose-limb fashion that either gave him the look of a short basketball player or an indifferent cretin. Beth chose the former persona and strode confidently throughout the house as though talking to a normal nice man in need of her services. Her professionalism put Benny at ease. Naturally, being a man, he nonchalantly peered sideways at the attractive realtor and envisioned her in his tiny house. After a thorough going over, he decided her clothes appeared fussy and well-detailed, no doubt, requiring an enormous amount of closet space, which would be lacking in the tiny house. And besides he thought, she had built her business on the south shore of Boston. Why would she want to tie her life to his? So far, he still had little to offer. Perhaps, he needed a hobby.

"Mr. Swan, your house has solid bones but could do with an update. I would suggest removing the carpet to expose these lovely solid oak floors." Benny felt a slight shock when the brazen realtor pulled up a corner of his mother's carpet to show him the wood underneath. His fantasy of their living a harmonious lifestyle crumbled in seconds.

"My mother was very excited when she had this carpet put in. It's wool, you know." His attention became fixed on the burgundy carpet, overlooking the frayed edges and large faded areas that gave it a shabby aspect.

"So sorry, Mr. Swan, but today's buyer likes a sleek interior tending toward grey and neutral tones. I would even suggest refinishing the oak in a darker hue and having the walls painted a Benjamin Moore color, possibly Edgecomb

Owl if you decide to stay with the oak's natural golden hue or Gray Owl if you decide to have your floors darkened. Shall I pick up some samples?" She peered under his hooded eyes and waited for an answer.

"I would be happy to pay extra if you would make all the arrangements. Esther and I will be busy in the garden and well, frankly, decorating is not my forte." Benny felt himself breathing heavily and disappeared in the kitchen for a moment to pull himself together. Esther looked sympathetically at her Cat-Dad and in her overzealous need to comfort him, leaped from the windowsill onto his shoulder forgetting to retract her claws. Loud screams brought Beth Hanson to the kitchen at the same time Benny gasped in pain and felt the life go out of him. The next thing he saw were the faces of the attractive realtor and Esther looking down at him.

"Of course, Mr. Swan, I'll take care of everything. Don't you worry. Now, let's wipe the blood off your shirt before it stains." She let the water run cold while Benny righted himself.

"Thank you."

"You're welcome. It's been a pleasure." They shook hands and Benny breathed a sigh of relief when hearing the door close.

TWO

A few days later, another woman appeared, frightening him slightly for no apparent reason. This one was dressed in men's overalls and had a small paint brush sticking from a wooly cap of hair. She looked to be in her mid-thirties. Benny and Esther had spent the better part of the day pulling weeds from the flower gardens and putting down fresh mulch to give it a clean look. Benny felt exalted over precisely cut borders and spent hours edging the grass with hand clippers. He thought a person's lawn reflected the tidiness of their mind. He often wondered how his neighbor next door ever managed to get through his day when little effort was given to lawn maintenance. He considered his neighbor's yard to be a blight on the landscape. This thought amused Benny and caused him to laugh out loud at the same time a feminine voice disrupted his interior delight. (Benny enjoyed spending time rollicking quietly in his own sense of the absurd. This penchant for idling happily in his imagination gave great importance to his imaginary wife possessing the ability to laugh easily.)

"Mr. Swan, Beth Hanson sent me to paint the inside walls and stain the floors. Outside looks pretty good for a vintage clapboard."

Benny and Esther turned to stare at the woman. Their eyes moved to the paint brush stuck in her hair, leaving them both speechless. Seeing a woman with a tumble of tight red curls instead of the fashionable bob caught Benny off guard. Esther wondered what else was being housed in the rat's nest on top of her head.

He shyly extended his hand, "Pleased to meet you. Ms. Hanson didn't mention your company name." Benny expected her to produce a clever business card with a paint brush logo, several swaths of pretty colors, and her name embossed in wood tones.

"Terry McMillan. Sole Proprietor."

"You're painting the entire house without help?" Benny felt pained to wrap his mind around the idea of a woman contractor. The ones in his field were a rough bunch who thought nothing of shooting holes in the tires of any male they found offensive. Benny took great lengths to avoid them and as a consequence they called him names, mostly harmless names like, 'shy boy' and 'dynamite Benny'. But these insults alone worked his nerves and sent him home tied in knots and looking forward to relaxing in front of a British sitcom with Esther. He especially enjoyed *Fawlty Towers* but took great care never to tell anyone for fear of being laughed at. Most men shriveled when hearing a woman laugh at them. They would rather be nagged, cajoled, suffer irritations, and other minor annoyances, than being laughed at by a woman. Benny felt certain righteous laughter caused more volatile exchanges in marriages than infidelity. Again, he led a solitary life and wasn't privy to what really went on inside a woman's mind. He just hoped to find one who would be kind to him.

"I have a couple of college students for helpers. They're good at cutting neat lines along the windows and ceilings. I also have one who enjoys sitting on a small stool and painting the baseboards. He calls it mindful meditation. Whatever the hell that is." She smiled sweetly, which caused him to glance in her direction and open his mouth in a full smile.

Usually, a woman swearing prompted him to sweat from the familiarity of it. He also found it disarming. Afterall, what other manly traits could she be harboring, he thought, dressing in men's boxer shorts? Benny remained clueless that this particular fashion had already taken place during the nineties hip hop era and was making a comeback. This time more for comfort than a fashion statement. Sometimes, Benny realized how little he knew about women and wondered if he should buy several books on the subject. This was such a time.

"Well, if you'll let me in, I'll take a look and give you an estimate including materials." She ran up the backstairs quicker than Benny and Esther could put away their garden tools. Instead, Benny leaned the tools against the house and eased Esther, who was tethered to his belt, and himself between the door and the sweet-smelling contractor.

"I'll give you a set of keys so you can come and go at your convenience."

"Alrighty, thank you, Mr. Swan."

Now, within a few short days, two women called him Mr. Swan. Benny smiled through his embarrassment.

Two weeks passed, the yard was lovely and all the flowers stood looking happily at the sun shining down on them. One of the oval gardens was filled with his mother's blue vervain she used to harvest for medicinal purposes. She swore it gave her the persona of a Greek goddess complete with supernatural powers no one could explain. His mother, a large woman, often gave voice to extravagant statements, which amused both Benny and his father. They twinkled when Mrs.

Swan swooped into the room holding a bouquet of her favorite flower expounding on their divine purpose and pressing upon her husband and son the importance of understanding God put flowers here to help us. "Much like women, they are not just a pretty face," she would often say and then quickly waltz out of the room to hang her bouquet from the cupboards to dry. The kitchen heaved with the aroma of flowers, especially during the fall.

Benny recalled all the times his slender father put his arms around his mother's waist and exclaimed, "Acres and acres and all mine." His mother would titter and the next thing Benny knew his parents clung to each other in a passionate embrace and then began their ritual salsa dance to the master bedroom. Benny wondered what they did up there when he was a small child but later with the help of the popular book *The Joy of Sex* his parents often left open on the coffee table, he was able to glean where all their parts went. But, when trying to imagine his own parents becoming that familiar with each other's naked bodies, it shocked his shy sensibilities and put him off the idea he might ever want to engage in such a lusty activity.

Now though, he leaned on the garden hoe and imagined the house painter without her overhauls giving him a come-hither expression.

Seconds later, he gasped and hung off the garden hoe for support such was the intensity of his passion. He glanced at the blue vervain and considered making some tea for the painter. He quickly dismissed this thought as being overly familiar. Besides, yesterday Benny saw another woman pay a quick visit to his painter. She gave her a thermos of soup and a spoon, then hopped on a motorcycle and left. Their exchanging mouth kisses shocked him, but Benny being somewhat naïve did not know if this meant they were close friends or lesbians who cared deeply for one another. He decided it might be prudent to spare himself the embarrassment of being rejected and so continued cleaning his garden tools.

Benny, of course, realized fantasizing about a woman before settling into his new home seemed a fruitless pursuit and his time would be better spent winding up the business of selling his parents' house. He also needed to close the deal on the picturesque tiny house down south and order his new furnishings from the *Sundance Catalogue,* which he thought possessed a masculine air that would suit his personality or at least the one he wished to have. He scoured the internet and discovered a program called *Tiny House Nation* on Netflix. He found the concept fascinating and became involved in the lives of the people who envisioned themselves living an eco-friendly lifestyle. He noticed most buyers wanted to hibernate in the woods surrounded by nature and some settled on beachfront property away from the general population north of Sidney, Australia. This seemed drastic to him. He wondered if such people thought this through, or were they spontaneous types who later regretted their decisions and happily moved onto something else. The more he dwelled on this notion, the more he realized these same people could possess obsessive compulsive leanings with the tendency to thrive on upending their lives in such ways it required a constant move forward that put them in new surroundings. He didn't know whether to envy them or feel sorry for them.

Upon reflection, Benny had lived in his parents' house for his entire life and never once considered moving for the sake of changing the scenery. He took comfort in glancing out the kitchen window and seeing his mother's flower beds. Memories of her dancing in the gardens with his father put a smile on his face but also caused a twinge of nostalgia. What happened to time? he often asked himself. If still alive, she would only be a seventy-year-old woman, probably standing in the same packed classroom inspiring her students with the works of the Eastern philosophers, urging them to live life to the fullest, treat every day like it's your birthday, and glory in the now. "It's all we have," she would shout at them. She had challenged her students in the most inventive ways, often times taking them to the fields and clocking them on how long they could stay present without mental forays into the past or future. She told them to raise their hands the minute a thought entered their heads. Those who failed she set on the sidelines to spend five minutes listening to the birds sing. No one ever lasted more than a minute. She laughed heartily on these occasions. Then a month later, they would find themselves inside the nearby mental institution for the criminally insane, where again she asked them to raise their hands the minute their attention strayed from their surroundings. No one ever did.

Mrs. Professor Swan often used her husband and Benny as test subjects for her focus experiments. One day she placed a piece of chocolate cake in front of them, clicked the oven timer, and told them to stare at it for forty-five minutes before eating. She then went off to run the vacuum cleaner. Benny learned self-control on these occasions. He also learned to occupy himself by calculating the number of crumbs in a medium-sized piece of chocolate cake. Mr. Swan never lasted more than fifteen minutes and nearly wept when giving way to the first bite. If they had been allowed to talk, Benny thought, he could have helped his father by telling him about the latest scientific findings regarding cats being dropped out of an airplane and landing unharmed but tended to hurt themselves if they fell off a step ladder. Mr. Swan loved listening to his son's enthusiasm over the latest in scientific discoveries.

Unfortunately, his mother insisted on strict guidelines while conducting her experiments and creating a no-talking zone was one of them. He saw the sweat on his father's forehead, the furrows between his eyebrows, and the occasional shortness of breath from panic. Usually, the last symptom occurred just before throwing himself into demolishing the chocolate cake, which sent Benny into fits of laughter he regretted the second he heard his mother admonish her husband for giving into his desires. "Oh, but peaches, you are my most delicious desire. Shall we go upstairs and let Benny finish counting his crumbs?" She laughed, and they disappeared but not before she made notations in her journal. Benny plunged into the chocolate cake exactly forty-five minutes after it had been set in front of him.

The most stressful of these experiments occurred when she tested their resolve with a piece of pumpkin pie covered in caramelized pecans. He too began to sweat and felt himself heave from panic over giving into the delicious smell of allspice and maple syrup. Within fifteen minutes, Mr. Swan lost control of his appetite and devoured his piece and then spent the rest of the time coveting Benny's pie. This itself was an act of self-restraint, a conclusion he used to thwart his mother's dismay when coming upon her husband's empty plate. On one occasion, Benny took pity on his father and pulled a candy bar from his pocket to satisfy his father's taste buds so Mr. Swan could make his wife proud. She buried his head in her large bosom and beamed with approval. A few notes jotted in her journal, and off they went to the bedroom leaving Benny to wonder if anyone would ever love him as much as his parents loved each other.

THREE

Beth Hanson called Benny to tell him his house was finished inside and to compliment him on the loveliness of his gardens. She waxed on about her own hydrangeas looking fretful and possibly in need of magnesium. She also expounded upon the old fashion plotting of his mother's oval gardens and dahlias alongside a trellis leaning from the weight of roses. She marveled at the smells and went on to praise her choices and then asked if his mother was a professional landscaper and had he inherited his mother's green thumb. He nearly begged her to stop talking. Benny's mind tended to be a private place that could not tolerate invasive questions. Talking about his family tree was like asking Benny if he enjoyed the missionary pose or does he study the Karma Sutra for ideas? All forbidden subjects in his mind of either polite or professional conversation.

Benny was not burdened with curiosity about other people's lives. He paid them little personal attention and lacked the intuitive power to differentiate between a saint or a thief in a police lineup. Everyone looked the same to him. He saw all people as simple, vulnerable beings in need of the occasional emotional tune up.

In fact, his limited curiosity caused him to forget to ask the reason why his pretty realtor was calling him due to all the digressions into nature and her wonderment over a mother who could teach philosophy and grow sunflowers for the birds to dine on.

Benny wasn't sure this tendency to talk a lot would be compatible with his perfect woman ideals. He decided to make note of it and let his mind linger a moment on what traits might be objectionable to him. Perhaps, he should go on a date and see if any peculiarities popped out at him that might be too intolerable for the confines of a tiny house. It wasn't an ordinary circumstance for the efficacy of finding a compatible woman. The process may take a while. Benny put away those thoughts and let Ms. Hanson wind up her monologue and move the conversation to the next step in selling his house.

"Don't you just love what Terry and her crew have done to the interior? Won't last long in today's market. It's a seller's market, you know. Shall we get the ball rolling?" Ms.

Hanson annoyed Benny further by assuming he knew anything about the real estate market and how could he be sure she wasn't just giving him the usual pep talk or would his mother's house languish in a sea of other houses all gleaming with new paint jobs and filled with expectations. Benny knew only one thing. Nothing was for certain.

"Yes, thank you, Ms. Hanson. That all sounds nice, but exactly what are your plans?" He and Esther puttered in the shed while talking on his cell unaware his realtor was calling from the main house and, in fact, she was now hurrying down the back steps to take another tour of the gardens. They bumped into each other when Benny stepped from the shed ready to gather up his tools and return to his and Esther's temporary quarters.

"There you are," she called to him in a light-hearted voice that had an appealing tone if only she didn't talk so much and worse, she mostly talked about subjects of little consequence or so he thought. He had never sold a house and still wasn't at ease with the notion he actually owned a piece of property. Having inherited the family home after his parents' early departure made it difficult for him to feel comfortable in a place once filled with happiness. On the other hand, there was nothing he cherished more than the memories of his parents, except possibly Esther who stood by reading his thoughts.

"Hello, Ms. Hanson." Benny felt himself quiver when in close proximity to all her smiles drifting through the air causing his head to spin from someone else's joy. He wondered if it were real or does she have an attachable helium pump that gives her a lift when she feels the need to appear perky.

"Beth. Please call me Beth. And shall I call you Benny?"

"Yes, of course, Beth." He smiled displaying two bright and shiny rows of teeth, enough to cause the realtor to lose her perkiness for a moment and wonder what her handsome client would be like in bed. She turned red before dismissing the thought as unprofessional.

"Shall we go inside so you can have a look?" Beth's habit of using the word 'shall' as her go-to verb annoyed him and the excessive use of 'so' diluted the importance of her words.

Once inside, Benny marveled at the difference. Everything gleamed and gone was the musty smell of old curtains. In fact, there were no curtains. They had been replaced by wooden blinds, which pleased him with their symmetry. However, he couldn't remember discussing new kitchen cupboards and granite counter tops, and the bathrooms stripped of their flowered wallpaper and covered in Italian tiles came as another surprise. He noticed quite a few changes he couldn't remember as being part of the beautification project. When turning to his realtor, he saw a happy smile waiting for his approval. They stood at the new picture window in the breakfast room, which Beth thought a nice touch for creating a vista into the beautifully cultivated gardens. Even the shed possessed a quaint old-fashioned appearance. They both stared at the landscape, each thinking their own thoughts at the exact moment an explosion occurred causing the shed to implode and land in a neat pile of rubble. Once the dust settled, Benny stared at a banner attached to two poles saying Dynamite Benny punctuated with bright red hearts.

"Oh no, the shed is listed as part of the property. We'll have to replace it with either a prefab one or go to this lovely furnishing house called *Architecture Appointments*. They are bound to have something vintage that would fit in that very spot once the remains are cleared. Let me get my people on this. Don't you worry one iota." She patted Benny's shoulder and rifled through her contact list.

Benny heard only silence while her words spun around him. He slipped back in time and remembered Elena, the beautiful explosives expert, who often teased him for taking his job too seriously. Being a literal man, he thought she meant exactly what she said and felt the sting of it as being an insult. Now though, he wondered if her teasing had been said with affection.

FOUR

Benny and Esther hit the road excited over their future suspended before them. Neither one had ever lived seconds behind a future filled with uncertainty. Benny's government position entailed the same basic job at different locations. He always came home to a familiar bed, Esther, and a house full of memories, except when being sent to other countries, which often required him to be gone for extended periods of time. His mind turned to the possibility of creating new memories with Esther, who sat harnessed in her car seat next to him staring out the window, taking the occasional cat nap to rest her nerves from the fast-moving cars. She thought it unnatural for people to travel in a plastic box instead of on all fours.

Benny envisioned them living in their cob house enjoying the sweet smell of nature, lake water, and the straw between the walls, made of dirt and sand. They looked at the many pictures on the *Lost in Sunshine* website and felt giddy over the uniqueness of their custom house carefully constructed by loving hands. Even the front door enjoyed a splash of turquoise paint that shimmered in the sunlight next to the pale pink surface of the adobe cottage. Yes, Benny thought it looked more like a cottage than a tiny house on wheels. It was square and set on a slab foundation. He bought the extra acre of land next to his house for large flower gardens and other optimistic possibilities. Benny had become a man of vision. His soul surfaced and to his delight he discovered it to be a poetic soul with the heart of a husband hidden inside. Just then, he and Esther were startled by a loud noise a hundred feet to the right of the interstate. He shuddered when seeing a large tree flying through the air along with a bedraggled banner that read *Dynamite Benny*. His and Esther's nerves began wrestling with their new reality possibly having a few bumps along the way to a peaceful future.

Benny continued driving past the debris, gingerly down the highway in hopes of avoiding the police, fire department, and the likelihood of being pulled over and questioned by a burly officer, who would scrutinize his driver's license only to notice the bedraggled sign now draped over a power line has the same name as the diminutive of Benjamin. His name surrounded by hearts resembled a histrionic valentine message that would surely be featured on tomorrow's front-page of the local newspaper. Or worse yet, all the passersby snapping pictures and posting them to their social media platforms might intrude upon his quiet lifestyle and tendency to avoid attention of any kind. Not a minute later, a flash of flames from a burning tree appeared in his rear-view mirror. Finally, Benny eased his car among the row of cars that had already been parked, allowing the drivers to get a gander at the commotion. Just as Benny feared, most stood snapping pictures of the magnificent sight, which further distressed his nerves now hanging from a thread.

Benny's emotions had been clamped shut for most of his adult life. He finished high school at age sixteen, college at eighteen, followed by two years in the armed forces and another twenty-five years contemplating the number of dynamite sticks it would take to bring down a multi-story building in place. Now, in his mid-forties, he let go of his emotions and nearly wept parked along the highway suffering from a heart that ached for love but was confronted by the possibility of disaster. Even Esther hung over the front seat staring at the bright flashes of light beginning to drift down and torch the dry grass and cornfields.

Esther's pinched, unhappy face then glared at Benny expecting him to do something brave. Naturally, Benny couldn't live with being a disappointment to his cat, so he eased the SUV away from the crowd and once out of sight shifted to fifth gear and sped late into the night, arriving sleepily into the next state in the early hours nearing dawn. They both breathed a sigh of relief when tucked under the clean white sheets at a Hampton Inn. Later, he would pick up a to-go order and bring it back to the hotel for Esther and him to enjoy, giving them both a moment to contemplate the week's events ending with a bang.

Esther began to question her Cat-Dad's limitations. She was a highly perceptive, telepathic feline who could transport her astral form to take a peek at others running amuck trying to prove their relevance. She saw the crazed woman chasing after her Cat-Dad, pretty by human standards if you like the disheveled bedlam look of messy hair and masculine sweatshirts, khaki, and boots tied past her ankles. Personally, Esther preferred soft women, demure women, who loved animals and enjoyed the company of their house pets over that of humans.

Most humans, Esther noticed, lacked refinement and tended to speak in loud voices and blow their noses at the dining table. They gobbled their food instead of eating one pea at a time. They piled them on spoons and then shoveled them into open mouths in a toothy display of grinding that worked Esther into a state of anxiety sending her to bed where she remained hidden underneath her small coverlet for hours. She loved her Cat-Dad and felt fortunate he kept himself neat and tidy and even washed the sheets once a week, including Esther's bed covers. His table manners were impeccable along with the delicate movement of his hands. She supposed all people handling dynamite on a regular basis required the delicate touch of steady hands. She saw the evil woman Elena lighting the fuse and throwing it at a lovely oak tree standing majestically along the side of the road so passersby could glory in the stateliness of nature. And then suddenly, the tree was propelled through the air silently screaming from sadness over the human condition. The tree saw humans' careless attitude toward their environment as being driven by greed and an obliviousness to the consequences of cow dung and plastic.

Esther crept into her Cat-Dad's thoughts and became confused among all the excitement over their destination combined with an undercurrent of fear at being the object of a desperate woman's acts of violence. He wondered how he had managed to get himself wedged into Elena's chaotic mind. He remembered the time she asked him to go for a beer. He declined. His mother had told him beer wasn't worth the malt used for fermenting a vat of the wretched stuff. She poured him sips of wine at the dinner table and told him it would help aid his digestion. He wondered if drinking wine was the reason he never had digestive problems, or was it because at only seven-years old, he was less likely to be prone to ulcers? Esther lingered for a while, but realized she could do little to comfort him except crawl onto his lap and purr.

Benny often wondered if Esther read his mind and even how invasive her telepathic powers might be. Did she plumb the depths of his insecurities and think less of him for sitting paralyzed on the edge of the bed with a firm grip on her large feline body? Sometimes, doubts crept along beside him asking if he were normal. Did other men need something soft to hold onto for comfort? His thoughts were cumbersome things, especially when turning to Elena. He thought she might be trying to capture his attention. Or maybe she was trying to kill him for not joining her in a dark tavern to down a beer, pretending to be a masculine man who watched football and might often have flights of fancy or scenarios of choking the life out of his neighbor for letting the weeds grow in the cracks of his sidewalk.

He noticed men seemed captivated by his occupation and kept asking what it felt like to blow up buildings. Benny didn't blow up buildings so much as he brought them down gently to land in a pile of debris on the ground. Others made him sound like a lunatic carrying sticks of dynamite in his briefcase and lobbing them willy nilly at any random eyesore. He never considered his occupation a masculine venture. He accepted his government assignment, perfected his trade, and collected his retirement at the end. He'd seen his coworkers become cocky with their fuses, stingy with the wiring it took to coordinate a perfect implosion, and even show off by inviting their friends and relatives to watch. Occasionally, the results of their carelessness ended in stone fragments flying everywhere, frightening his friends and relatives, and an unfortunate hard hat having to be taken to the hospital.

Elena, however, possessed a reputation for putting on flamboyant displays of destruction that made a grown man shrink from fear. They could hear her laughter after the last brick fell along with her trademark banner saying ELENA WAS HERE!

Previous to these events, Benny had never

been stalked. He considered going to the police and then quickly dropped that notion for fear of appearing cowardly. Or worse, would they laugh at him for being afraid of a little woman? It was true. Elena only weighed a hundred pounds at five foot three, although she gave off a masculine vibe that frightened all those who felt protective of their manly parts, which amounted to nearly half the population. Elena loved to frighten men. The company shrink wrote lengthy descriptions of her pathology in a sizeable folder, harboring the intention of writing a book about her someday. With all of his degrees and learned air, he had no idea she would rip his heart out when seeing herself in print.

Benny glanced down at Esther crouched in his lap trying to soothe his wounded pride. She knew him to be a gentle man. She herself would have a go at the crazy woman if given the chance. She could see herself shredding Elena's masculine shirt and ripping the tattoo art off her body. Esther held little use for humans who defiled their naked bodies with pictures of flowers and love for their mothers, sweethearts, and even their favorite country singer. She thought the human psyche a dangerous place to be so avoided venturing outside her comfort zone. Esther went along with Benny, not because she was eager to relocate, but because she enjoyed having him home wherever that might be. She studied the pictures on his laptop and agreed *Lost in Sunshine* appeared to be a paradise of sorts. Living on the edge of a lake didn't thrill her, but then she would probably be spending most days indoors looking through the window screens. Perhaps, an occasional foray into the gardens would be enough to placate her sense of adventure, although after the hot pursuit by a crazy woman, she couldn't wait to crawl into her little bed and stay there until her Cat-Dad told her it was safe to come out. For a quick second, she worried he might think she was high maintenance.

The following morning Benny and Esther crept from their hotel room, threw their suitcases in the back of the SUV, and sped down the highway traveling a mile under the speed limit. Eventually, Benny loosened his grip on the steering wheel and began to feel a sprout of enthusiasm return. Esther's enthusiasm, however, had been diminished by the ordeal and remained hidden under a blanket of dread. She found the average human an inadequate biped and often wondered what life would be like if God hadn't got the bright idea of adding such greedy beings to his creation. Her mind often drifted to pondering mystical questions like, 'Why does the chukar bird stare at the moon all night and sleep in the sunshine? Does the silly bird really think God can be found residing in the moon and if the moon, why not the sun?' Esther's thoughts ran deep, which accounts for the need to give her mind frequent rests from thinking too much.

"What do you say, girl, shall we pick up a burrito from the drive-thru coming up on the right?" Esther looked out the window. All she saw were giant signs cluttering up her view of the trees. She wondered why humans felt compelled to block a beautiful forest with a twenty-foot billboard reading: ALL YOU CAN EAT AT HERB'S DINER $9.99. This didn't apply to her, of course. Cat-Dad always shared his plate and let her choose whatever was to her liking. She considered him an anomaly among the other human life forms and showed her gratitude by allowing him to walk her on a leash much like a common dog.

Fifteen minutes later, the pair sat in the parking lot munching on a veggie burrito, not that Benny was necessarily a vegetarian. He considered Esther's feelings on the matter and figured Esther would be less anxious if her closest human wasn't chowing down on a cow's hind leg. Actually, Esther enjoyed the fish flavor in her kibble and wasn't above eating a can of chicken now and again. She considered herself a miniature lioness and only separated from her natural jungle habitat due to a clerical error made by government housing.

Benny had also encouraged Esther to use the dirt as her litter box when outdoors. He wanted her to feel at home in nature and remember her roots, which Esther thought was hysterical since she had never seen him do his business behind a bush and knew for a fact, he was so fastidious about his privacy, he closed the door when in the bathroom standing over a toilet bowl. However, she humored him and would squat to water the grass on occasion. She drew the line at muddying her paws unnecessarily in the parks alongside the road smelling of dogs and skunks. They compromised on the matter requiring Benny to put a portable litter box behind the driver's seat where she disappeared a few times during their long trip to paradise.

Benny didn't mind tending to Esther's wants and needs. He found the routine gave him comfort and created a sturdy scaffolding to hang his day on. He liked making Esther happy despite her periodic tantrums. Her refusal to cooperate sent Benny into peals of laughter, annoying Esther even more till finally one would find it easier to give in to the other, allowing both to get a peaceful night's sleep and continue their amiable companionship in a harmonious mixture of small pleasures and necessities.

Once in a while, Elena would flit across his mind and tug at his spirits trying to rattle them some with the notion life hung by a tenuous thread. He worried Elena might do something dangerous. Most people would find her recent behavior dangerous, but Benny's line of work had distorted his perception of danger and even peace only occurred during his lunch break. Benny, despite all of his lovely qualities, resembled a guitar with strings wound so tight, they could snap any second.

The pair meandered along the highway surprised at the open spaces and straggle of trees running along the ridge of the sheared off cliffs. Benny never particularly enjoyed blasting through mountains to put in a highway. He found it to be a crime against nature and felt guilty every time he watched the dirt and rocky bottoms fly through the air to be carried away in dump trucks. He could hear the animals moan from losing their homes and wondered if karma really existed, and if so, what would he have to pay to even the score for all the damage he'd done over the past twenty-five years?

Benny remembered the old general wanting him to rejoin the army to destroy human beings in much the same way he had burrowed through the hills. He worried about having contributed to all the destruction on planet earth. Unlike Elena, he never enjoyed his job but only headed in the direction of security because his father had spent many hours telling his son to work for the government and enjoy the security of receiving a paycheck for the rest of his life. Benny trusted his father, who valued serving his country above all else. He never thought to question him. He never considered what he wanted to do with his life beyond making his parents happy and enjoying the peace of his mother's gardens. And then they were gone.

The house stood empty waiting for his return from the army. Their old cat Rags stayed anxious at the neighbor's house growing sad over the loss of the elder Swans agitated by Benny's grief, and so one night, she couldn't take it anymore and died of heart break, further adding to Benny's bewilderment over what to do with the rest of his life. A sentimental journey through childhood listening to his happy father talking about the government with fondness had prompted Benny to keep his memory alive by taking his advice. The civil service exam seemed the likely step toward adding a foundation to his future. Now, he wondered what good was all the work for a secure future if he didn't have someone to share it with besides Esther. She heard his thoughts and cocked an eye, expressing some disgruntlement over his lack of gratitude at having his life graced with a superior being.

Benny shoved his thoughts aside when seeing a sign reading a hundred miles to *Lost in Sunshine.* In less than two hours, he and Esther would be settling into their new home. Suddenly, his spirits lifted, and he felt a flicker of hope. The most important thing his mother ever taught him was no one could live without hope.

FIVE

Maisie McRay, mountaineer and consummate storyteller, managed the tiny house village with an easy way about her and a penchant for harmony. She had been a smoking hot fiddle player in famous bluegrass bands and Greenwich Village coffee houses in her twenties and thirties. But Maisie was still relevant. Even while wearing blue jeans and peasant shirts, a personality like Maisie's never went out of style. Mostly, because the woman could throw a blanket of love over the most recalcitrant male and have him humming a sweeter melody in less than the minute it took him to feel wronged.

At night, the resident manager would lean into her fiddle and play a Chopin Lullaby with a sound so gentle it put the tree frogs to sleep and caused the residents to leave their laptops and lay down in their own dreams. She could transpose any music to the fiddle and often sent a fright to Gershwin when she plucked the clarinet's melodic line from *Rhapsody in Blue*. This bright and pretty woman brought a liveliness to the small village causing most residents to feel grateful and the others to deal with life's irritations without her salve to take away the sting.

Maisie lived in a four hundred square foot cottage built on a foundation with a wraparound porch. It begged the passersby to stay awhile and listen to her tell a story. After giving her guests a glass of lemonade, she settled into the recollections of her youth and a few mountaineer memories that would shock a city dweller with her candor involving some randy boys and a girl named Betty Lou.

Maisie loved tiny house living, the residents, and even drawing her water from a pump handle she had installed in her kitchen running to a barrel that collected the rain when it fell. The interior was all wood painted white and filled with lovely down-home quilts and a palm tree that looked like it belonged in a jungle. She never collected gewgaws but instead had accepted small paintings from famous artists in return for her affection. Their beauty turned the small house into an aesthetic wonderland of color and country charm.

She had already done a background check on the new resident expected to arrive any day. Benny Swan caught her interest, squeaky clean with every government clearance available except free access to the President himself. Benny possessed a soft-spoken phone voice and an ability to be charmed by her loquacious use of words and even when she waxed on about her granddaddy having been a preacher man, Benny hung in there and listened to every word with awe and satisfaction. She was a woman of character, a kind woman, he thought, making the move less daunting in its unfamiliarity. When he told her about Esther, she laughed with pleasure over another animal addition to their village. She spoke of cats, dogs, and a baby ball python that got lose on occasion and scared the neighbors, until they finally agreed to participate in a peace-loving snake handling ceremony. Not the rattle snake kind that fostered a belief in Jesus, but a getting to know all your neighbors, even the ones most people find objectionable. She described this event to Benny in great detail and went on to say it ended in success with the baby ball python being happy and loving the attention, although there were some problems with Manuel the little Chihuahua who enjoyed lounging under a weeping willow tree without worrying about a snake getting in his face. Finally, it was agreed when Manuel was outside, Charlie Walker would be secured in his aquarium. This decision satisfied everyone and afterwards they celebrated with homemade ice cream made even smoother with a jigger of whiskey. Benny listened enraptured by the manager's ability to glide smoothly from one subject to another without seeming to take a breath. His only concern was the possibility Esther may dislike Charlie Walker, which he knew wouldn't end well for either of them. Esther tended to hold onto a grudge and could smell someone she wasn't going to like the minute they entered her comfort zone, which was a small area with hardly room enough for a person, never mind something that slithered on the ground in silence.

Maisie remembered the Northerners from her youth, mostly loud and edgy New Yorkers liking a good time, high on pot, and talking nonsense about Nirvana being an acid trip away. She was a Southern Comfort girl and never veered from her drink of choice. Now, though at almost fifty, she found herself happy with a good cup of chamomile tea. In recollection, she had not encountered a true Yankee from New England but was always told they were a rigid, over-educated lot, who kept their CVs in their billfolds and exchanged ideas instead of falling into gossip on the behavior of their neighbors. They tended to categorize people disproportionately into little boxes of neuroses where they remained to be studied like bugs under a microscope. Maisie held a simple view of peoples' peculiarities coming from a need to be loved or a need to love. She had already concluded her newcomer fell into the category of needing love, and she looked forward to the challenge of helping him adapt to village life.

Maisie kept her private life in several suitcases hidden off-sight and away from the curiosity of the police chief hovering on the edge of the village property line. Still though, she thought you couldn't be too careful when dealing with the police. Coming from the mountains, she bore a natural suspicion to all forms of law enforcers and thought them to be high on authority without enough brain power to take a step back before whipping out their guns. Actually, Maisie didn't really like anyone carrying a firearm and had written *No Gun Zone* on one of the signs she had placed on the dirt road to the village proper.

Benny and Esther glanced out the window when turning onto the dirt road to their new village. They read the sign saying *No Gun Zone* and breathed a sigh of relief the residents wouldn't be toting firearms and tossing grenades hither and yon. Flowers grew along the roadside and more signs appeared indicating only three hundred yards to paradise. This pleased them both and when hearing each other sigh with relief, they both held a clear understanding the need each had for quiet.

Benny parked in front of Maisie's house where a small sign read, *Manager Inside,* ring bell for service. He placed Esther on the ground, encouraged her to squat near a bush, which was as useless as telling her to take a bite out of a cactus. She followed along next to him at the other end of a red leash attached to a rhinestone collar, which she thought set off her glorious combo charcoal and light gray-haired coat. Esther felt a rush of excitement at meeting the lovely woman who had been communicating with her for the last twenty miles. Mostly, she talked to Esther about looking forward to meeting her and what a pretty cat she was and even expressed her own excitement at having such an evolved being living nearby. This all went straight to Esther's head, especially the part about being evolved, which reassured her natural tendency to feel superior to humans and dogs. She did tell the woman calling herself Maisie that she considered her and Cat-Dad to be equals on most days. This caused Maisie to laugh with delight and even Esther enjoyed the melodious sound of the woman's voice and hoped it wasn't lost on Cat-Dad, who she knew had been moping for weeks wanting to add a human female to his den.

Benny reached over and lightly pressed the doorbell. Esther sat next to him looking regal with her bushy tail wrapped around her front legs and gold eyes tipped upward. A sudden gush of words filled the air coming from the prettiest woman Benny had ever laid eyes on. "Oh my, darlin' girl, you are a beauty." She bent down and paid obeisance to Esther before standing to slip a warm hand in Benny's hand. Esther could hear their hearts flutter from happiness. Just then a loud noise blasted through the paradisical setting and a tumble of skinny trees fell a few feet beyond a sign reading, *"When a cow jumps over the moon, where does she land?"*

SIX

Esther stared at Cat-Dad with a heavy expression of disapproval. Again, she expected him to step up and be brave. Benny felt relieved there was no banner flying around with his name on it. He tried not to look guilty when turning to Maisie.

"Should we call the police?" he asked.

"Oh, no need to bother. Our local Police Chief Earl has been hidin' in the bushes since dawn. For all I know he set off some charges for grins." She looked over Benny's shoulder at a tall skinny man rushing to the fallen trees. "Com'on inside and take a load off. Got some lemonade and the keys your realtor asked me to give to you." She opened the screen door further, allowing Esther to enter first, followed by Benny. They both settled on an overstuffed floral print couch, as though an old married couple, which didn't go unnoticed by Maisie. She sized up people in a few seconds and found Benny to be a sweet shy man looking to be useful. Esther, on the other hand, had a high opinion of herself and felt no need to explain her presence on a stranger's couch. To further show an air of possessiveness, she placed a paw on Benny's knee and turned her gold eyes to Maisie.

"You're a catch for anyone, darlin'." Maisie had read her mind, and after a few sugary words, Esther calmed down and draped her bushy tail over the edge of the couch displaying the beauty of a self-assured feline who looked like she would be comfortable bossing about a clowder of bobcats.

A few minutes later, Maisie set a tray with two glasses, a pitcher of lemonade, and a plate of cookies on the coffee table in front of Benny. "Didn't know whether or not you liked sugar so brought the bowl." She sat across from him in a vintage wicker rocker. "I hope you and Esther enjoy the homemade lemon cookies. Maybe hit the spot after your long trip?"

"Thank you. That's very kind," Benny said. He felt himself shaking inside, unusual for him, but then he had never been in such extraordinary circumstances. He expected the police chief to haul him and Esther to the precinct but nothing ever came of it. Eventually, he slipped into the easy, sing song voice of the village manager, listening to her stories and fond descriptions of the residents and their animals. His mood fell in sync with her words.

An hour later, Benny opened the door to his new home. Esther surveyed the large room and jumped on the queen-sized mango wood bed covered in a duvet so soft her body sunk down a few inches. Soon, she was fast asleep, resting from the long journey and the occasional blast of dynamite, which interrupted her dreams for a second but once past the rumble, she was floating on a cloud made of downy feathers. Meanwhile, Benny opened the pine cupboards and pulled out a plate to examine the fine quality of earthenware. In fact, every plate and cup were made of earthenware he had found in a potter's catalogue bearing price tags that would boggle the minds of most people, but Benny saw the value in filling his new home with all things handmade. He could feel the popular term 'organic' in every nook and cranny, every object, and even the limp snoring body of Esther added her natural essence to the handmade environment.

Benny glanced around at his *Sundance* furnishings, appreciating their masculine quality and woven upholstery. A Moon Garden Kilim loveseat and nearby ottoman made a comfortable seating arrangement for Esther and him to stare at their attached acre of land through a large picture window. He could see the corner of Maisie's cottage from across the weeds giving him a rush of oxytocin, which caught him off guard but settled around him like a fine mist. Then, Elena popped into his mind and the easy feeling he had been enjoying dissipated into a world of fear.

Benny couldn't bring himself to examine the damage of the last explosion. He hoped she would remain anonymous or at least stay out of sight. Not that she was keeping a low profile by any means, but even Benny knew his tendency toward optimism was often misplaced.

She must have detonated small charges of explosives or a hit of nitrogen causing the trees to fall at precisely timed intervals one after the other. He caught himself admiring her artistry and then a second later he succumbed to worry. Finally, in a state of exhaustion, he crawled in bed and fell asleep next to Esther. They slept the rest of the afternoon and then decided to unpack the SUV. Maybe, he thought, with their personal possessions scattered about and a few groceries in the kitchen, they would feel at home.

Benny spent the next few days surveying his land and making frequent trips to the hardware store for tools and garden supplies. He even bought a rototiller to plow through the soft earth, creating flower beds that waited for precisely cut edges. Bob, a professional landscaper, came by and laid turf around the areas marked off by stakes to designate the gardens. Benny had already worked hours on building a stone walkway from his back door to both ends of the lot where it meandered in what appeared to be a haphazard way but ended neatly at a small gazebo where Maisie's lot met his own. Benny's thoughts ran around the large backyard noticing it bore a striking resemblance to his mother's own gardens. This gave him comfort. He envisioned Esther lying in the small gazebo where cushions had been strewn to add a touch of luxury. Newly placed rambling roses hung off the trellised sides smelling like the old-fashioned sweet roses still lingering in Benny's childhood, not the no-scent hybrids only designed for beauty.

Benny's delicate demeanor allowed little room for lusty thoughts causing Maisie to go by the wayside. Sometimes though, she tripped through his visual landscape when he stopped to remember her lovely smile and laughter that sounded as gentle as her nightly violin lullabies. During these times, he thought he had died and gone to heaven.

Everything had run smoothly until Esther decided to join him in the garden to watch Bob put down the turf, unfolding it like a velvet carpet. The turf felt good on her feline body. Suddenly, a snake appeared and slithered across the greenway grabbing a small runaway dog yelping from fear. The snake wrapped its body around this tiny Chihuahua named Manuel and then suddenly a small boy appeared and began to cry. Two adults ran out the door of their trailer but stood at the edge of Benny's property afraid to trespass.

Esther and Manuel had spoken often to each other in their silent animal language since her arrival, and once confident he wasn't going to be an annoyance, she decided to meet him outside where the men were putting down grass. Neither one thought to check on the whereabouts of Charlie Walker. Esther had not seen the loathsome creature since moving to her new home so hadn't given him any room for consideration as an actual sentient being. However, Esther's fearless nature took over when spotting the snake about to choke the life out of her new friend. Esther leaped in the air like a she-cat and came down on Charlie Walker sinking all of her claws into his tender body. He loosened his grip on Manuel and then suddenly Esther sank her teeth into his neckless head and dragged him a few feet and flung him onto his own front yard. A gnarly man came running out the door of a tiny cabin with a bottle of whiskey in one hand. He wore a T-shirt with *Daddy Guitar Band* written across the front.

"Hey, neighbor, see yer met Charlie Walker all right." Esther hissed at the man and ran to the little dog and wrapped her arms around him in hopes of calming the tiny Chihuahua before he died of a heart attack. Everyone stared at Charlie Walker's dad hurrying across the yard with his hand extended toward Benny and a big grin splattered across his face. Tobacco spittle ran down the sides of his mouth leaving a permanent stain.

"Pleased to meet you. I'm Benny Swan and that's Esther. This is Bob from Bob's Nursey." Benny politely introduced everyone as though at an ice cream social. This prompted his neighbor to offer the men a swig from his half empty bottle. They declined.

"Jus' call me Bo. Yer met my better half, Charlie Walker. Not goin' grow much more on accounta bein' a ball python. He only eats and shits once a month so needs little in the way of upkeep."

The small family disappeared, which didn't go unnoticed by either Esther or Benny. He thought about introducing himself later and maybe taking them a pretty pot of mixed flowers filled with calibrachoa, starflowers, lilies, and creeping Jenny, with some salvia sprigs growing for accent. Several large pots of mixed flowers had been placed in the bare spots waiting to be planted. "Well, now, I'll let you boys git back to work. Give me a holler, Benny, if'n yer need anythin'. Also, my band plays at *Duke's Rye Bar* ever' Friday night. If'n either yer boys have a hankerin' to drop by, a drink 'll be on me." Benny thanked him, but doubted if he would be idling away his time on a bar stool. This quickly brought back memories of Elena until Bob interrupted his wayward thoughts.

"Actually, his band is pretty good but the nights he plays usually end in a fight with the band running out the back door to high-tail it home. Too bad, Bo Walker used to be famous in these parts for his original haunting lyrics but then suddenly he just dropped out of the limelight. I reckon to live off his royalties and enjoy himself playing for pleasure." Bob began whistling, which broke the tension that felt thicker than island fog. Benny chuckled and the two men went back to work while Manuel and Esther settled themselves on the gazebo benches.

~

Once finished several hours later, Benny took a quick shower and called for Esther to come and pay a visit to Manuel's family. She resented having to wear a harness to go next door. Afterall, any cat who could mangle a python deserved some respect and shouldn't have to suffer the indignity of being hitched into a fancy black leather buckled affair similar to the ones they put on horses attached to chariots pulling tourists on a fantastical sightseeing journey of every major city. Esther knew this because she watched Netflix with Benny and noticed he lingered a lot in London and New York where these forlorn horses stood on street corners like common hookers satisfying customers by wearing out their bodies. Esther thought both to be undignified professions and again dwelled on the human perspective, considering their vantage point askew when it came to kindness.

Mostly, she humored Benny knowing he meant well and couldn't help suffering on occasion from the same density as his fellow man. She stood stiff as a board and let him place each leg in its appropriate loop while telling her how happy she makes him feel every single day. He went on to talk about her bravery and marvel over not knowing she loved Manuel so much she was willing to risk her life. Benny's last sentiment rattled Esther's nerves when dwelling on the fact she may have feelings for a dog. She thought Manuel an easy-going creature who grinned enthusiastically when she said something that amused him. For instance, when lying on their respective pillows in the gazebo, she mentioned Charlie Walker's dad being as dumb as his own snake, a man who slithered instead of walking, no notion of hygiene, and a yellow grin that was an affrontery to a cat's sensibilities. Manuel didn't understand half of what his new friend said but thought her pinched face and haughty air hysterical in view of the fact she had taken on an uncommon snake. He was grateful and was about to ask if he could lay next to her but when seeing her tail twitch in annoyance, he thought better of it.

Benny carried the potted flowers in one arm and pulled Esther along with the other. He wondered why she appeared disgruntled and slightly out of sorts over wearing her harness. He knew she preferred her collar but not wanting to take the chance a strange environment might cause her to slip from her collar and bolt, he had decided on something more secure. She had run away once in their old neighborhood. Benny never recovered from the grief of nearly losing her. Fortunately, a fire fighter lived on the same street and knew enough to walk the neighborhood carrying a can of *Fancy Feast*. The smell alone brought several cats out of their hiding places along with Esther. Benny spent the evening clutching the six-month-old kitten while she gobbled the fancy cat food and licked her tiny chops. He shook off the memory and knocked on Manuel's door.

High pitched barking sounds startled both of them. Who would have thought so much noise could come from such a little dog? He glanced at Esther's unhappy face and sighed from worry she would forget her manners and spend the evening in a corner staring at everyone with an expression of superiority. Whenever she gave Benny one of these haughty disappointed stares, he laughed, causing her to forget her latest grudge. The inter-feline family stood on the stone sidewalk in front of the Airstream trailer a full minute waiting to introduce themselves. A lot of scurrying about could be heard along with an excited conversation in Spanish ending with "Halo" the second a dark-haired woman opened the door and invited her guests inside where the little boy and Manuel sat on a tattered chair. The father extended his hand and introduced them all in his broken but reverential English, as though he himself were the guest.

"Bonita and Mateo," the man said pointing to his wife and then himself. He also introduced Hugo who appeared to be about six years old but looked wiser. Manuel knew he was of small importance and was lucky to have a water bowl on a placemat near a small wood stove. The family had climbed off a boat at the bottom edge of Florida, except they weren't originally a family. The couple stumbled across Hugo on the beach kneeling next to a campfire he had made from driftwood.

The small boy had hidden behind a rock while his parents were dragged away by border patrol. His American birth certificate had been stuffed in his pocket and a locket with pictures of his original parents inside hung from his neck like a priceless medallion. Both Bonita and Mateo eagerly took the boy with them, although they had no real plan. They had faith God would care for them. Eventually, they stumbled into a small village where a beautiful woman invited the family to sleep in her cottage. She threw sleeping bags on the floor and made a pot of chili and sliced a loaf of French bread, which Mateo declared the best chili he had ever eaten, failing to tell their hostess he hadn't eaten in days so anything given to him would naturally be his best meal. Fortunately, she understood a few words of Spanish, which allowed her to deduce they were in need of a place to live and some work to make ends meet. She gave them Mr. Maren's abandoned Airstream, made a call to the local motel asking for cleaning work and the next day the grateful family set about living the American dream. They always remembered Maisie in their prayers every night and thanked God for bringing her into their lives. Their prayers often lasted a half an hour, which tired out Manuel, but Hugo took to heart the significance of feeling grateful, and so thereafter was attentive to his devotions. Even throughout the day, he could be seen kneeling at the feet of nature silently thanking Mother Mary for the pretty flowers and a little dog who suddenly appeared by his side and never left. Needless to say, Manuel became part of the family where he thought life couldn't get any better until meeting Esther, the most beautiful cat in the world. And while the grownups stood talking, he invited Esther to sit on the arm of the chair. He knew such a regal being deserved to be elevated over her lowly, slobbering servant, such was Manuel's humility.

"Please, sir. You eat with us and little kitty, she too eat?" Mateo said. He and Benny stared at her perched on the arm of the chair looking down at Manuel and Hugo. Benny felt relief she was making an effort to be neighborly.

"Yes, thank you," Benny responded.

Mateo pulled out a rickety straight back chair and indicated for his guest to make himself comfortable but first hurried around the small space to find a pillow to put on the chair. The little family shared a can of heated refried beans spread neatly on soft tortilla shells. They stumbled through a lively conversation and looked forward to being neighbors. Hugo also ate with the grownups while Manuel entertained his guest by dragging out all of his toys to share with Esther. He felt honored over her presence and his heart swelled with pride at having such an elegant friend who made him feel important, while at the same time, he really did believe himself to be her humble servant, except he had no idea how he could be of use to such a goddess as his new neighbor.

SEVEN

B enny sat on his new couch remembering the time when his parents enlivened the days. He contemplated their sudden loss and crushed his own soul with tears that never fell from his eyes but stayed inside turning him into a pool of sadness. His sergeant, usually a hard ass, cried when giving Benny the news while reassuring him transportation was being arranged to return home under such unusual circumstances. The word home stuck in Benny's mind that day and caused him to pummel the life out of its meaning when understanding his beautiful happy parents were his home. Not the large eccentric house or the gardens but his parents' gaiety brightened his young life and created a cheerful safe haven of unending blessings so abundant he often felt like a hoarder. All that disappeared the day his Sergeant dampened the telegram with his own tears, never allowing Benny free from the wiry man's excess of emotion to take in the enormity of his own grief.

Esther could hear him from the large bed. She had shoved her small canopy bed out the front door when moving into their new home and took up residence on the soft down comforter next to her Cat-Dad where life settled nicely around her. But this evening she could hear his heart cry. Sometimes, she understood the association Benny's heart made from his lonely life to the seemingly happy family units that surrounded him. This night appeared to be such a time when he became fraught with the understanding he had failed to create the makings of a happy home filled with children's voices, a few dogs, and Esther who would be a delightful comfort in his middle-age.

She jumped from the bed and sprinted to sit next to Benny with her elbow nudging his side pressing him to use her as comfort in a cruel world made up of loss and harsh people. Benny wrapped her in his arms and nuzzled his face against her soft fur. She purred so loud Manuel could hear her from the Airstream trailer. He looked up from his tiny bed and caught a whiff of her sweetness before she shoved her attention aside to minister to her Cat-Dad, the one who put food in her bowl and called her beautiful. So far, Manuel had only proven to be a distraction. He went back to sleep wishing his goddess neighbor will someday offer him a modicum of the devotion she felt for her Cat-Dad.

Benny grabbed hold of Esther's comfort and called her his precious girl, a sentiment he considered deserving when glancing around his new adobe house and noticing he was alone with his cat in a place empty of laughter. He thought of Maisie. He wondered what it would be like to have such a pretty woman in his life. Would she love him forever? Or would she leave the day after tomorrow and wasn't everyday potentially the day after tomorrow? His mind filled with worrisome, nonsensical thoughts that held no more importance than the fluff floating from a dandelion. Thoughts seemed to breed more thoughts, until he fell asleep on the couch while clutching Esther and dreaming about Maisie running naked through his newly planted garden. Her pretty hair hung in loose curls to her shoulders and her lady parts were covered with tiny curls in a matching color, rousing him in his dreams. The next morning, he remembered Maisie smiling at him and motioning for him to follow her to the peony bed where they laid down under the cover of large pink flowers. He spent the entire night wrapped in her arms.

While recalling the loveliness of her naked body, he saw the real Maisie, wearing a white peasant shirt tucked in tight fitting jeans tapering to a pair of sturdy boots walking in the direction of his house. This would be her first visit, the one he had been waiting for without knowing he was waiting. He was a reticent man, well-hidden in his shyness. A light tapping at the door brought Esther from her food bowl to stand next to Benny excited to see the one human person who could hear what an animal had to say on life in general. Naturally, Esther began excitedly expounding upon her adventures with Charlie Walker, his no-account dad, and new friend Manuel. She ended by saying the little boy Hugo sits in sadness. Maisie assured Esther he would be all right and the best thing Esther could do would be to offer kindness to both Manuel and Hugo explaining how they suffered from the sort of exile only those separated from their mother country could understand.

Esther walked off slightly perturbed something was expected of her, especially since grown-ups could trace all their misery back to the ones in charge of their sorry lives. Then she saw herself running free in the jungle accountable to no one. Life couldn't be better for Esther when realizing she was exactly where she was supposed to be or some new-agey clap trap, but when pondering her position, she realized sleeping in the big bed with Cat-Dad was about as good as it gets. Then she remembered the sign at the vet's office saying: Life is Good. She thought this also bordered on new-agey claptrap and why do people feel the need to surround themselves with signs reminding them they are living in the human condition? Whatever that is. This brought her thoughts right back to the innate greediness of the top-of-the-heap humans who simply couldn't accumulate enough wealth to satisfy their pathetic sorry asses. Periodically, Esther fell into the unladylike habit of swearing. Manuel found every word ushered from her mouth endearing. Afterall, she was a goddess.

Benny invited Maisie inside and asked if she would like a ginger ale and some vanilla wafers. He felt slightly embarrassed at offering wafers from a box when remembering his mother telling his father they were a common cookie sold to the gullible masses with little in them except sugar and white flour. He wondered why he had bought them. His own taste leaned toward chocolate but then recalled the time he ordered a chocolate ice cream cone from the ice cream truck after a hard day's work. Elena began calling him chocolate boy, which he thought inappropriate but the more he objected, the more she had teased him until he began to avoid Elena altogether feeling somewhat embarrassed for dropping an anonymous complaint about her bullying the men with cruel words and laughter. Nothing changed. The men still cringed every time she walked by.

"That sounds lovely. I brought you some warm corn bread fresh from the oven. Thought you and Esther might enjoy something downhome." She smiled and his dream came back to him like a spool of film spilling images in an evocative manner, all slightly haphazard but arousing. This embarrassed him and he hurried a few feet to the kitchen.

"Thank you. We could share a piece now. I bought some homemade butter from a local creamery. Might taste good." He turned and smiled at her pretty face, so fair with a light pink hue just underneath her skin and eyes so blue he could get lost in them.

"Yes, that sounds lovely. I also brought a thermos of coffee. She reached in a large straw purse slung over her shoulder and pulled out a tin thermos. An indoor picnic, Benny thought and then he remembered the gazebo.

"Why don't we put everything on a tray and carry it into the garden?"

"Splendid. You do know how to make a girl happy. Nothing like getting lost in the sunshine." They both laughed, and Benny knew he would remember that moment forever.

Once sitting comfortably with coffee and cornbread, they began to ask each other questions. Maisie wanted to know how he and Esther were settling into their new home. Naturally, this required quite a few words for Benny to sling together into amusing anecdotes on the antics of Esther, Manuel, and Charlie Walker. Benny never mentioned himself personally but usually expressed his moods through Esther, even though she wasn't always nearby. Benny, similar to most people, assumed Maisie's full-time job was being manager of the small village. He had no idea she ran a side business that brought Officer Earl out to sniff around the grounds like an overzealous hound dog chasing a good scent. Maisie enjoyed hiding the other aspects of her life. She considered herself to be a demure wild woman of few vices, little regard for the law, and leanings toward benevolence. Her personal assessment, while accurate, failed to express the raw sexuality vibrating underneath the peasant blouse and blue jeans persona. Benny would have to travel to her front door and into her bedroom before experiencing the full extent of her offerings. Being a shy man, he would wait for an invitation. Unfortunately, this tended to leave his unrequited desires pulsating beneath his polo shirts, which often left him exhausted and in need of a cold shower.

The cornbread chat suddenly became overwhelming for Benny. He hurried his guest politely through her last bite, thanked her for coming, and when she was gone, he sat morosely on his own couch missing her presence and wondering exactly what was wrong with him.

Benny often wondered why he wasn't more like his mother, a robust sort, full of life, and so expansive, she took in the world and let it flow over her like water coming from a garden hose. Not Benny, he inherited his father's introverted personality. Mr. Swan, however, at least had the wherewithal to wrap his arms around the one woman who could make him feel like a real man full of vitality even though he suffered from a timidity that thwarted his secret ambition of being a fighter pilot. Instead, he settled for a government job where he sat in the corner at a great big desk going over government munitions inventories, keeping perfect records and a long list of figures that would dazzle your average accountant.

Benny stared out his picture window and watched Maisie walk lightly through his garden smelling the flowers as she passed by. He also saw Hugo kneeling in front of the rose bushes with his hands folded in prayer. Maisie smiled sweetly in the boy's direction and continued walking to her back door.

EIGHT

Hugo appeared to be an odd child with hands folded praying earnestly for Mother Mary to bring back his original parents. He told Mary he didn't want to seem ungrateful for the substitute parents, but he missed the sweet smell of his mother, her smile, and the father who had large hands and knew how to use them to dismantle a car engine and build a makeshift house out of scrap lumber. He thought his father a brilliant man, so admirable, in fact, he wanted to grow up and be just like him. Except as he told Mary, his father had disappeared in the middle of the night leaving him without a role model. Leaving him without love.

Benny saw Manuel and Esther appear next to the child, also praying. Manuel's prayers consisted of muddled ramblings of a lovesick dog full of longing for the company of his beloved friend Esther. She on the other hand, prayed for sardines on a plate of crackers served cold. She also wished God would do something about all the ignorant people who failed to see her as a feline princess, especially the tobacco-stained neighbor, a man so objectionable he got on her last nerve.

Just then, Charlie Walker slithered up to the three kneeling figures and once again wrapped himself around Manuel. The little dog managed to yelp weakly before passing out in a dead faint. This allowed Charlie Walker to tighten his grip around Manuel's limp body and reach down to swallow him whole. Just then, Benny grabbed him by the tail and yanked so hard Charlie flipped up in the air and hurled over backwards to land at the feet of his owner. Bo picked up his beleaguered snake and began apologizing to everyone, using words slightly slurred from too much whiskey and exhaustion after playing three sets at *Duke's Rye Bar* the night before.

"Man, I'm so sorry fer the little guy gittin' hurt. What can I do but maybe take 'im to the vet who could revive him with some oxygen or somethin'. Maybe I should call Earl. That sombitch bin standin' over yonder fer days. Not understandin' why we git the pleasure of his company on a regular basis." Bo turned and yelled at Earl, motioning for him to hurry.

Meanwhile, Benny leaned over Manuel administering CPR and comforting Hugo with soft words, telling him everything will be all right. Telling him the little dog is suffering from fright and will need extra care to help make him feel safe again. Hugo piped up, "I never feel safe Senor Benny, but I feel better when Mateo puts his arm around me." Hugo scooped Manuel in his arms and held him against his heart. The little dog opened one eye and spotted Hugo. He raised his head in a half-hearted way and then closed his eye again until feeling Esther rub her cheek against his belly. He woke up startled by his own feelings, except his easiness dwindled some when realizing he probably looked like a coward in front of his goddess. Then he felt shame. Esther knew and rubbed her face against his cheek, which electrified his entire seven-pound body and suddenly he was ready to have a go at his nemesis Charlie Walker.

Earl reached in his holster and pulled out a gun, telling Bo to put his snake on the ground, so he didn't shoot him by mistake. Earl had a history of taking pot shots at suspects before even getting them into the patrol car. Sometimes, he took pot shots at the passersby from his front porch. The locals knew he won the national sharpshooting contest five years straight and hardly winced when a bullet went over their heads, but the tourists took exception and naturally hurried to the police station to report a crime. The other officers spent much of their time covering for their boss with elaborate stories and occasional mention of his having spent time in the local sanitorium for nervous exhaustion. Some of the tourists felt sorry for the man shooting at them and others took to their Facebook page and sent out posts on nearly being shot dead on their vacations.

"Nobody here is pressin' charges. I promise to keep ol' Charlie in his aquarium where he won't be a bother." Bo begged Earl to put away his gun but the police chief enjoyed shooting anything that moved and was reluctant to miss the fun of sending that cold-blooded reptile straight to hell.

Benny joined the men and, in an effort, to bring them all together to see the light of reason, he began to speak slowly using logic as the basis for his argument, "If you shoot the snake, and I'm not saying he isn't objectionable, you will traumatize the little boy and frighten Manuel even more than he is already."

Earl gave this some thought and decided the newcomer had a point. He put his gun back in its holster after first threatening to shoot both Bo and Charlie Walker if he ever saw that miserable reptile again. Bo didn't think this was fair on the chief's part being as how he spent most of his days trespassing on private property but then he also knew Earl was prone to walking the perimeter of their village to avoid such an accusation should he ever find himself in court. Benny nudged Bo until he finally agreed to the police chief's demands. Everyone went home sullen except Manuel. He laid in Hugo's arms pondering his mortality and the beauty of Esther, his goddess, causing his heart to sigh with happiness.

NINE

Maisie often found herself glancing out the kitchen window at the little gazebo where she and Benny enjoyed cornbread and coffee, topped with a lively conversation, until suddenly her host gathered up the dishes and abruptly ended their good time. She sensed a lot of baggage traveled behind him. Maisie was not inclined to pry. She fought the desire to rub up against him, pull him to the ground, and roll over together in the grass where the leaves of the weeping willow tree filtered the sunlight and the birds could watch in awe. She mused on it having been a long time since a man had warmed her bed, however briefly. But Benny seemed a solid sort of man, possibly husband material, or maybe a long, true bond would be nice until their bodies dwindled and their minds fell in sync and spoke in silent pauses. What a lovely life, she thought.

Meanwhile, Maisie's prescription drug supply for her clients was running low, which required a trip to Canada. Driving straight through took forty-eight hours, plus another two hours for pick up, and then right back home. Altogether, she would not be gone long enough to raise suspicions, but Earl had always been a suspicious sort and a cause for aggravation the last several years. She glanced sideways out the front window and saw his scrawny neck, head tucked under a cowboy hat, and body cinched inside a pair of black skinny jeans, which gave him the air of a maverick in his own mind, but to the typical onlooker, he appeared to be an extra on a Quentin Tarantino film set.

Maisie began to purchase drugs in Canada years ago when her now deceased mother was diagnosed with cancer requiring four thousand US dollars a month in medications, which upon investigation she discovered was more than ten times what the pharmaceutical companies paid for manufacturing costs. The lack of humanity in the pharmaceutical world pressed her to pursue a life of crime, especially when she discovered the demand was high and old Doc Martin would facilitate her transactions to at least half of his cancer patients. The other half were rich and didn't mind the cost, only the feeling of well-being they received when on the opioids Doc added to the mix of pills to ease their pain.

Her mother joined several cancer support groups and solicited business for her despite

Maisie asking her to stay at home and rest. The poor woman spent most of her time listening to sad stories even worse than her own, all victims of the medical machinery, disheartening stories she passed along to her daughter, which allowed Maisie to see herself as a modern-day Robin Hood, never mind she took ten percent of the adjusted price. She ran it like a business and even had a secret compartment custom built beneath the wheel well of her car to accommodate all the little vials, a two-month supply for her regular clients.

Her mind wandered back to Benny and their imaginary marriage. Would she tell him? Would he mind? She resigned herself not to care what a man thought of her personal morality, after all she was the one who had to live with herself and she had long ago rationalized her actions as charity work with overhead.

Earl's haggard face now stared at her from the front steps. She kept the screen door locked and stood waiting for him to explain his presence. "Maisie, I knowed yer home. Have some questions. Yer bin seein' anythin' unusual like? We got ourselves some kinda terrorist blowin' up things and then disappearin' like we was all stupid. Startin' to reach the end o' mah rope. What you seed?" He looked hard at her with an expression of malevolence she learned to ignore over the years. It helped knowing Earl in grade school and watching him come to class every day banged up by his father beating him for no apparent reason, according to Earl. Even then, she considered him an annoyance to his own father and those around him and probably deserved a good thrashing once in a while. The teachers usually rolled their eyes and sighed with despair when seeing Earl wrapped in a head bandage, a blight on their classroom.

"No, Earl. Only that day all the little trees shuddered and then fell over. Suspect it was an earthquake shaking things up a bit." She laughed and closed the door.

Earl was one of the many redneck boys who cluttered her memory with their predatory stares and hands that touched her body every time she walked by. Eventually, she ran from the bus to her classroom and then back to the bus at the end of the day. They tried to dampen her poetic thoughts and hamper the lovely riffs she heard coming from her violin. Fortunately, Maisie hung in rare circles where the ugliness surrounding her was diminished by her expansive need to see beauty in all things. On occasion, she saw a light in Earl but it darkened with each passing year and now she found him to be a nuisance and possibly dangerous if he uncovered her secret life and stepped inside to investigate. A little bit of fear swept over her every time she saw him walking the perimeter of her village. These were the times she wished she had a man to soften the hardships, warm her bed, and listen to her muse over life surprising us each time we turned a corner.

What if Benny scrutinized the signatures on her paintings? Would he assume she had the money to buy fine art or would it occur to him she may have exchanged each piece for her favors? Maisie being a loving woman shared herself where her heart took her. She rarely felt guilty, probably from growing up on a mountainside where satisfying one's lusty nature was a pastime and often considered a biological function the way a bull takes to a cow. Her love of beauty came from enjoying the freedom of nature, no manicured lawns or chemical trucks obstructing her view of the dirt road that ran past the shanty house where her mother died one night, alone and without a daughter's comfort, tormented by a disease that could ravage the soul of a Hampshire pig.

Maisie shook Earl's visit from her mind and drafted a memo to leave on the porches of the villagers, ten in all, each of their houses set in an enclave of trees on an acre lot. Benny was the only resident who bought an extra acre, which she found slightly excessive until watching him turn the trampled weeds into flower gardens punctuated by several diminutive Japanese maples sprouting dark red leaves and an enthusiasm for life often lacking in your average forsythia bush. That was the day Benny came to mind as a romantic possibility, but she noticed his shyness may be an obstacle and Esther was also a force to be reckoned with. She knew Benny's cat could smell insincerity and lacked the patience to overlook it. She found herself working hard at getting on the good side of the cat and wondered for a moment if there might be something wrong with her mind. Usually, a cat's way of being went unnoticed without the need to comment or even pausing a moment to scrutinize an imperfection. Esther did not have an imperfection.

Once packed, she hurried to the gas station and then hit the road for another forty-eight-hour trip. After each visit, Maisie and her Canadian connection passed notes with codes on them to communicate the pickup point and a date for the next exchange of money for drugs. Men rarely stopped a pretty woman at the border except for some idle chitchat and an awkward pause to enjoy the sexuality emanating from her body. They often acted like fools but Maisie kept on smiling with the slyness of charm used for manipulating the minds of weak men. Occasionally though, she would find herself stopped by a judicious sort whose clipboard appeared permanently attached to his arm and his thoughts spilled out in long check lists instead of a jumble of useless words. Maisie hid her anxiety well and continued on her way when finally viewed as harmless. Fortunately, men never ceased to underestimate women, which most women knew would eventually result in the downfall of the masculine gender.

~

Occasionally, Maisie felt a wave of disappointment when seeing her own gender leave casseroles on Benny's front steps. Lori Clyde had already been to his doorstep three times and hovered around the edges of Benny's gardens watching him work. Esther let out a howl every time she caught sight of the sex-crazed woman. Maisie found it amusing, but still, it appeared undignified and lacked the wherewithal of knowing you have value with or without a man in your life. Her thoughts paused a moment remembering she too took a dish of cornbread to his house and was she any better than the others? Upon further thought, she knew her visit was purely neighborly with the intention of leaving the cornbread rather than having a romantic repast in his gazebo until their good time ended and she found herself back home wondering what had happened.

And too, Earl's frantic palavering over the possibility of a terrorist wrecking his jurisdiction caused her mind to wander over to Benny. She saw the tree roots dangle from their trunk a split second before each tree fell on the same day Benny arrived and smiled sweetly as though butter wouldn't melt in his mouth. Then she grabbed hold of her mind, preferring to let it stay focused on the business at hand. While her mother was no longer of this world, Doc Martin depended on her to provide his patients with their much-needed medications. Hours later, she sat in her car on the edge of a Canadian parking lot waiting for her contact to pull up in a van. The exchange was made in the middle of the night with the help of a flashlight, a clandestine affair worthy of a high-quality British mystery. She wasn't privy to Benny's preference for British TV rather than the blandness of American films. Besides, it didn't seem worth pondering at that very moment.

Maisie knew little about her contact until one day finding herself alone in Earl's office with his computer. He had already logged in and was open to the site listing persons of interest. She ran through all the mugshots but found nothing until flipping to the page with the heading Pharmaceutical Crime Ring. She saw a picture of her contact in a dimly lit alley-way unrecognizable to most law officers. However, Maisie recognized his right ear hanging at an odd angle unlike other people's ears. She wondered if she should tell him. She decided it seemed more prudent to keep her mouth shut and find out who stood on the top rung of the ladder in case Earl ever became smart enough to track her contact down. She knew the U.S. enjoyed reciprocity with Canada so neither side was immune to an arrest. This discovery also alerted her to the reason why Earl kept sniffing after her like an overzealous hound dog. She then realized the need to be wary of Earl and rethink her life of crime.

The entire ride home, she visualized her future and considered talking to Doc Martin about no longer aiding in a drug smuggling operation. She would have to face the unsavory aspect of her Robin Hood days and come to terms with the idea it may be time to quit. If Earl continued creeping around the borders of *Lost in Sunshine*, it was only a matter of months before he stumbled across the bright idea of following her car all the way to Canada and then what would she use as an excuse for her impromptu visit to a foreign country? Afterall, he knew all of her kin folk resided in the hills. She considered asking her Uncle Cyrus to have a heart to heart with Earl, but there was always the risk of it ending in bloodshed similar to when he was thirteen and laid down on the school room floor to look up her dress. Uncle Cyrus, the principal of their small country school, nearly yanked one of Earl's arms from its socket when he threw him out the second story window. Earl cracked his head open from a hard landing on the sidewalk. No one ever knew for sure if his crazy behavior was a result of that incident or from all the times his father began knocking him senseless. Either way, Earl always managed to remain obnoxious.

Once home, she rested for several hours before meeting with Doc Martin. She again pondered whether or not to continue leading a life of crime. While she wanted to be helpful to cancer patients, it didn't seem worth her peace of mind. Doc could find someone else, allowing business to go on as usual. While walking down the sidewalk of the small city-town known as Earl's jurisdiction, she bumped into Duke, owner of *Duke's Rye Bar.*

"Hey sunshine. Ain't you the perttiest thing I've seen all day." He smiled a broad grin that invited a girl to lay down on the sidewalk for him, but Maisie, startled by the whimsical notion, shoved aside his comment and returned the smile.

"Thank you, Duke. You do have a way with words." They stepped onto the grass and stared at each other for a second. Maisie appreciated his virile good looks but couldn't see herself with a man prone to flirt.

"I was 'bout to call you, Maisie. Business stuff." Still grinning, he leaned closer to her when he talked. Nearly irresistible to someone whose bed has been empty for a long time. Maisie heard herself sigh and even Duke knew she yearned in his direction if only for a minute.

"Business! Yes, of course, how can I help you?" Maisie assumed he wanted to buy the cottage for sale at the village.

"The town ladies have been bothering me for a teatime. Yes, hard to believe, but out of respect for women, they tell me, the *Rye Bar* owes an afternoon a week to the town ladies for a tea and crumpet affair. They even want Friday. Not some slow day during the week but it's got to be Friday afternoon till six at exactly the same time all the exhausted workers just want to sit down and have a drink after a long week." Duke appeared to run out of steam once coming to the end of his predicament, but Maisie still didn't understand how she fit into the mix.

"Yes, that sounds lovely. Maybe I'll come. What a wonderful idea." Maisie could see herself feeling energized by being in the company of other women and wouldn't it be nice to have her *Women in Business* meetings there. Her mind went crazy with possibilities.

"Well, that ain't all." He changed his stance and tilted to the right looking serious as a mule pulling a load of lumber. He appeared burdened, Maisie thought.

"Yes."

"Well, they want the tables gussied up with real tablecloths and flower buds in the center, homemade pastries and China tea service. Plus, Maisie, they want music playing in the background. I was wondering if I could hire you to play your fiddle on Friday afternoons. Heck, I'd pay you real money if you'd arrange the whole thing and play your fiddle, too. Maisie, would you think about it?" He nearly begged.

"Oh, I don't have to think about it. I'll do it if you give me a long leash from two to six on Fridays and an hour to clean up."

"Oh, Maisie. God bless you, darlin'; you saved some marriages and made a lot of people happy, includin' me. And don't worry about the money. *The Rye Bar's* a gold mind what with the poker game in the back room. Thank you, darlin'." He reached out and hugged her at exactly the same time Benny and Esther drove by on their way to Bob's nursery.

"Not sure that's professional but it was nice. I'll stop by later to look at the space and then work up seating arrangements and make a list of necessary items. Naturally, I'll bake the crumpets, which will cost you more." Maisie studied his face to see if it went rigid from the noise of the cash register. Nothing.

"No worries about the cost, my little buttercup. Besides the ladies will be paying for their tea and crumpets." They both laughed and parted ways feeling better than when serendipitously bumping into each other.

Given the new circumstances, Maisie broke the news to Doc that she wouldn't be making any more trips to Canada. He shocked her by saying there had been inquiries about the position.

"You're being vague, Doc. Need details. It's me, Maisie." He knew she would coerce him for a name.

He muttered, "Earl," and then turned away.

"What? And you trust him?"

He muttered again.

"He's an officer of the law. That's illegal."

Doc began guffawing. "Oh Maisie, I can't help myself."

"What's so funny. The man's a supercilious nitwit whose been hanging about the village for weeks now spying on me. And suddenly, he wants my job?"

"Don't get high and mighty. You know how fuzzy the law is with hill people where you and Earl come from. So, don't blame him.

Besides, it's a lot more complicated. Breaking confidentiality goes against HIPPA laws but his mother's got cancer and he's desperate for a way to pay for her medication. Figured you would understand." They both looked at each other with sadness. Earl's mother was the best of the entire family.

"I'm so sorry. But doc, I'm not stupid. He knows what I've been doing and was going to threaten me if I didn't stop. He could then slip easily into my position and help his mother out and make extra cash for his own pocket."

"That's about the size of it."

"There's more?"

"He got mean and said to put a bug in your ear about quitting or he would see to it you were jailed for your crimes. Sorry, Maisie, I was going to fire you today."

"Fire me? That's rich coming from you."

They both began to laugh and then sat down to enjoy a cup of coffee in Doc's office. Maisie told him about the coincidence of being offered a sweet gig at Duke's and they both lingered for a few minutes in happiness.

"Sometimes, life surprises you in ways you don't see coming," Doc said.

"Just had that realization myself earlier today." Maisie mused on Benny and Esther, now always seeing them as a couple. She decided to go to Bob's and ask for a weekly order of dainty flowers for the tea tables. She and Doc parted on friendly terms. Maisie gave him the codes for the next Canada rendezvous to pass along to her replacement.

TEN

Bob's Nursery was a display of country charm combining acres of wildflowers behind the area of cultivated showy flowers that would enliven any cottage garden. Maisie loved looking at all the varieties and watching the happy people drift through the rows of succulents, herbs, annuals, shaded plants, and perennials with perky faces waiting to be permanently placed in an amateur gardener's front yard. Her own cottage plants all came from Bob's Nursery. They enlivened the delicate yellow clapboard house trimmed in white with a bit of New England bric-a-brac running along the roof line. Whenever she arrived home, she felt her spirits lift the second she laid eyes on the loveliness of charming flowers that she was convinced leaned toward her with appreciation and the understanding their caretaker treated them with reverence. She loved them all.

Just then she heard a cat meow and recognized the sound as coming from Esther. Her meow was followed by several complaints over Maisie's absence and something about a nosey neighbor leaving abhorrent food for Cat-Dad and why hadn't Maisie come by to do something about it and wasn't wrangling all the sex-crazed women her job. After all, she was supposed to be the manager, so why does a nut job get to run loose in a people-compound bothering the innocent residents who only want to be left alone? Maisie heard herself apologize in cat-speak for at least a full minute, which allowed Esther to calm down and forgive her, although with a slight annoying tone suggesting Maisie might want to do better. It required self-control to keep from laughing. In fact, the entire day seemed surreal and now coming across a loquacious cat at the local nursery caused her mind to veer off center.

"Maisie, you okay?" Bob suddenly appeared along with Benny and Esther. The latter grabbed her by the ankle and wouldn't let go. Fortunately, she was wearing heavy cotton socks and ankle boots.

"It's been an interesting day. Duke just offered me a job arranging a Friday tea affair for the town ladies along with playing what he calls fiddle music. I thought I would look for some small annuals to put in bud vases. It's nice to see you, Benny." She smiled at them.

"What?" Bob responded. He looked surprised

"Yes, it's true much to Duke's chagrin. Every

Friday the bar is to be opened for a ladies' tea. It's a lovely idea but Duke, being the hard living, he-man sort, is having trouble wrapping his mind around the idea of adding any feminine frill to the place."

"If you ask me, a good cleaning would be a start," Bob retorted.

Both Maisie and Benny laughed while Esther got busy rubbing her face against the soft part of Maisie's leg.

"Cleaning is first on the list. I already hired a crew to come in after hours. Same ones I use at the village. Well, enough about me. How are you, Benny? Getting all the help you need here from Bob. You're in good hands." Benny dismissed the image of a handsome man hugging Maisie as a friendly business gesture.

"Yes, thank you for asking. Bob's been really helpful. I wouldn't be as far along as I am without his help."

"I'm going to have a look-see for some mini carns. I think they'll do the trick, Maisie." Bob hurried off and let the two continue talking.

"I've been meaning to knock on your door but didn't want to seem forward," Benny spoke softly, appearing slightly embarrassed at committing an oversight.

"You're welcome anytime. No one stands on ceremony in this neck of the woods," Maisie responded with a broad smile that disarmed Benny even more.

"Oh, of course not. I mean that's neighborly in the nicest way. Well, what I wanted to suggest was our either going out to dinner or you coming over for some veggie burgers on the grill and potato salad as a side. Or anything you like."

"Oh, are you a vegetarian? I put an egg in the cornbread."

"Well, part-time at least. I try to be sensitive to Esther. Not eating animals in her presence, although frankly I think becoming a real vegetarian might do me good along with the planet. Esther and I watch the *Discovery* channel a lot." Benny hadn't a clue what he had said might be construed as eccentric.

Maisie again felt her life take on a surreal aspect when imagining a man and his cat watching television together. Perhaps, she should rethink her interest in Benny. She couldn't possibly compete with someone as gorgeous as Esther. Never mind, the cat had years to tunnel her way into Benny's heart with the intention of staying there for the duration.

They both glanced down at Esther who at this point had her arms wrapped around Maisie's leg, purring. "Well, perhaps we should go to a restaurant. Might be more private. Would you like to go out somewhere, or am I being presumptuous?" Benny appeared ridden with doubts. Maisie decided to give him a try.

"Yes, I would love to go to dinner with you. I know a place with a lake front view if I may make a recommendation."

"I'm grateful if you do. How about Saturday later in the afternoon, maybe take a walk if you're inclined? Whatever you want." Benny could hear himself prattling on like a lovesick schoolboy.

Bob interrupted, "Lots of minis. Just let me know how many you need and when, I'll put some aside." He seemed pleased with his announcement. In fact, everyone seemed pleased and parted ways smiling at each other, except Esther who was reluctant to let go of Maisie's leg.

Maisie stopped at Duke's on her way home to measure the space and make a list of everyone she needed to contract in order to have the place ship shape in two weeks. She liked giving herself deadlines. Working inside a flow chart felt comfortable in its orderliness. Her entire life drifted by like one long flow chart. She remembered all the men she loved and left with only paintings to show for their good time. Her love flowed freely and then moved sweetly into a period of entertaining the coffee drinkers and the intoxicated listeners, hanging onto the melody drifting from her violin. Images appearing from the past caused her to hum a little tune at the recollections. Finally, she settled down at *Lost in Sunshine* and built a small house that fit the confines of her desires. She seemed pleased at her life and when viewed objectively, she could see it was lived fully in decades of productivity that left her feeling good on the front steps of *Duke's Rye Bar* about to take another turn into the future. Life always had a way of handing her delightful surprises. She saw herself as a fortunate woman.

She walked easily into the bar and glanced around the large front room full of booths and bar stools. She asked a waiter to take her to the backroom. She expected to see musty, cramped quarters with a round table in the middle cluttered with poker chips. Instead, she walked into an expansive room with windows across the side and back walls, French doors opening onto a brick patio with a few wooden chairs circa 1950s scattered about the edge of a creek running along the back of the building. Two weeping willow trees and a blue heron stood nearby looking like a painting removed from the *Expressionist* period. Maisie's ideas jumped onto her flow chart and mingled till they turned into an enchanting tearoom spilling onto the brick patio shaded by tiny leaves moving gently in a soft breeze.

"What're ya thinkin', Maisie?" Duke came up behind her.

"I'm thinking of taking over your backroom one day a week. You'll be pleased with the renovations and it won't interfere with the poker game you got going, 'cause you and I both know the ladies have husbands sitting at your table and these husbands want their wives happy."

"I got ya. Here's the business credit card. Knock yourself out my sweet petunia." He grinned. "Just leave the poker table some place where we can find it."

Maisie agreed and was left alone to study her surroundings. Occasionally, her thoughts landed on Benny and their Saturday afternoon date. Life couldn't be any better.

~

Benny and Esther continued to work with Bob at the nursery. Benny envisioned a small pond with some exotic fish and lily pads in the center of his gardens but didn't know how to go about creating one. While heavy in conversation, Bob's wildflowers suddenly flew into the air in a long rapid-fire succession of small charges detonated in such a way dirt and petals came down like the frogs talked about in the 'Good Book', frightening people and distressing Benny and Esther and confusing Bob. He ran to the gardens to look for the cause of his wildflowers exploding like rocks in a war zone.

Benny conceded it was time to talk to Earl. He dreaded the prospect of admitting he knew the woman who was terrorizing his jurisdiction. He dreaded the consequences and worried Maisie would think less of him for being associated with a loose cannon of a woman stalking him all the way to Maisie's village. He worried about Esther now hanging over his shoulder and shaking from fear. He heard the faint sounds of Earl's siren and then the man's irritating voice shouting through a megaphone telling everyone to take cover and don't leave the property until they've been questioned. Fortunately, he had parked nearby and could sneak behind a row of privet hedges to his car and move on down the road to home. He needed time to think, time to make a plan that could ease him out of his predicament with some discretion. General Howser came to mind.

ELEVEN

Maisie noticed Earl wasn't hanging around outside and cluttering up the landscape with his skulking figure. She felt sure the other residents were also relieved, although no one ever complained about it, except Bo Walker and he really didn't expect her to do anything to rectify the situation. He mentioned taking matters into his own hands if the scrawny redneck put one foot on his property line. He even mentioned letting Charlie Walker have a go at the man, although feared Earl would shoot him just for grins. He did ask Maisie to come up with one reason why that man wasn't fired from his job for being a danger to the public at large. Bo went on in this vein until exhausting himself, saying he had a gig in a couple of hours and didn't have the energy to deal with one of God's rejects. He then apologized for his rudeness, mentioned something about Charlie Walker feeling left out of the social circle. He said Manuel and Esther often trotted by his screen door while Charlie was stuck taking a time-out in his aquarium for misbehaving. "It doesn't seem fair, Maisie. Those two spending their days lolling about the grounds enjoying the same freedom as a pair of Rhode Island Reds while poor Charlie Walker is stuck behind glass watching their good time, flaunting themselves. It's a damn shame when ever'body can't git along no matter what their species." Again, he mentioned leaving but couldn't seem to let go of the source of all his aggravations. He alternated between Earl's limitations and the smug duo upsetting his reptile, working on convincing her even snakes have feelings, "Possible, Maisie, jus' damn possible snakes have souls like people do and think deep thoughts. Jus' cause they have tiny heads, don't mean they can't have big thoughts." He left Maisie to see Charlie Walker in a different light, briefly though, her mind suffered from a long day full of surprises and a demanding cat who may stand between her and the possibility of romance. Life certainly did turn around on itself often leaving a person in an uneasy state.

Maisie flung her body on the couch and let her mind drift backwards to a childhood largely spent in the company of a beautiful mother. She considered her mother a wood nymph holding her hand while they walked among the trees. Her mother insisted 'they can hear us, Maisie.

They can hear the quiet chatter of our voices marveling over their elegant branches and a drapery of leaves that shade our house in a green silk canopy of tranquility. It's all God's doing, Maisie, and we should be grateful every single day we weren't born in Siberia or some such place where nature turns cold or sometimes dies altogether like in the Sahara Desert'. Maybe people looked at them like hillbillies, but her mother was convinced they were indeed the luckiest people to be living on 'God's green earth' where nature danced and people could enjoy the wildlife scampering alongside the heels of their shoes.

Recollections of her mother always brought sadness to her heart when dwelling on the most tender-hearted woman living every moment expressing gratitude for all that had been given to her. When a child, Maisie glanced around their house and saw chipped dishes, two broken burners on the stove, and a clothesline that sagged from Monday's washing. The gate to their yard always creaked when opened and the bottom step lost a couple of nails and had to be propped up by bricks. Even the house leaned sideways, and the front porch looked tired from years of neglect and a futile attempt at trying to appear happy under the burden of wood rot. Maisie thought her mother saw the world through rose colored glasses, but the day she died a note laid next to her on the bed with Maisie's name written in pretty lettering at the top.

Dear Maisie,

I knowed I couldn't give yer much bein' only fifteen at the time o' yer birth but I love yer baby girl and will miss yer when I'm gone. God bless yer for bein' the best daughter a mama cud ever want. I love yer more than the moon when it shine on my pillow at night. Remember, when yer lookin' at the sky, I'll be lookin' back.

Yer Mama forever.

Doc Martin had taken care of Maisie's mother the day they found her holding a note in her hand. He gave the grief-stricken daughter a tranquilizer to calm her nerves and lessen the anguished screams of loss that echoed inside his jeep and let loose to frighten the trees once comforted by the presence of her mother. The world lost another bright light that day, and in her heart, Maisie knew she was a pale shadow of the woman who had given birth to her. Weeks turned into months and even Earl grew irritated when hearing her cry at night while making his rounds. When he complained to Doc about doing something to make her stop crying. Doc asked, "How close were you to her window?"

"Well, close enough, I reckon, to hear her but watching for any lowlifes hanging around that commie commune Maisie calls *Lost in Sunshine*. They's all lost if'n you ast me. Buncha hippies past their prime. That's what they is. Gonna come to a bad end, yer watch and see. No good comes when people decides they need to live off grid."

Doc shook his head in frustration but his thoughts wandered over to Maisie with sympathy. He increased her antianxiety pills in hopes it would alleviate the pain of loss. He remembered the day a little girl came to his office, all skin and bones with a large belly ready to give the world a little tow-headed baby who smiled when she was born and was the spitting image of her mother. They always looked like sisters, he recalled. The little girl had no parents, her baby's father did a runner, leaving her with nothing but a hand-me-down shack from her gramma and a heart that embraced the beauty of her surroundings with wonderment. Even through a bout of cancer, the woman never lost her smile. She talked sweetly to those around her about God living everywhere and even inside of us if only we would close our eyes and wait for him to appear and take us back to the glory of our original home. The woman never went to church but instead sat on a tree stump in the front yard for hours communing with the one who gave her so many blessings that filled her heart to the brim and then let it overflow onto other people, most especially the pretty little daughter gliding through the air on a swing tied to a tree branch. Doc brushed his tears aside and went about his business of curing people.

Meanwhile, Maisie let go of her past and brought Benny back as a prospective companion of some sort. She allowed her intuition to take over in order to keep the man somewhere nearby to examine him for flaws. So far, Esther presented the only obstacle to a lovely romance and the possibility for permanence. Benny's face passed by her line of vision, a rugged but lovely face expressing tenderness every time he glanced in her direction. She wondered if he had a story and also worried the baggage from his early years might be too hard for him to carry with a woman thrown in the mix that would require satisfaction. Afterall, Maisie thought, it had been a long time and she was suddenly aware that waiting for the right man had become a tedious business. Her intuition told her Benny was the right man and somehow she and Esther would work out their differences. Fortunately, Maisie could tune into the cat's thoughts and right now knew she had become caught up by her friendship with Manuel and was enjoying the freedom of living off leash around the compound. Except, for the constant complaints of the neighbors interfering with her solitude and vying for her Cat-Dad's attention, she found life to be a peaceful respite from the loneliness she endured when Cat-Dad would be gone for hours earning a living to put fancy food in her bowl. She was a cat who lacked gratitude but beautiful in her adornment. Perhaps, looking at Esther's natural beauty would always be a reminder of her mother's belief beauty only made itself seen to the most discerning eye. Yes, Esther could serve as her reminder and an opportunity to practice patience. Maisie sighed and let the world enfold her in the most delightful daydreams of desire.

TWELVE

Benny's nerves took a beating every time his mind imagined an intimate dinner with Maisie. His dreams of finding a loving woman in his future may come true if he doesn't ruin it by talking about Esther too much, confessing to being stalked by the unknown terrorist, or mentioning he had spent his adult life blowing up things instead of gardening, which he now discovered comforted his soul like a hand reaching from a passing cloud patting him on the back, and reassuring him he really does have value. He began to understand his mother's inclination to putter in the garden singing Leonard Cohen songs with the same gusto as a prima donna. How his father loved sitting on the backsteps listening to her sing. "Voice like an angel," he would often say, but to Benny she sounded like a gruffer version of the balladeer himself. Remembering his father's happiness lifted his spirits, but he wasn't ready to talk about his parents to anyone, not even a therapist as suggested by his sad sergeant when delivering the news.

Finally, Saturday arrived sending him to the closet in search of something nice but not too formal and not too casual. Actually, he hadn't a clue what to wear in the heat of the southern sun so decided on linen slacks and a loose silk shirt in a soft rose color that set off his silver hair and tan face. Esther watched him with great interest. She knew exactly where Cat-Dad was going and assumed she was going with him. She went straight to her basket to rummage for her leash and once found, she dropped it at Benny's feet only to be disgruntled by his laughter.

"Not tonight, Esther. You be a good kitty and I'll bring you back a doggie bag." He bent down and fluffed up her hair, a loving gesture she had always appreciated until now. She felt betrayed. People always think lesser of animals than they do of each other, which is a joke in most animal circles when considering humans are the ones intent on destroying the very world they inhabit. The inner recesses of the human mind were fraught with chaos and a mess of contradictions, Esther thought, when hearing her own Cat-Dad mention the words doggie bag. It ruined the appeal of a midnight treat. She found the human world to be dog centric and pondered how they ever came to the conclusion dogs were the superior pet, perhaps because they were more amiable, gave slobbering unconditional love, and fetched. She concluded these attributes reflected badly on how little it took to make a human happy. They preferred blind obedience to intelligence and subservience to beauty. Esther jumped on the big bed and turned her back to Benny's gentle goodnight and his closing the door lightly so as not to disturb her.

Benny's worrisome thoughts over leaving Esther in a sad state disappeared when seeing Maisie step onto her front porch wearing a buttery linen shift with a small silk rose attached to the edge of its Nehru collar along with a green crystal bead necklace spilling nearly to her waist. He saw a vision of loveliness and caught himself staring at her like a love-struck lion, which nearly caused him to roar, but instead he settled down and opened the car door for her, silently purring in the process.

"You'll have to give me directions," he said, but again he lost his mental bearings and began to stammer.

"Go to the end of the lane and turn left for four miles and then right onto Lakeside Road." Maisie continued with a light patter of words in hopes of putting Benny at ease. She picked up on the low level of worry he kept well-hidden from those around him. His father would often say, 'Lighten up son, life is a beautiful place to be'.

Once they were seated on the veranda surrounded by a lovely view of the lake, Benny sighed with contentment while staring at the shimmer from the fading sun cast on the water. He turned his attention to Maisie and gazed at the prettiest face he had ever seen, with lips full and pink, a broad smile and perfectly pointed nose similar to a movie star's only with more distinction. He could fall in love at that very moment of absorption in the beauty of a woman he knew he had met before if only in his dreams or a past life scenario mystics hold forth as a place where we can walk freely from one realm to another.

Benny remembered his mother pontificating at the dinner table on the joys of the mystical realms inviting us to visit anytime we could sit still and rest in the divine spirit who carries our burdens and only asks that we remember where we came from. His father held onto her every word and beamed with the possibility they would always be together. "And you my little rosebud, will you take me with you when you go?" She kissed his hand with enthusiasm and replied, "Of course, my darling, how could I ever live without you. Even my soul yearns for the constancy of your companionship. And surely God will absorb our love into his." They smiled at each other causing Benny much unease at being in the midst of an intimate moment not intended to include him. Even the meaning of their words was foreign to him and the possibility of them going off to yonder world rendered his heart a useless thing barely beating underneath his polo shirt. Now, he found himself discovering such a love was possible if only Maisie saw him with the same urgency as his parents expressed toward each other on a daily basis.

"Thank you for inviting me to dinner. It's beautiful here." Maisie raised her water glass and touched Benny's glass with a light clink. He smiled and did likewise.

"What's good here? Do you have a favorite?" Benny asked and waited for Maisie to glance up from her menu. Her brows furrowed causing her to appear deep in thought.

"Actually, I've never been here but heard great things about it. I'm glad we came. What a lovely view. We're fortunate. Don't you think?" She beamed.

"Yes, very fortunate." Naturally, Benny considered being with Maisie his good fortune and Maisie thought of all the choices on the menu. It would take the entire summer to taste the sauces alone, she mused.

The waiter appeared with a wine menu and asked if they would like to begin with an appetizer. Maisie said, "The Alsatian cheese tart looks good." Benny agreed and they both decided on a Hampton Water Rosé.

"Benny, how are you and Esther getting along with your neighbors. It must be a little bit exhausting meeting all new people when you're used to living in the same house your entire life. I remember you told me on the phone when you called to inquire. I have lived in many places so was captivated by the notion of being born in a house and never leaving until suddenly it seems like a good idea. Seems like the time. Am I close? I don't want to intrude." Maisie's smile caught hold of Benny's breath and left him nearly speechless for an answer.

"I was a few days away from retirement, when I glanced at one of my mother's magazines and saw this pretty village that said 'tiny house available'. I was smitten by the possibility of romance. I'm sorry. That sounded silly. I mean it seemed time for a change and there wasn't anything tying me to Boston, and I also thought Esther might like the warmer weather." A quick recollection of what he had just said brought the word 'mother' uppermost to his mind. In his effort not to mention Esther, he mentioned his mother and her magazines. How was he going to tell Maisie he kept up Mrs. Professor Swan's subscription to *Better Homes & Gardens*?

"Oh yes, one of the reporters at *Better Homes*

& Gardens was here last summer taking photos and asking numerus and personal questions. Most of our residents came to get away from something or find peace of mind off the beaten path. Needless to say, they were upset when discovering their homes had been featured in a home décor magazine, especially Bo Walker." Maisie glanced up from her appetizer and smiled at Benny.

He nearly melted from seeing his reflection in her bright blue eyes, knowing her smile could mean anything and then immediately his mind jumped to the last image of Esther sleeping in the middle of the big bed. How would she take to his bringing home a woman? Would she consider Maisie competition for his affection or would she be the affable cat he snuggled at night while watching the *Discovery Channel* reruns?

"Bo Walker? Charlie's dad. Oh, he appears rough around the edges but still seems a nice sort. I can understand his wanting to live a quiet life, although musicians are by nature performers so would think he'd consider it good marketing. Being pictured in a display for *Better Homes & Gardens* wearing his *Daddy Guitar Band* T-shirt."

Maisie laughed out loud. "You would think but he's an odd one. Kind, though. Cares deeply about animals despite his snake's tendency to give over-zealous hugs to Manuel." She laughed again.

"Yes, I noticed. I don't want to come off as prissy, but he does need a good scrub once in a while and the tobacco stain? It doesn't come off with a little soap and water?" Benny enjoyed the appetizer and made a mental note to put some aside for Esther. Asking for two servings seemed a brilliant idea in retrospect.

"Some of us are from the hills, so we grew up with rough men and don't give it much consideration," Maisie responded.

"Oh, I'm so sorry I was being critical, and frankly I'm not sure what growing up in the hills has to do with not bathing."

"We were poor and got our water from a spring when the rains were plentiful. During a drought, we saved what water we could get for drinking." Maisie heard herself sounding defensive and regretted the words the minute they fell off her tongue.

Benny put his hand over hers and gazed into her eyes. She was overwhelmed by his tenderness and wiped away a tear threatening to spill onto her linen dress. "I was being unkind and spoke out of turn. Mr. Walker is a nice man and doesn't deserve my criticism. I hope you'll forgive me." A tear slipped onto the tablecloth. The waiter handed her a napkin.

"No, you weren't really. It's just that sometimes I miss my mama who died in those hills where I grew up, knowing she would walk miles to bring me a glass of water. How about your mama? Did you learn to garden from her? Will she be visiting us?" Maisie collected herself and continued on what she considered to be a lighter note.

"Oh, no, sorry I gave you the wrong impression. My parents passed away when I was nineteen. I don't know why I haven't cancelled their magazine subscriptions, except well, I've learned a lot from my dad's *Fine Woodworking* magazine over the years. He looked forward to retirement and starting a full-time woodworking business. Several of his pieces were featured at *The Workbench Gallery*." He prattled on without curtailing his anxiety over the flood of recollections that came rushing back to him. Beautiful memories and expectations that would never be. He grew sad. Maisie took his hand in hers and caressed it gently to alleviate the pain.

"I'm so sorry. Perhaps, we should order and when finished go for a nice walk around the lake. They have a garden path and all sorts of charming wildlife." She made an effort to brighten the atmosphere. Benny nodded in agreement and soon they found themselves walking and laughing together like old friends becoming new lovers.

Later, Benny spent the night dreaming of Maisie settling in his and Esther's life with the ease of a butterfly landing on an Amazonian tree leaf. He overestimated the size of his tiny house and never worked out the exact living arrangements, especially when hearing Maisie say she was going to the shelter soon to pick out a puppy needing a home. They would have to toss around some ideas for joining households where everyone finds a comfortable nook adding to the harmony of melodic love. His dreams continued into the night in this sweet-honey fashion until being interrupted by gunshots and a woman screaming. Esther leaped to the windowsill and Benny tossed on his linen pants and ran out the front door to see Earl dragging away Mateo and Bonita.

THIRTEEN

Benny saw Maisie in the distance running toward Hugo who was coming back from the lake with Manuel. She swept him up in her arms at the same time Earl began to drive away with the people pretending to be Hugo's parents handcuffed in the backseat of Earl's patrol car. Benny ran after Earl's car and jumped on the hood just as he was about to make a grand exit. Earl slammed on the brakes to shake him loose but Benny held onto the wipers, ripping them both off before hitting the ground.

"God damn you Yankee piece o' shit. You got no bidness vandalizing poleece property." Earl yanked the wipers from Benny and examined his car for scratches.

"Where are you taking them?" Benny demanded.

"Thar illegals and are 'bout to be kicked back to where they come from. Now git out the way fer I shoot yer." Earl waved his gun around and just for grins shot a hole in the nearest tree, which brought Bo and Charlie Walker out of their cabin in an angry mood. Bo's gig last night ended abruptly in a fight, a tiresome event, especially when he and his boys weren't even midway through the first set before tempers flared from too many beers and too little sense.

"Damn it, Earl. Yer disturbin' the peace. You ain't above the law." Bo bent down and looked in the backseat. Charlie hung from his neck and also appeared curious.

"Like I said to the Yankee. Thar illegals and are goin' back to whar they come from." Bo stepped back when realizing the gravity of things.

Everyone's thoughts leaned in the direction of Hugo and wondered why Earl had overlooked the little boy. The second Earl pulled out of the driveway, the residents came together to comfort Hugo but he didn't appear upset.

"I have papers." He reached inside his back pocket, pulled out a neatly folded envelope and handed it to Benny. While Benny looked over Hugo's papers, Maisie admired his well-toned chest, a man you could call buff. Her mind wandered to a large bed where they laid together but quickly shook the image and returned to the distressing business at hand.

"He was born here to different parents," Maisie said.

"Yes, si, Senor Benny. They take my madre and padre in Florida where we live on the beach. Mateo and Bonita found me and they pretend to be my parents. But I miss my own." Maisie put Hugo down but held onto his hand, understanding the boy's grief occurred a year ago when he heard his mother scream and his father beg for the mercy of allowing his wife to stay in this beautiful country. Now, Hugo found himself alone again but this time not without friends. He, of course, included Esther and Manuel among his friends and felt Maisie and Benny to be kindred spirits who would do their best by him. Hugo was not afraid and took Benny's hand in his and stared into his eyes.

"Would you and Manuel like to stay with Esther and me until we can get things sorted out?" He sat on his heels to be at eye level with Hugo. The little boy threw his arms around Benny and even Manuel licked his bare feet. Bo offered to move some of Hugo's belongings into Benny's house. Maisie created a small private area where she arranged his dresser and twin bed. She brought a rice paper screen from her cottage adding a touch of privacy and also enhanced Hugo's space with a handmade quilt and a few decorator pillows that added a homey touch to the back corner of Benny's living room.

Esther could tolerate everyone being in her territory except the reptile hanging from their neighbor's neck. She hissed with such vehemence

Bo tossed Charlie Walker out the door where he could be seen slithering back home. Soon Manuel, Esther, and Hugo settled on his bed and played together. The adults stepped outside to discuss a permanent solution.

Benny thought for a moment before saying, "I can hire an immigration lawyer to help track down Hugo's parents. I mean if everyone agrees. I may be able to work out a sponsorship arrangement to keep his parents here and start the visa process." Maisie and Bo were awestruck by his generosity, but they did not really know their new neighbor learned kindness from his parents and often lived with what he and his father called 'mom's strays' when referring to a steady stream of strangers ensconced on their downstairs' couch. Most of these strays were foreign students short on money and filled with fright until coming under the loving umbrella of the Swan family where they too learned the meaning of kindness. Taking in Hugo held little weight for Benny except doing right by a fellow human being and his dog. Maisie now watched him with more than a casual interest. Perhaps, she could put her concerns over Esther's willful nature aside and learn to share the man who would fit nicely in her future.

"Why don't I whip us all up somethin' for breakfast. We can eat on my front porch. I already made a pot of coffee and a pitcher of iced tea." Everyone agreed to be there in half an hour. Bo alone could drink the entire pot and Benny looked forward to being in Maisie's company. Tomorrow he would search for a good attorney and start the process of uniting Hugo's family. He noticed the empty trailer where Bonita and Mateo once lived, considering whether or not to buy it with the hopes Hugo could remain in his own home.

Meanwhile, Maisie dialed Earl and began barking at him the minute she heard his voice. "You and I go back a long way. I know your secrets. People would be interested in that little honey you had on the side while Laverne was in rehab recovering from a car accident caused by your lackadaisical attitude toward car maintenance." Brake fluid dribbled from the lining while Mrs. Earl Hubbard was driving down a steep hill. The poor woman never made it to the bottom. Took town locals an hour to retrieve her from the wreckage.

"What you want, Maisie?" Earl sounded scared.

"I want you to take your passengers to their sister in Jacksonville. I have the address. I expect it to be done by nighttime."

"Not sure 'bout that Maisie. Immigration comin' tomorrow to pick 'em up. 'Sides yer astin' me to commit a crime." Earl sounded hard done by but realized he hadn't much of a leg to stand on when hearing Maisie laughing on the other end of the line. "Ok, but don't be tellin' nobody. Makes me look weak." Maisie agreed and a few minutes later she told her guests Mateo and Bonita would be living with her sister in Jacksonville. The news made breakfast taste better and the day unfold with an easy Sunday peacefulness that would cause a duck to smile while floating on a sun speckled pond.

~

Attorney Jones explained the immigration laws and loopholes, and ways of sponsoring Hugo's parents, who they had no doubt been stashed in a detention center this past year. The attorney expounded on all the people requiring payment to locate Hugo's parents and then to extract them from their current place of residence. Benny indicated he could absorb the cost of greasing the palms of government officials to bring Hugo's parents back into their son's life. Attorney Jones smiled and continued explaining the process of sponsorship. It seemed all Benny would have to do is provide them with employment and a place to live while waiting for their papers to be processed, which might take several years and more money depending on the expediency of the local bureaucrats. Benny understood what the attorney implied but didn't realize his own representative would be skimming off the top. He thought Jones's exorbitant hourly fee to be more than fair. Benny's naivete was a charming attribute for a man who had carried dynamite and nitroglycerine in his toolbox every day for twenty-five years and never blinked an eye when a building landed in the dust of its own rubble.

Attorney Jones went over the profiles of the local investigators, each charging upwards of five-hundred dollars an hour plus expenses. Once again, the crooked attorney failed to mention he took a cut of the investigator's fee as was common in what Maisie called her 'neck of the woods'. Naturally, it was also common in Benny's neck of the woods, it being where graft abounded and the taxpayer lived in ignorance as a government victim.

Benny had no idea how to choose an investigator but thought a former police officer in Miami as well as being an ex-Marine in Iraq might be up to the task, especially when he noted in his file the investigator mentioned he loved dogs and meditated two hours a day, was a vegetarian, could bench press two hundred pounds, and was also happily married to a man named Cecil with two children under the age of ten. He sounded perfect, the sensitive sort with a black belt in martial arts also helped Benny make the decision to hire Neil. Jones groaned silently. Neil resented having his paycheck dismantled before he received it by the nefarious attorney but figured all attorneys were alike so continued taking work from him. Neil really did lead an exemplary life and only became an investigator to help people much like a social worker, only more hands on.

The two men shook in a gentlemanly fashion once Benny handed Jones a sizeable retainer fee. Jones promised to put Neil on the task immediately without knowing his availability. He figured if Neil was too busy, he would use a more affable investigator without bothering his client with the details. Fortunately, Neil was available and eager to bring together a small family, which he figured would take two days' work and five thousand in expenses. Neil always tucked Jones's fee in his own bill without feeling a twinge of guilt. Afterall, he had a family to support and never liked denying Cecil and the children anything their hearts desired. Next month, they intended to visit Alaska.

Once finished, Benny hurried to Maisie's cottage to pick up Hugo and Manuel. She greeted him with a smile and Hugo jumped into his arms while holding the tiny Chihuahua.

"Any problems?" Benny asked.

"No, mostly we pulled weeds in the flower gardens and drank lemonade in the gazebo. Also, Bob arrived to put in a small lily pond. Sounds lovely. I had no idea your garden was going to have a water feature. How delightful. All that's missing is a Mexican chimenea." She giggled, a sweet sound to Benny's ears but his sentimental lapse was interrupted by Hugo's squeals with delight.

"Senor Benny, my madre used to roast marshmallows in our chimenea. So delicious for the senor," Hugo responded.

Caught up in their enthusiasm, Benny agreed to talk to Bob about it. "Do you have your key, Hugo?"

"Yes." The little boy pulled out the chain around his neck and showed Benny the key to his house.

"Okay, good. Would you and Manuel check on Esther and make sure she has enough water and is happy today?"

"Oh, si, it is best to keep Esther a happy kitty. She can be grumpy as a desert gator." Hugo ran off leaving Benny stumped over the meaning of a desert gator.

"Means alligator among other things. I would discourage him from using the term. Not particularly complimentary." Maisie frowned and then asked Benny to come and sit on the porch to enjoy a glass of iced tea. He couldn't think of a place he would rather be. He told her about his meeting with the attorney looking hopeful, although more involved than he had originally thought it would be, so he didn't want to get Hugo's hopes up and went on to say, he was without a plan B, except to adopt the boy himself if all else failed. Maisie didn't have the heart to tell him the slower the process, the more money those involved made at his expense, but the end result would no doubt be the safe return of Hugo's parents.

FOURTEEN

Benny surveyed the attached acre and looked for ways of blending the two lots together while allowing the main gardens to appear friendly but separate for everyone to enjoy. He spoke to Bob about adding a chimenea. Bob suggested designing a stone grill island fired with liquid propane, which could be nicely placed on a matching stone patio directly behind Benny's house. He also suggested Benny invest in Brown Jordan patio furniture. Anytime Benny heard the word invest when referring to an object, he knew it was going to be expensive. He didn't want Maisie sitting on a chaise lounge made of plastic webbing, but he had noticed she was a downhome woman with simple but refined tastes. He considered making his own furniture as a surprise for Maisie but knew his skill level was amateurish. He recalled his father promising to teach him when Benny returned from the service with a view toward one day hanging out a sign saying Swan & Son. Benny liked the idea of working alongside his father for the rest of his life, but his dreams were cut short and his hope of enjoying the company of his parents into their ripe old age ended the day his sergeant wept all over his army issue shirt. The memory laid heavy on his heart and to this day he suppresses a tear whenever seeing a sign with '& son' written on it.

Benny's father, being an enthusiastic man, had already visited the local sign maker and given him a pencil drawing and a calligraphy book with his choice of lettering circled in green ink. The package arrived the day after his parents' funeral. Benny wept inside the backyard shed underneath his father's sign that he had mounted on the wall as a tribute to a man of dreams. The beautiful hand-carved sign turned to ashes in Elena's dramatic attention-seeking implosion. His mother was right about Elena. She lacked refinement, unlike Maisie, who now had a firm grip on his heart and an easy way of assuaging his grief. Listening to her sweet voice and the melodious pull of her nightly lullabies covered him in moondust glistening through his bedroom window. Even Esther purred with contentment.

The following week, Hugo and his amigos, as the little boy liked referring to Esther and Manuel, followed Benny all over the gardens surveying the work that needed to be done if they were to erect a partial wrought iron fence to separate the properties and add a costly stone barbecue grill to his little oasis. Benny took a mental peek at his bank account, which included a large inheritance, 401K, savings, Fidelity investments, and Esther's trust fund. Satisfied, he ordered the Jordan Brown patio furniture and succumbed to all of Bob's suggestions on the extensive yet practical beautification project. Hugo enjoyed the words beautification project. Benny overheard him expound in great detail to his two amigos on the 'beautification project' unaware their eyes had glazed over, but out of politeness the pair remained seated until the little boy finished keeping them in the loop, another term he also used frequently when talking to Manuel and Esther.

Benny's life had now become a magical place to be. He put together a makeshift family, found himself frequenting an expensive beauty salon, and using hair products to keep himself stylish in the way of a *Gentleman's Quarterly* model. Esther smirked when noticing Cat-Dad's hair rivaled her own in color and perfection. She considered humans to be fussy creatures without taste and a tendency toward cheap opulence. Maisie often tuned into Esther's thought processes and was amused by her knack for combining words like smugness and oxymoron resulting in a comical outcome. Sometimes, Esther could hear her laughing.

Benny remained clueless the two females in his life tuned into their private grapevine to natter about unimportant things: Benny's industrious nature, Charlie Walker's whereabouts, and the police chief poking his head above the tree line bent on being an annoyance for no apparent reason.

Several neighbors viewed Benny as a capable man and took him aside to ask if he would carry Charlie Walker on a stick all the way to the woods on the other side of the lake. This sounded like a dangerous task to Benny, so he politely declined, but suggested they ask the police chief lurking not thirty feet away. He watched them hurry in Earl's direction but then found himself worrying about Charlie Walker being shot. Since taking to the road, Benny noticed the amount of violence surrounding him had increased considerably, which caused him to spend some time stewing over damage control. Something would have to be done about Elena and Earl's constant presence. It was beginning to make him anxious.

He joined Bob and together they studied the plans to an eight-foot by ten-foot backyard lily pond. Bob had suggested buying a kit rather than purchasing the parts individually to make it easier and also the desirability of having a warranty in case the pump or skimmer didn't work properly or the lining ripped after a harsh winter, which rarely happened in the Southern hemisphere but Bob liked to keep his customers happy and free from worry. Besides that, he enjoyed Benny's easy-going manner and found himself amused by his relationship with Esther. None of his other customers had ever arrived at the nursery with a cat on the end of a leash. The two men shook hands and exchanged pleasantries.

"I see you started already." Benny appeared lighter than air, which Bob noticed and wondered if there had been a new development with his love life. He had also noticed the way Benny tipped backwards a few degrees every time Maisie appeared within viewing range. Bob, although married, succumbed to Maisie's charm and often found himself feeling lighter when in her presence.

"Yes, digging the hole is the most labor-intensive part of putting together one of these ponds."

"Shall, I help?" Benny asked.

"Actually, I need you to draw a sketch of how you would like the rocks to be arranged around the pond and what plants you think would enhance the overall look. We can build a slight incline on one side to give it some depth and mix the size of the rocks from pebbles to ocean boulders. Using different shades like pink and gradations of grey granite would make for a natural look." Benny retrieved his notebook he carried with him when working with Bob and jotted down his instructions. It was a habit left over from his government employment, although he supposed it was time to invest in an iPad, something he heard one teenager say to another when standing in line at the coffee shop. A teenager using the word invest made him laugh out loud resulting in all heads turning in his direction, which prompted him to apologize, but then Benny further caught their attention when he laughed at the notion of having to apologize for laughing. His mother could lecture for an hour on *Humor and the Uptight American.* Professor's Swan's pontificating on this topic resulted in her essay being published and freely passed around the campus for all to enjoy. The students loved Professor Swan and would rush to take her classes with extraordinary enthusiasm the likes unseen by the school president.

"Are you all right, Benny?" Bob asked and was surprised at Benny's response when he admitted to missing his mother. Again, the man's unusual proclivity for being authentic gave Bob pause for a second.

"She was larger than life in all ways. Thousands of people came to my parents' funeral. It had to be held outside in the rain but nobody left and everybody cried. It was a long time ago." Bob patted him on the back and sympathized with his loss. Usually, when a person makes a sad confession, the listener feels the need to sympathize by telling an equally daunting story proving a useless way of cheering up the one telling the original story. Instead, Bob remained silent. Fortunately, Maisie, Hugo, and his two amigos, could be heard coming in their direction. Benny wiped his face on Bob's handkerchief and the two men got back to work, leaving Bob to wonder why so many people would want to go to someone's funeral and then he remembered Benny had said 'his parents' funeral' causing him to be even more curious as to why they died together.

"Hi, thought we'd bring a pitcher of tea for you boys and some cookies." Hugo passed around glasses of tea and cookies on a napkin. Maisie was teaching him manners in a fun and loving sort of way. Even Esther seemed to settle down in her presence or maybe she took such a shine to Manuel, she considered it in her best interest to curtail the diva routine and act like a regular cat. Benny made these observations while sniffing Maisie who smelled like honeysuckle, such was her sweetness.

FIFTEEN

Esther and Manuel spent the heat of the day lying near the screen door where they caught a breeze from the weeping willow tree nearby. Esther found herself lost in the swaying branches empty of thoughts and lazing in a moment of pure pleasure. Peacefulness was a place she rarely went lately what with adjusting to the new house guests, which was further aggravated by Manuel snoring most nights. She studied the movement of the leaves when suddenly noticing Charlie Walker's tiny eyes staring back at her. Charlie had been a lonely guy since being banned from the grounds. He harbored no ill will toward Manuel but had to admit to being afraid of Esther's nasty temper. Addled from flash backs when remembering the time her claws sank into his tender skin, he thought for sure he was now suffering from PTSD.

When Manuel opened his eyes and saw his nemesis staring at him from a tree branch, he threw an arm around Esther, buried his face in her fur and began whimpering. In a flash, Esther stretched her body full length against the screen with her claws grabbing hold of the lightweight mesh ready to yank it out of its frame to have a go at Charlie Walker. He slithered back down the tree and up to the screen door where he rested on his midsection within full view of his neighbors, who by now had worked themselves into a frenzy but didn't know quite what to do with their state of befuddlement over being nose to nose with a needy reptile. Up close, he looked harmless, pathetic even, Esther thought, when hearing him beg to hang out with them, also asking why she found him to be such an objectionable creature when he considered himself to be a good-looking snake with a kind heart but had to admit wrapping himself around Manuel probably wasn't a gentlemanly thing to do, especially knowing the poor dog suffered from an anxiety disorder that really should be treated with holistic medicine. When hearing Charlie Walker babble on in such a self-introspective manner, Esther nearly opened the screen door and let him inside, but then Manuel began to sob, bringing Hugo to check on the little dog. He shooed the snake away and carried Manuel to his bed where he gently tucked him under his coverlet hoping it would make him feel safe. Hugo empathized with his dog. He, too, had never rested easy in his own circumstances and was dependent on the generosity of Benny and Maisie. The little boy came to the sad conclusion at age six, living the good life was never a sure thing.

~

Maisie threw herself into high gear preparing Duke's backroom for their first Ladies' Tea. She had a small tasteful sign made to direct the customers, who would rather avoid entering the bar, down a path around the side of the building where they could enter the backroom through French doors, installed by her contractor who also painted the interior and hung flowery wallpaper above the wainscoting. The small round tables covered with linen tablecloths were set with fine China and the poker table had been placed in the corner for parties of six to eight, also covered in linen. Maisie had ordered an Italian espresso maker complete with milk steamer, along with individual China teapots that held two cups of tea for those who preferred tea to fancy coffee drinks. Mary Lou, a townie working at the local coffee shop, agreed to come by every Friday afternoon and act as their barista while Maisie played sweet melodies on her violin designed to soothe the nerves of her customers who had untold chores and rancorous husbands to deal with all week and wanted nothing more than a respite with their own gender so they could benefit from a boost in their serotonin levels along with some oxytocin thrown in for love. Even the patio looked inviting for those who preferred to sit creek side and enjoy a riparian afternoon where solace could be found.

Opening day turned out to be a festive occasion with the exception of Duke sticking his head inside the door and asking everyone if they were having a good time. The room turned silent and even Maisie stopped playing her violin to stare at the man who thought he had a right to interrupt the Ladies' Tea. Afterall, he considered it was only due to his good-natured generosity they had a place to meet. Actually, Duke never did like to be left out of anybody's good time, which is why he opened the bar in the first place. Once feeling the chilliness in the air, he quietly closed the door and asked his female bartender to hand-deliver the individual treat bags filled with chocolate and locally baked cupcakes with *Duke's Rye Bar* written on the top in pink icing. Everyone calmed down and let their hearts be softened by an edgy male trying to get in touch with his feminine side. Duke, on the other hand, knew it was in his best interest to keep the wives of the poker players happy and if that meant letting them have their privacy, well so be it.

He appreciated Maisie's transformation of his backroom but did think it leaned slightly on the frilly side.

Later that evening, Benny asked Maisie numerous questions about her first tea, mostly wanting to know if she enjoyed herself. She did, which made him happy, although like Duke, he too, would have preferred to be there to watch everyone having a good time. However, understanding the concept of boundaries, he never once suffered the inclination to poke his head where it didn't belong. Working alongside a group of testy females had taught him to go silent and pretend to be invisible while they insulted every male walking within yelling distance.

An hour later, he received a call from the chief of police about a request to pay bail for a 'long-lost friend'. In his excitement, Earl had gone straight into mountaineer-speak, confusing Benny, which prompted him to tell Earl he needed to make a few phone calls to settle the matter without it becoming front page news. Earl conceded to keep Elena locked up before pressing any charges, but thought the scrawny bitch needed a good slap upside the head. Benny agreed without saying as much, but asked Earl to be patient that the matter would be resolved soon. He quickly made a call to the General's office. He had kept the number on speed dial in case this very situation arose where he would be at a loss to explain why a potential felon was wreaking havoc in his life.

General Howser's assistant understood removing Elena from police custody in exchange for another stint in the army could work to their advantage. He put the old General on speaker phone, allowing him to hear the gravity of the situation being an opportunity to add an explosives expert to his arsenal. The old 'five-star' yelled into the speaker phone at Benny, "Hold tight Benny boy, I'll have my assistant put together the paperwork and gas up the army jet. We'll be down to extract our asset from the town jail in no time. Good job there."

"Thanks, General. I know you're short-handed and am glad to help." A sense of lightness overcame Benny when weighing what it meant to be relieved of the constant threat to his new romance.

An indiscernible heaviness had settled on him the day the old General paid him a visit at his final implosion. It had taken three months to prepare the building and three thousand sticks of dynamite. Elena and two others worked on the job under him, but she found it difficult to take orders and became a constant nuisance to him and a threat to everyone nearby. Benny had never met anyone with rage so intense, it was an effort for her to exchange pleasantries. He heard the men say 'hello Elena' in passing only to be called a 'buncha tiny-dick losers' by a delicate-boned female. Finally, he took her aside and told her the harassment laws applied to women, too, and if she didn't treat her coworkers with respect, he would write her up and then fire her after the second warning. His words stung Elena. She had always considered him a handsome mama's boy, underestimated his inherent strength, and laughed at him for having a cat instead of a Rottweiler like her dog Rex.

"Thanks, General. I look forward."

"Same here, Private Swan. Over and out." The phone went silent.

Benny stood staring at it wondering if the General was firing on all of his cylinders. The phone rang.

"Sorry about that Mr. Swan. We'll be underway tomorrow and should touch down by noon with a short car ride we should be there by 1300 hours and meet you at the town jail, which I believe is under the jurisdiction of a Chief Earl Hubbard?" the assistant said.

"Yes, and thank you for calling back. I look forward to meeting you." Benny knew most titled people would be nowhere without their assistants. He appreciated the need to keep the exchange a clandestine affair but didn't know how to stick a metaphorical sock in Earl's mouth that tended toward braggadocio.

"Same here." The phone went dead again but this time Benny had a surge of confidence they would show up with the paperwork in hand.

Minutes after receiving a phone call from a government official, Earl had blustered about the precinct hollering at his officers about fast becoming a police state. "Yer mark mah words, we gonna be carryin' water fer the Man. Uncle Sam, mah ass, he's nothin' but a muthafuckah wantin' to control us common foke. That's what they callin' us up North. Send us to the front lines 'cause we'as espendables. Yeah, now they want that thar sweet little girl in our jail cell to blow up the enemy. Well, if'n yer ast me, the enemy lives right here and is comin' tomorrow to show us who's the boss o' things." Previous to the phone call, Earl had referred to Elena as a dangerous bitch who ought to be locked up for good or made to be a housewife and have babies in the hills. After spending too much time on these thoughts, he decided to go have a beer and ponder why such a pretty thing would want to demolish the town garden project, Bob's Nursery, the pine tree growing in Town Square used as their sanctified Christmas tree and a tradition sacred to all good people, not to mention, the old abandoned Beatty farm house, which was an eyesore from the county road so nobody missed looking at the scrappy clapboard structure once home to the town blowhard. Earl remembered him as the bane of his existence when a small child. The old coot always called him the 'homeliest boy I ever done seed'. Earl took those words to heart and snuck in his barn one night and let his prize cow loose in the neighboring farm. A feud ensued resulting in multiple injuries and the cow being sold at auction. Things went downhill from there. But despite some heavy pondering, Earl simply couldn't grasp the subtlety of life's tendency to operate in a state of flux.

The next day, General Howser waited for his assistant to open the passenger side door to the Jeep Cherokee, the only car left at *Cut Rate Car Rental*. He considered it an inferior product and couldn't understand why a Hummer wasn't available. His request taxed the clerk's good mood and made his smile droop at the corners of his mouth. He had never seen a Hummer in these parts and thought the General must be suffering from dementia like his aged grandma who would know a Hummer was out of most people's price range and also tear up the lovely wildflowers growing along the side of the road. The clerk suggested they might want to take a taxi since they were only going to be in town for the afternoon. The assistant ignored the suggestion and said he would leave the keys in the drop box if they returned after hours.

Once the General accepted the reality of his transportation, he and two heavily armed privates made themselves comfortable for the short ride to Earl's precinct. Earl waited for them in a dark and vile mood that frightened those around him. Benny remained standing while the police chief ranted over his red, white, and blue privileges being usurped by a bunch of renegade bandits. Benny became lost in Earl's tirade and tuned out for several minutes, long enough for the four military men to enter the small office where Earl sat at a large desk cleaning his gun. He had never served in any of the armed forces and for a second nearly weakened at the knees when being surrounded by brass and camouflage causing him to feel caught up in guerrilla warfare.

"So, which one of yer, is gonna pay the little girl's bail?" Earl snarled.

Benny cringed and the assistant stepped up and said, "We're assuming you had the intelligence not to charge her with a crime so no need for bail. We will forget you brought up the matter. Although, we do have some papers for you to sign releasing her into our custody." The assistant whipped out a batch of papers and laid them on Earl's desk. Yellow arrows showed Earl all the lines requiring his signature.

Meanwhile, General Howser greeted Benny respectfully, shaking hands, and smiling with his dentures on full display. Earl wondered at the connection between the two men but thought better of asking to be brought into the loop.

"Benny boy, so good to see you. Sure, we can't talk you into using your talent for our side?"

"Thank you, General, I appreciate the vote of confidence. But I'm afraid my dynamite days are behind me."

The assistant piped up, "You're a legend Mr. Swan. It's an honor to finally meet you." The two shook hands, further aggravating Earl with all the friendliness going toward someone he considered an outsider and an obstacle to the object of his affection. Naturally, his 'affection' cringed every time the man came in her line of vision. Earl suffered from a vivid imagination and misplaced devotion seeing as how he had a wife. Caught up in a brief fantasy of Maisie naked by the lake, he inadvertently picked up the gun he had been cleaning and waved it about. In one swift action, his left hand laid crumpled on the pile of signed papers and a Glock was pressed against his temple.

"My boy. Watch your manners. My privates will escort the prisoner to a waiting vehicle. Now! If you please," the General barked, not realizing he had offended the two soldiers and caused his assistant to hold back a snicker. "Hunker down on him. Better yet, go with him."

Benny noticed the whole affair lasted less than five minutes without any formal introduction to the police chief or respect given to the office he held. Benny almost felt sorry for him but remembered Earl played fast and loose with his power and caused Maisie to be in a state of discomfiture every time he walked the edges of her tiny village. He also wondered if Elena knew she had the right to reject the General's offer and remain in Earl's custody. She must have weighed her right to choose whether she wanted to serve time in a penitentiary or on the front lines in Afghanistan. She may have waived the right for a fair trial when realizing she would be at the mercy of an overzealous police officer who would see to it she served at least ten years for destruction of property or wrap up her offenses into a tidy bundle of domestic terrorism with the possibility of serving twenty years.

Elena appeared from her cell looking bedraggled and screaming at the two soldiers for man handling a little woman going on to say they ought to be arrested for assaulting a harmless female. Then she saw Benny, "Hey, handsome, finally got your attention. What's the matter you ain't man enough to take me on? Had to call for backup. I been watching you moon like a lovesick calf over a woman who couldn't hold a candle to what I got to offer." She laughed while struggling with the two privates who were having difficulty getting her under control without breaking something.

"Put the itty-bitty thing in shackles." The old General reached into his briefcase and pulled out enough hardware to subdue a bull. He handed them to his assistant with a self-satisfied look of a man who knew how to get things done. The privates hesitated before following orders. Soon Elena's small body was laden with fifty pounds of steel. Benny nearly found himself protesting until recalling the shed his mother loved so much being reduced to a pile of wood chips. He stepped back and let them pass.

"Well, I'll be darned if'n yer ain't a buncha bullies trussing up that little girl like she a threat to society. Nobody here's gonna miss anythin' she blowed up 'nuff to want her dragged out of our town like some kinda wild thing. I'll report yer to the authorities!" Benny admired Earl for his compassionate outburst. He wondered if this was the best solution. Maybe they could have reasoned with her without involving the military, but once again he recalled an unpleasant incident when discovering one of his workers trapped in the men's sanitary station with several sticks of dynamite and a timer duct-taped to the outside of the door. The makeshift bomb required the local bomb squad to dismantle and an investigation that strangely led nowhere. Later, Benny discovered Elena had been sleeping with half the local precinct, which disturbed his moral compass and made him dream about his retirement. And now, he was trying to enjoy his retirement only to watch it turn into a nightmare. He concluded the right decision was made and waved goodbye to the Jeep Cherokee as it sped down the road and out of town.

"Yer reckon the little blossom be alright?" Earl came up behind him and stood on the sidewalk watching the General and his entourage drive away. Actually, several people gathered on the sidewalk and pressed Earl for some answers on why he let a woman be mistreated in his jurisdiction.

Fortunately, Benny saw Maisie walking across the street on her way to *Duke's Rye Bar* to tidy up the backroom. He hurried to her side, slipped his hand in hers, and for the first time made a motion toward taking love where he thought it might be offered. "You seem happy to see me. What have you been up to?" She smiled brightly and waited for him to answer.

"Can I tell you when we have some time?"

"Of course. I'm on my way to finish up at Duke's. Want to have dinner later. We could fire up that new grill I saw Bob installing yesterday." She beamed, causing Benny to go warm all over and for a second he forgot the unpleasant business on the other side of the street.

"I'll pick up some veggie burgers and vegetables. Hugo has been preferring his veggie burgers and now eats carrots like a champ." Benny grinned.

"In that case, I'll make a salad. Later!" Benny nearly bent to kiss her but caught himself when realizing the small crowd across the street was staring in his direction. He turned away and could hear himself sigh from happiness over anticipating the good time he knew the evening would bring.

SIXTEEN

Meanwhile, Manual and Esther reached an understanding with Charlie Walker. They decided to let him hang from the planter hook three inches to the left of the screen door, specifically outside with a pleasant expression on his face and not a menacing look he was given to expressing in an effort to look dangerous. Esther had been communicating lately with the sad snake, which quickly turned into therapy sessions where he began reaching back to childhood in an effort to find understanding. Charlie Walker came from Central Florida slithering happily along the Everglades when a human trapped him in a net with the idea of including the small python in his petting zoo. Being a handsome reptile, he was soon stolen from the zoo by a desperado who later lost him to Bo Walker in a poker game. He continued recalling his unfortunate childhood, telling Esther the whole affair left his nerves shredded and caused his spirits to sink from despair over his current imprisonment. He missed the days of gliding along the Everglades. She inserted empathy in their dialogue but thought the snake lacked the wherewithal to get himself out of his current predicament. She told him Bob the landscaper made periodic trips to the Everglades to pick up plant specimens and went on to suggest he hitch a ride in the back of his truck hiding among the bags of dirt? Charlie Walker confessed to being afraid of vehicles having nearly got runover by Bo several times when he backed out of their driveway drunk on whiskey and failing to say goodbye, otherwise he would have noticed Charlie was asleep under the wheels and might have known enough, even in his drunken state, to move his long body onto the front yard to safety.

Esther tired of listening to his woes and the incessant whining she thought unbecoming a reptile, told him to be ready at a moment's notice and she would arrange for him to hide in a gunny sack during their next trip to *Bob's Nursery*. This event happened the following day. She instructed Charlie to jump out when they arrived and hide among the foliage until Bob prepared for his trip. Esther also advised him to keep a low profile until arriving at his destination. Charlie whined some more over his loneliness and if only she and Manuel would include him in their family circle, he promised to be a good friend and bring them field mice for dinner. This disgusted Esther. She enjoyed her diet of *Hill's Science*. Thank you very much! She promised to discuss it with Manuel but the little dog threw a tantrum and hid in his bed until Esther dropped the subject. So, the following day, Charlie Walker found himself at Bob's Nursery residing in a huge plant pot among the shrubbery with a price tag stuck on the side. He was asleep when finding himself being checked out at the cash register frightening him and the clerk whose screams brought Bob running. He recognized Charlie Walker and thought he was doing the little village a favor in returning him to his front yard.

Esther frowned when listening to his latest tale and decided it was time to take Manuel in hand and include him in their therapy sessions to practice trust exercises. Eventually, trust was established and now the foursome frolicked in Benny's gardens and hung out at the gazebo with the added rule Charlie Walker was to keep a distance of six feet from Manuel. Hugo enjoyed their togetherness and thanked Senor Benny for expanding his life. Now, all four could be found praying in the gardens to Mother Mary for the safe return of Hugo's real parents. Even Charlie Walker felt the little boy's heart ache and bowed his head in prayer adding an addendum on his own behalf promising to be a good snake if only Mother Mary would bless the man who fed him every day and make him happy without all the bottles occupying their coffee table. He was disappointed when not receiving an immediate response but thought the lady must have a busy schedule and he should practice patience. Hugo stroked his head when they finished paying respects to the blessed virgin. This made Charlie Walker feel special and allowed him to stop dwelling on all the negative things in his life but instead practice gratitude. Afterall, gliding in the Everglades had its downside, leaving him prey to alligators.

~

Finally, Benny received a call from his attorney telling him where Hugo's parents were being detained. Some more money changed hands to facilitate the paperwork. Benny bought the Airstream from the Maren estate and prepared the interior to accommodate a lovely family of three plus dog.

The ICS Detention Center was located a few hours south of *Lost in Sunshine* and would require a two-day round trip. Maisie offered to take Hugo, Manuel, and Esther until he returned from his trip. She also told him not to worry the trailer would be spic and span and Hugo would be prepared for the big event the minute she received Benny's phone call saying they were safely tucked in his SUV and headed home. When life is beautiful all things seem possible, Benny thought. He gazed at Maisie's pretty face and kissed her and his little family goodbye.

The attorney had made the arrangements for Hugo's parents to receive their sponsorships from Benjamin Swan, Proprietor of Sunshine Gardens Estate. The paperwork further stated they would be given housing along with jobs maintaining the gardens. Benny's foresight in buying the extra acre left him buoyant every time his mind lit upon the possibility destiny existed in the natural order of things and while some of his life hurt so much it would bring a bull elephant to his knees, these glorious days of sunshine brought tears of joy to his eyes. He finally let the tears stream down his face the moment Juanita and Eduardo hugged him in the parking lot outside of the Detention Center. Everyone cried in anticipation of being reunited with Hugo, even Benny who had only been gone a day.

When noticing Juanita's and Eduardo's clothes hung in rags, Benny insisted on taking them to a nice store where they each bought a new wardrobe and some new clothes for Hugo who no doubt had grown a size or two since they had last seen him a year ago. Benny further insisted they each buy five complete outfits plus work and dress shoes and undergarments.

"Bless you, Senor," Eduardo kept saying, still in a state of disbelief over his newfound happiness.

"Si Senor, I make rice and beans like you never taste before," Juanita added with a pretty smile.

It was at that moment Benny realized the couple were only in their twenties but looked care-worn from the anguish of being separated from their only child. Occasionally, Juanita burst into tears while trying on clothes, but she kept her terror hidden when fearing another Americano would throw her in the back of a dark van and drive to an unfamiliar place where she would spend her remaining days in grief.

They stopped at a motel for the night with adjoining rooms and left early the next morning only pulling over at fruit stands along the side of the road. They delighted Benny with songs and entertained him with stories of their homeland in broken English. It made the time go by and a few hours later they pulled into the driveway and parked in front of the Airstream where Hugo stood beaming along with Maisie, Esther, Manuel, and Charlie Walker. Not even a snake could keep Juanita and Eduardo from running toward their little boy, swinging him around, crying more tears, and laughing over their reunion but acutely aware of the strange turn life takes when you only want it to stand still long enough to breathe.

Maisie and Hugo showed his parents inside the tiny Airstream. The table was ladened with a full meal of grilled vegetables, rice, beans, tostados and every recipe south of the border Hugo knew his parents would enjoy. They showed his parents a refrigerator stocked with all of Hugo's favorite foods, Manuel's dog bed, Hugo's bed, their bed and a small couch plus a woodburning stove, which delighted the little family. Benny brought their belongings to the doorway and told them to make themselves comfortable, further saying Hugo would show them the grounds where they would be tending the flowers. He suggested they take off the next few days and relax.

Maisie pointed to the guest parking lot where Bob had left an old pickup truck for the family to use as their business vehicle and personal transportation. More excitement followed this announcement, leaving Benny exhausted from emotion and Maisie happy from experiencing the joy of others. They left Hugo and his family, walked to Maisie's house, and sat on her couch together along with Esther beside them and Charlie Walker peeking through the screen door, smiling.

SEVENTEEN

The following day, Benny and Esther stared out the picture window in awe of their new surroundings. The change of neighborhoods and cultivating his own flower beds brought a sense of wellbeing, surrounding him with the glorious memories of his early years where the air was abundant with butterflies, the smell of French toast, and his mother singing Rigoletto, a sound that could shatter glass but to him it was the musical notes of enthusiasm pervading his happy days before beginning a reluctant life into manhood. The finality came when hearing the news that shook his soul and made him question the existence of God.

His mother had used many names for God. She impressed upon him the importance of hearing the inner music. She encouraged him to read William Blake and visit the stratosphere. Benny often wondered if his mother really was a goddess. Other mothers did not talk about the heavenly realms or encourage their children to sit quietly and visit the stratosphere, as though they were taking a trip to New Zealand. He sat baffled on a little pillow she had given him covered in peace signs on heavy tie dye material reflecting the seventies where his mother, no doubt, was in her glory making love not war and objecting to the establishment. She still objected to the arbitrary use of rules. She said all people were born free like lions, except others felt the need to control them, mostly the establishment, she would say. She impressed upon his seven-year-old self to marry a woman who lets him roam the desert in the winter and climb Mt. Everest in the summer. He had no idea what she was talking about until now when meeting a woman he would like to marry but was hesitant from shyness. He wondered if it was too soon to ask? Maisie would let him go to the desert and climb Mt. Everest, but he didn't feel the need to go anywhere. He found the stratosphere in her presence, an oasis shimmering with the possibility of love. His thoughts leaned on his soul for answers helping him realize the greatest gift is love, but it seemed intangible to him, an unknowable energetic state of joyful vibrations coming from the One his mother called by many names. Still though, Benny hesitated to acknowledge such a sanctified life was being offered to him and succumbed to sadness.

He heard a knock at the door. Maisie saw

him and Esther on the couch, pushed Charlie Walker aside and entered with a carefree air that dispelled his sadness and caused the corners of his mouth to turn up and smile at the lovely woman coming toward him. She sat next to him and asked to talk.

"Of course. Yes, let's talk," he said.

"I have to tell you something in an effort to make full disclosure."

His heart sank. "Yes, please, but if you have secrets, they belong to you." His mother had emphasized the importance of secrets. She said people were entitled to privacy and their most urgent secrets should be cherished as a reminder our life is already being shared with God.

"Thank you, but I don't want Earl or Doc Martin telling you I was a cancer prescription drug runner for years and while doing some good, I also made a small profit." She glanced down at her pretty hands. He saw a tear of shame splash onto her fingers. He laughed. She stared at him in surprise, but relieved he would not judge her. They both laughed without concern for Esther who grumbled at the excessive noise.

"I thought you were going to tell me, you found someone much more handsome, thoughtful, and a list of other things along with a tally of my faults, beginning with my overbearing attachment to Esther, and then possibly you would want to know what I've been doing these past forty odd years." Benny's words filled the small room and echoed off the plaster walls, shaking him with their indiscretion and causing him to back pedal to recount all his blunders.

She reached over and hugged him with such tenderness, he melted against her soft bosom feeling himself sink into satisfaction so torturous only his heart knew the consequence. With love follows loss. He sighed, lifted his head, and kissed her softly on the lips, ready to take the few steps to his bed but at that moment, Esther jumped off the couch and walked over to the bed where she stretched her twenty-pound body against both pillows. How could he disturb her?

"What have you been doing with these past forty odd years? You never talk about your childhood, work, or why a five-star general arrived and greeted you like a knight from the king's court. Yes, Earl told me. Told me about the woman Elena who likes to blow up things." She moved herself into a comfortable position against the pillows to listen. He saw a sliver of a smile cross her lips. It gave him hope.

"I may have downplayed my profession."

"You said you worked for the government. I pictured you behind a desk writing important memorandums."

"I pictured myself there, also." Benny sighed. He sighed a lot when in Maisie's presence much like a dog who either sighs from happiness or resignation.

"Oh, what did they have you doin'? Nothing dangerous, I hope." She moved closer.

"Yes, as a matter of fact, I spent my work-life tending to the details of bringing down unwanted buildings, mountains, and discharging both dynamite and nitroglycerine, sometimes working with engineers constructing dams. I've made a few trips to Afghanistan and other warring countries to help the military with their missions, the latter top secret. But never mind, here I am, all safe and sound." He forced a smile.

"Elena? She must figure in your work life somewhere seein' as how she has a bent toward destroying things. Mostly, pretty trees and flowers. How come she was here?"

"I can't say I really know for sure. Stalking, maybe. She worked under me. Asked me to go have a beer once in a while, which I politely declined. My mother didn't believe in drinking beer. She thought it a crude substitute for wine."

Maisie appeared surprised. "And that's why you didn't go out with her? Because of what your mother said?"

"My mother was an unusual woman. Refined but robust, larger than life, and a force of nature.

I believed everything she said. She was never wrong. Plus, Elena is dangerous. And I'm not a person who cultivates danger."

"Oh, but danger must follow you. You're every girl's dream bad boy." Maisie laughed and put her hand on his knee. "Your mother sounds wonderful. What a loss for you."

"Yes, unfortunately. Both my parents are deceased but at least they died together." Benny tired of the conversation and suddenly felt the need to be alone with his thoughts. "Would you like to go out to dinner tonight? That is if you're not..."

"I would love to have dinner with you. Come by at seven but let me cook for you." She threw her arms around his neck and kissed him passionately. Benny responded until nearly bursting into flames from the heat of his body. He could hear himself groan silently from happiness. It caused him to remember the dog Maisie had mentioned wanting to adopt. She had mentioned a maternal need for a little Beagle.

Benny shook all thoughts from his mind and remained on the couch sniffing the sweet smell of Maisie. How could someone so lovely want to share her life with him? Did he have a low opinion of his worth or did she seem too good to be true? Both, he thought. But one thing he was learning about mountaineers that distinguished them from other people. They spoke their minds and were what they appeared to be. Earl was a case in point and Maisie buying drugs for cancer patients was a tribute to her generous and kind nature. Authenticity gave him comfort, a place he could rest in reliability, and feel like he was standing next to an oak tree growing on solid ground. No subterfuge or inuendo to fill his mind with doubt.

Suddenly, Esther ran past him to the screen door. Manuel and Hugo stood on the other side waiting for her to come out to play. They had developed a daily routine of spending at least two hours together before the sun hit high noon and beat down on their good time prompting them to lay under the weeping willow tree to enjoy the easiness of the day. Often Charlie Walker would join them within the boundaries that had been set for him by Esther. If he remained on the ground, he couldn't come any closer to Manuel than his boundary of six feet but otherwise could hang from a branch on the weeping willow tree so long as it wasn't directly above them. Usually, he curled up in a ball nearby and fell into smug satisfaction over having been invited into the small circle of trust. Even Bo noticed they had worked out their differences. He no longer had to listen to

Charlie's fretful moods that brought his spirits down while at the same time he harbored the worrisome notion his animal companion might die of loneliness. He had read about such things happening in a magazine and thought it was the saddest thing he had ever heard prompting him to register the formal complaint to Maisie. He thought animals working out their differences was a much better solution than getting adult people all fired up over the behavior of their respective pets. In short, Bo's mind preferred to idle on a hypnotic melody than be cluttered with his snake's feelings. He didn't even know snakes had feelings until acquiring Charlie.

Benny opened the screen door for Esther to go outside to join her friends. He spoke to Hugo. "How's your family settling into their new house?"

"Senor Benny, we are all happy together. They love working in the beautiful gardens and they, too, thank you Senor Benny and the Blessed Virgin Mary every day for bringing us together." Hugo still kneeled in the garden along with his animal kingdom and prayed to the saint he called Mother. Benny saw the angelic expression that often flitted across the small boy's face and lit up the animals who followed behind him like he was St. Francis of Assisi.

"Hugo, I've enrolled you in the local school.

I think you will enjoy first grade. I'm happy to take you myself."

"Oh, would you, Senor Benny? Madre, she very embarrassed about her English."

"I forgot to mention, I found an English class perfect for both of your parents. Tell them I'll drop off the directions, or if they like, I will take them." Benny smiled at the sweet face staring back at him.

"Oh, thank you, Senor Benny. I will also teach them what I learn from first grade. Si?"

"Yes, excellent." Benny watched Manuel, Esther, and Hugo walk toward the gardens with Charlie Walker following behind them. He smiled and thought moving to *Lost in Sunshine* a heavenly stroke of good fortune and then felt embarrassed for gushing.

EIGHTEEN

Benny noticed the postman had dropped off several packages across the way. He stepped outside and ambled over to pick up his mail. A letter from his former neighbor was among the pile. She had forgotten to give Benny a three-page message from his mother dictated to her while Mrs. Swan lay dying in the hospital. Mrs. Swan was a verbose woman with a jolly sense of humor but also a need to seek closure and consider the feelings of those nearest to her. Despite being married to her husband for twenty-five years, she felt closer to her son and her sense of responsibility triggered the need to offer an explanation over the shock of not being there to greet him when he arrived home on his next furlough.

Benny tossed the letters on the dining table to go over later, but now he felt the need to walk along the outskirts of the village, sit on the bank of the lake, and wait for the evening to arrive when he would be in the company of Maisie.

~

Benny knocked on Maisie's door at exactly seven o'clock. He had picked flowers from his garden, handed them to Maisie as he bent to kiss her, and then drew back when noticing her tear-stained face.

"What's wrong? Not bad news, I hope." He led her to the couch and pulled her down beside him.

"It's Earl. He's been here. Gloating in some sick way. Brought me this envelope full of newspaper clippings about your parents." She picked up the packet from the coffee table and showed the contents to Benny. "I was going to throw them away and not mention the incident, except something told me you'd know what to say. Earl wrote this note."

Benny read the note. *Yer got yersef a broken man.* "I'm sorry you had to see this. I would have told you when I was ready. But even after all these years, it's painful to talk about." Benny glanced at the headlines.

The Daily Herald read: HUSBAND DIES TRYING TO SAVE WIFE FROM SHOOTER! The New York Gazette read: HUSBAND THROWS HIMSELF BETWEEN SHOOTER AND WIFE! And the one that caused Benny to sob from long suppressed grief: WIFE SUCCUMBS TO GUNSHOT WOUNDS! *Mrs. Swan was shot two more times after her husband fell to the pavement from a shot to the head. He died instantly. Mrs. Swan is now fighting for her life in the ICU. Police suspect lone sniper on top of the McDow building and are now in search of a man wearing a red baseball cap.*

Mentioning the red baseball cap always bothered Benny for reasons he couldn't grasp but suspected it was stupidity on the part of the reporter who failed to grasp the sniper would remove his cap the second he saw himself on the nearest tv and what sniper with half a brain would wear something so blatant. He asked the police if a profiler had analyzed the mentality of the alleged killer. He was told the profiler had come to the same conclusion, a not very bright male with low IQ and possible self-esteem issues. She also concluded it was a random killing and not an intentional act to harm Mr. and Mrs. Swan. Later that day, three more people were gunned down from a roof top in the same manner. Benny wept for himself, his parents, and the others who suffered at the hands of a madman. Yes, as it was revealed, the gunman was mad as a hatter, having just been released from a state facility for killing his stepfather twenty years earlier at age sixteen. He received life imprisonment without parole for his recent crimes.

Mrs. Swan died three hours before Benny

arrived at the hospital. She didn't mind dying but minded leaving her son motherless without her as a rudder to guide him in the direction of goodness. She would have to trust the Divine Potentate to care for her boy and take her husband to heaven where she may be joining him shortly.

"Benny dearest please tell me if I've done the wrong thing in showing you these but some part of me thought the pain might be less if we shared your grief. Maybe I'm being a fool, kinda high on myself in thinking I matter enough to soften your past hardships." Benny wiped away Maisie's tears with his handkerchief and held her against his chest.

"You mean more to me than life itself. I love you. I love your way of moving, smiling, and I love the sweetness that follows you everywhere you go. I'm a lucky man for having found you. You are my heart. My everything." Benny wondered where this fluttering of words came from. He had never offered his affection with such an unabashed showering of sentiment. But it would have disappointed him if he hadn't let himself loose to feel what Maisie helped him see. He was capable of love.

"Oh dearest, let's put these clippings away and enjoy the evening." She kissed him sweetly. They lingered on the couch past dinner and slowly moved to her bedroom where they spent the night. Occasionally, Maisie would soothe Esther with a few reassurances her person would be home soon and wasn't it lovely to share. Esther didn't feel the same way and periodically relayed her disgruntlement to Maisie's ear, but it went unheard and eventually everyone fell asleep.

The following day, Benny sat at his dining table going over the mail. He picked up a bulky envelope and noticed the return address was from his former neighbor Mrs. Simmons. A note fell out apologizing for having forgotten to give Benny his mother's last message dictated to her from Mrs. Swan's hospital bed. She asked him to forgive her absent-mindedness. The dear lady's flowery hand-writing startled Benny with its familiarity and sent him back to childhood to revisit the times Mrs. Simmons sat down with him to improve his penmanship. Fortunately, he had omitted the loops and curls in his own cursive style but smiled when noticing she had gotten carried away and the S in her name covered the bottom half of the page and now resembled Baroque calligraphy with intersecting loops. He smiled at the thought she still enjoyed the art of penmanship. He then picked up the three-page letter addressed to him.

My Darling Son,

I apologize for our abrupt departure from this earthly world. If I don't get to say goodbye, an unanticipated event occurred taking us all by surprise. I had no idea it would be quite so dramatic or even pedestrian (excuse the play on words, especially a pun of all things, which in itself is pedestrian. You know how your mother delights in words) as walking across the street only to be riddled with bullets and bombarded by the sound of people screaming. Your dear father threw his body on top of mine like a soldier on the battle front. You would have been proud, darling child. He sacrificed his life in an effort to save your mother. Unfortunately, the doctors here are such pessimists. They say I only have a few days to live and chatter nonstop about internal bleeding and the risk of surgery. From my vantage point, I can see numerous tubes sticking out from under the bedcovers. Never a good sign, so I harkened to Mrs. Simmons who like a dutiful neighbor put herself at my service to compose what the doctors insist will be my last words. (Oh God bless the optimists. I could use one right now. Even the nurses frown from dismay, hovering nearby like tiny grim reapers, waiting.)

I want you to know how much your father and I have loved you since your inception. I won't mention it was in the backseat of his old Plymouth, an ugly car in my opinion, but the seat was big and well, we were smaller in the days of our youth and fit snugly together knowing we would never be apart. Until today. And who knows what God has in store for us. Perhaps, he will keep us together in one of those many mansions Jesus waxed on about without details as to their appointments. Another adventure, I suppose. But darling boy, we loved you so. Our world circled around your tiny self and grew as you grew. I hope we returned a modicum of this same happiness that lit up our lives by your very presence.

I know you will mourn us. I can see you crying now, fat tears of grief so intense it will cause your knees to weaken and burn a hole in your heart where our love resided and now seems extinguished. But I believe we will love you forever. You have only to give away our love to others. Pay it forward, as they say. Find yourself someone to love and never let them go. Worship the God in them, the all-pervading immanence of joy so heartfelt, you don't realize it is the divinity that exists in all of us. Do not hide behind your work. I remember the nights you burned the midnight oil in a desire to graduate early. You were always in a hurry and overlooked the need to dally in the arms of a deserving companion, who would make you laugh, yes, put a smile on your face and bless you with happy days together talking about love and other things. I worry you will continue with your studious ways and never smell the sweetness of freshly shampooed hair.

Your father didn't suffer, which could give us some relief, but at the moment, the loss of him seems too much to bear, but then I only have a few days to linger here and you have a lifetime to miss the quiet man who gave us comfort in his solidity and was always there to cheer us on when we stepped into the spotlight. His reserved nature allowed us to shine while he sat basking in our light. He was a treasure put here to help others and now has become the world's loss. I know you will miss him; you will miss both of us. When you step into the empty house, cry until we come running to hover nearby, two souls who remember you were a part of them. Let your tears water the plants and wash away your grief.

Oh dear, the doctors have become annoying things. At first, I thought they wanted my hospital bed, but I now realize they're hem-hawing around about giving my organs to patients in need of transplants. Never mind, I'm not done with them, yet. I suppose they have to be pragmatic about my impending death, but I prefer they do it out of earshot. Now, they want me to sign something giving them permission to take your father's organs, too. Thus, the need for expedience as one doctor put it. A nurse glared at him for his tactless manner. I suppose I should make these decisions now, otherwise, they'll be chasing you down the hospital corridors brandishing a clipboard for you to sign away all our organs. They're talking about giving the remainder of my body to science. I'm drawing a line here. I know you won't want to think of your mother being tossed about in a cadaver barn for years of scrutiny by med students. I waved them away when asking for this last impertinent request. Your father and I want to go up in a blaze of fire and smoke. No need to waste a burial plot. Just throw our ashes in the nearest river and let us float out to sea.

That reminds me. I forgot to tell you that we rented a houseboat last summer for a couple of weeks to see if we should hold onto our dream of touring the edges of the world in a yacht during our retirement. I wouldn't recommend it for those who need intellectual stimulation and enjoy planting bulbs in the dirt and watching them flower in the spring. Two days of staring at the water and waving at the passing motorboats prompted us to change our minds. The only time we really enjoyed ourselves happened when we parked the bulky floating house next to a blackberry patch and spent the afternoon picking berries and making ourselves a lovely, plump cobbler. No need to worry about our retirement, which brings me to my point. Life is short, darling son. You must live every moment in happiness, which you will find above the fray of mediocrity. Stay humble and give the best of yourself to help others along the way. Keep a half smile on your face and let your eyes twinkle and all good things will come your way. I may sound as trite as a Hallmark card, but I'm bent on cramming my pearly wisdom in a few platitudes that will serve you well, knowing I won't be around to ease the vagaries of a haphazard world. If your father were here, he would tell you to take a government job, but since I have the last word, I'm telling you to go where your heart takes you and bring a dog to remind you there is such a thing as unconditional love.

Mom and Dad

Benny read the letter several times. He memorized every word to be played back in times of need. He cried when imagining his mother pouring out her heart hours after her husband had died saving her life. How hard it must have been for her. These thoughts ran around inside his head until his only relief came when hearing

Esther climb through her cat door, followed by Manuel, and then a few seconds later followed by Charlie Walker who had become a conscientious guest quietly settling in a corner. Benny smiled when remembering the last line of his mother's letter, 'bring a dog where your heart takes you'. His thoughts turned to Maisie and her desire to adopt a dog. The subject kept coming up. He wondered if his mother's words had traveled through time on an ambrosial breeze emanating sweetness and reminding a person there's more to life than what one sees.

The animals laid in their respective places and fell asleep, tired from the heat of the sun. He wondered if there was room for another dog in his life, but then Manuel really belonged to Hugo and now Esther had claimed ownership of his good nature. She appeared satisfied with the status quo. Benny smiled at the trio and promptly imagined a little puppy among them. Would they treat him well? Would they even accept him or would they find him a nuisance in need of training and possibly a tiny tyrant at the food bowl? All things were possible but still it wasn't the time to question either Maisie's desire for a dog or his mother's prophetic words.

Benny turned his thoughts to the irony of his parents being shot by a domestic sniper while he labored in the army learning to become a sharpshooter, part of his training for the time he may need to use a weapon to protect his country. These thoughts brought more tears and caused him to doubt the decision to join the army. If he had been home with his parents, perhaps they would still be alive contemplating their retirement. His tears dampened the tile and made puddles in the crevices. He became tortured with regret.

"Benny, dearest, what's wrong?" Maisie stood on the other side of the screen door. He looked at her with relief. The second she stepped inside, he put his arms around her. "But dearest, you've been crying." Maisie had rarely seen a grown man cry. Mountaineers didn't cry. It never occurred to them. Her own father wandered off one day, before she was born, without explanation. Feeding a family had become too much for him. The possibility they might go hungry had become even more of a hardship. There seemed no recourse but to leave his family to fend for themselves. He left without crying over abandoning what made life bearable on a bad day. Maisie's lovers had never cried either, but then she had always kept her affairs brief and somewhat orderly lest they become messy with emotion. A moment of concern rose when finding the man she hoped to be her constant companion crying the day after they consummated their love for each other.

"I'm so happy to see you. Please excuse this dramatic display. I'm not given to tears but a letter arrived from my mother. My old neighbor had forgotten to give it to me." He showed Maisie the letter and suddenly she began to cry.

"I'm so sorry. I'm also sorry I will never meet such a beautiful soul. Benny, do you see what she said about wanting you to get a dog? She must have known people are incapable of giving unconditional love. They always want something or need something. Small things, mostly. But really dearest, I would cherish such a letter as I cherish the one my mother left for me." She smiled at him through her tears.

"You know what this means?" Benny said, trying to lighten the mood.

"What?" They sat on the couch together. Somehow his small house seemed happy to accommodate all the occupants. What was one more, Benny thought.

"Let's go to the shelter this afternoon and look for a dog."

"Yes, a dog to share?" Maisie asked.

"Of course, shall we live in one house or shall we build a breezeway from your house to mine? We don't want to confuse the poor thing. Turn it into a latch key dog." They both laughed.

"There's nothing in the by-laws that states

we can't put on an addition to accommodate an expanding family." Maisie surprised herself.

Benny kissed the top of her head. "Why not? I'll get an architect on it. Anything you want? Shall we use your house as a 'she shed'?" They both laughed again.

"What a great idea. I could use it for storing all the baking equipment I need for Duke's Friday tea parties. I forgot to tell you, it's become such a hit, Duke said we could include Tuesdays. This will keep me busy making scones and other pastries. I will get fat."

"And I will love you anyway." They fell into each other's arms. Later, the topic of marriage would come up but first they would adopt a Beagle puppy and call her Arabella.

Benny reread his mother's letter often and felt satisfied he was living a life of goodness. He settled happily on the notion love came to him at the right time to be treasured for its abundance.

Part II
Gloria Dobbins & Pete

ONE

Professor Gloria Dobbins tended to get on every man's last nerve simply for being smarter than ninety-nine percent of the population, half of whom are male. She also possessed the uncanny ability to remain oblivious to their strident voices. Unfortunately, the Dean couldn't take her tendency to employ the facts in committee meetings rather than supporting his personal goals, which most times were out of sync with the facts. The moment he heard she was combining the contemporary philosopher Aaron James's book *Assholes a theory* and Eastern philosophy's spiritual theory of Oneness, he saw an opportunity to bring her classroom antics into question and enforce a sabbatical. He suggested she use the time to put her opinions in a book.

Gloria delighted in the idea and took to the road with her cockatoo St. Peter, Pete for short, and headed to a village down south called *Lost in Sunshine*. She bought a newly built tiny house next to Bo and Charlie Walker. She liked the idea of having a musician for a neighbor due to Pete's love of dancing. And, too, the manager Maisie sounded like a sweet soul already enlightened to the concept of Oneness. Gloria did overstep her bounds, as often happens with people oblivious to propriety, when asking Maisie if there were any assholes in her haven and if so, were they kept under restraint. Maisie thought about it for a second and said, "Yes honey, and rest assured we got him under control now and besides, darlin', he doesn't live here but dawdles on the sidelines." Gloria's spirits soared with the notion a kindred spirit waited for her in the village she was about to call home for the duration of her sabbatical.

She shoved Pete's favorite CD in the player of her Audi station wagon. He danced on the customized railing built in the back seat allowing him plenty of room to stretch his legs to music. He had mastered twelve dance steps and continued to marvel Gloria with his rhythmic gyrations. The guy knew how to shimmy, shake, and strut up and down his railing and then fly to the dashboard to dazzle her with his plumage. Every hundred miles, he perched on Gloria's shoulder so she could kiss his beak and reassure him her love was as deep as a bottomless reservoir. He was a needy little guy.

While Pete danced on his railing, Gloria's

mind ruminated on the comparison between contemporary American philosophy and the Eastern view of living in Oneness with every living being inhabiting the Universe. She impressed upon her students the need to see assholes for what the writer put forth, as morally questionable in their belief only they are special and the rest of us should be quiet while they talked, which seemed to be all the time. She posed her own question to the students, asking if the asshole could be persuaded to embrace the concept of Oneness. A bright student in the back row had hollered, "Only if he's in the company of a saint." Gloria agreed and asked him his name, "Elmo Bond from Kentucky, Miss Professor. Where I come from an asshole can make your life a misery, mostly male, mostly suffering some kinda affliction of thinking they're right all the time and nobody else has got a brain in their head. My daddy is one for sure." Gloria liked Elmo from the get-go and didn't mind his hanging around her office asking questions. He took her words to heart and pontificated on everything from Krishna to Aristotle, mostly in the cafeteria to a captive audience.

Gloria shoved her thoughts aside and smiled when seeing Pete in the rear-view mirror dancing to Michael's Jackson's *Thriller*, combining the moves of MJ and James Brown. He tended toward sweeping gestures displaying his plumage much like James Brown when wearing a cape. Pete tripped in a world of his own while caught up in people music but had discerning taste when it came to the beat. He disdained the long melodic line of new-aged music meant for massage rooms painted botanical green and soft people who floated through life as though carried by a slow breeze without a care in the world. Pete needed music to speak to him, ruffle his soul, and set his mind right.

Born on the wings of the divine, Pete, a mystical bird, stuck his beak in the nectar found only on the higher realms where the saints sat in meditation and the flowers grew as large as an elephant's ear swaying along a jungle path. Pete possessed the power to see beyond the windshield and get a peek at Maisie looking pretty in a garden full of dahlias and small animals scampering after a smiling boy. This excited Pete who became ecstatic the moment Maisie tuned into his airwave and said, "Well, hello there. You must be Pete." He chortled causing Gloria to glance once again in the back seat. Her bird was jumping up and down on the railing, flapping his wings, and singing *Barcelona* like he was Freddy Mercury. She assumed he was happy going for a drive in the car unaware Maisie was a passenger in the back seat talking to her bird.

Pete recognized the frailties of humans but had more patience with them than Esther who believed they were God's afterthought. He lived in the world of Oneness his Bird-Mom chattered about while they were alone at night. Fortunately, Gloria could read her Eastern philosophy books unbothered by Pete's music playing in the background. Most of what she told him when repeating the words of the saints, he already knew from experience. He loved her for this need she had of understanding her surroundings and taking it up a flight in the belief there might be more than desolating sadness. Pete understood the limitations of the human brain requiring empirical knowledge before they were willing to entertain the God's honest truth.

Maisie said she looked forward to meeting him and Gloria when they arrived and wanted to introduce them to the other animal inhabitants and a few people they might enjoy. She asked if there was anything in particular he would like her to get for him. Pete mentioned seeds and berries, the organic kind without pesticides preferably grown in Northern California. Maisie laughed at the funny bird. She could see him spreading his wings and rocking back and forth but couldn't hear the toe-tapping music playing from his favorite lineup.

After a few more exchanges, they disconnected and went back to their respective tasks. Maisie marveled over the beautiful white bird and Pete smiled that silly grin he often gets when thinking life could be a blessing on the earth plane when least expecting it to evolve into something lovelier than a homeless beggar sleeping in an alley way. Pete could also hear his Bird-Mom singing along with ABBA, her head swaying to the beat, beaming with satisfaction everything was going to be an easy ride. Pete knew better. He had lived with Gloria for twenty years and had become accustomed to her inherent tendency to 'stir the pot' as humans say.

TWO

Elmo Bond sat mystified in the back row of Gloria's class now taught by the Dean himself. Mostly, the Dean droned on about whether or not a falling tree made a sound in the forest if there was no one around to hear it. The class agreed it made a sound and all the philosophers had to do was ask the animals who heard the crash, which would make quite a racket depending on the size of the tree. They argued sound was comprised of vibrations and could be heard by anyone with an ear. They also considered the possibility there might not be any animals in the woods that day, and therefore the vibrations would bluster silently through the mist and disappear into the quiet spaces between the air waves. One girl insisted the world was an illusion, and so naturally if we are all imagined, then it really doesn't matter. Elmo dwelled some on the girl's grim worldview but didn't have the patience to pursue her line of thought and besides he was busy stewing over the loss of his favorite teacher.

After class, he approached the Dean and asked, "What did you do with Miss Professor Dobbins?" He caught the tweedy, sanctimonious, tiny man by surprise and at a loss for words. Elmo pressed further, "If'n you don't commence to tell me directly, I'll go to the poleece? And I'm not talkin' shit here."

The tiny Dean didn't appreciate the student's tone of voice and was about to dress him down for being impertinent. Yes, he thought, a good dressing down was warranted here. Even his thoughts presented themselves as spectacularly arrogant much like the Dean himself when trying to push his own agenda through committee meetings. He studied Elmo's tattered jeans and flannel shirt realizing the young man wasn't wearing them as a political statement but rather as standard dress of Kentucky mountaineers. He noticed a Louisville Brecks sticker on Elmo's backpack and a slight rounding of his words similar to the natives in Eastern Kentucky. The Dean was proud of his gift for regional sounds and never missed an opportunity to point out a person's place of origin. Most of the other professors found it to be a tiresome practice and would rather not be pigeonholed in a locale, especially if it betrays their bogus British accents, an affectation that tended to run rampant in academic settings.

"My dear man, I'm not happy with your manner of speaking to me. Afterall, being a student at this hallowed institute doesn't just present you with the opportunity to learn from the finest minds but rather as an opportunity to become both a gentleman and a scholar. I suggest you start with your attire." The Dean's contradictory statement caused Elmo to laugh out loud. A gentleman would never criticize another man's attire, especially one of small means who is about to earn another Masters in the natural sciences, all from well-deserved scholarships. A gentleman would also show compassion over another man's distress at losing his favorite teacher. "As for Professor Dobbins, ask the neophyte archival librarian where Dobbins spent most of her spare time when not with that deranged bird."

The Dean had met Pete when Gloria first began teaching at the University years ago. He was smitten by her extensive vocabulary and pithy rejoinders. He showed up at her house one night slightly drunk on wine with the firm belief he was irresistible to women and quite a catch for someone who placed little importance on other people's shortcomings. Yes, he knew his small size often hindered him from being a dream boat, but he had inherited a nice house and was convinced he would eventually be chancellor, altogether making him a good catch. Unfortunately, Pete became agitated over the sudden interruption of his and Bird-Mom's usual quiet evening at home. The second the Dean stepped into the living room, Pete squawked, "Forsooth, who goes there? Forsooth, who goes there?" Gloria found it amusing but her visitor suffered an anxiety attack and had to be taken to the hospital. He shuddered at the memory.

Elmo thanked the Dean and walked to the library, showed his card, and was directed to the downstairs' hinter regions where books waited patiently for scholars who spent an excessive amount of time there getting high off the musty smell rising from their yellowed pages. After scurrying amid the stacks for what seemed like hours, Elmo came upon a prim little woman sitting at a large metal desk, reading. He cleared his throat several times while taking in her neat and tidy appearance. He considered her a pretty little woman, gentle like his mama, except she wore wire-rim glasses and her clothes, while old, appeared made of expensive wool even though it was a bright and sunny day outside. He supposed spending one's life in the library catacombs would cause a person to lose track of the seasons. He then wondered what she wore in the winter.

The librarian finally looked up from her book surprised to see a student hovering over her. She peered under his lock of curly black hair and saw an intelligent nearly handsome face with a wide grin and pretty teeth similar to a girl's, all fresh from frequent brushings. Elmo assumed she was reading a scholarly tome written by a dead historian but the prim librarian's taste tended toward Jane Austin considering her the world's finest romance novelist. The head of the English department held a loftier opinion of the writer's work, which often bothered her when thinking him shortsighted and out of touch. Actually, they were both out of touch. Only Professor Gloria Dobbins kept herself up to speed on current trends in the hopes of understanding the philosophy of your average present-day human and their shaky morality.

"So sorry, I didn't hear you. Have you ever read Jane Austin?"

"No miss," Elmo answered politely.

"Well, I don't suppose she would appeal to a young man." The librarian sighed.

Elmo saw her face fall and couldn't bear to be a disappointment to someone who reminded him of his mother. "Recommend one of her books, and I'll read her right quick." She found his grin endearing.

"*Pride and Prejudice.*"

"I'll grab a copy on the way out. You wait and see." They both laughed.

"Oh, I'm sorry. You came here for a reason. I'm not very good at my job. I've only been here a couple of years fresh from graduate school. My aunt's the head librarian and decided this would be a good place for me to spend the rest of my life." She groaned quietly.

"I'm so sorry. Better to get a job working the fields in the sunshine where the butterflies light on the new mown hay and the grasshoppers gnaw on the wildflowers."

"You do have a way with words. What is your name?" The librarian, not much older than Elmo, became intrigued by the soft-spoken young man, a lanky sort emanating boyish charm.

"It's Elmo Bond."

"Penelope. You may call me Penny. Named after my copper hair."

"That's a pretty downhome name for sure." Elmo wanted to say something nice about her hair but it was cinched tight against her head with a clip in the shape of a lobster's leg.

"Thank you. And you were about to tell me the reason for your visit." She glanced at him expectantly.

"Oh yes. I'm searching for my favorite teacher, Professor Gloria Dobbins. The Dean of Philosophy told me you might know where she went off to."

"Oh Gloria, she's a real sweetheart. I loved our chats. She left suddenly in search of assholes for her book, but I told her she didn't have to go any further than her own department. We both had a good laugh over it. But she was serious and bought a little house down south in a village, let me see, oh yes. It's called *Lost in Sunshine*. I do miss her. Actually, I'm not sure I'm supposed to tell anyone." Penelope's face went white from the sudden realization she just revealed the whereabouts of her own favorite person to a stranger.

As though reading her mind, Elmo responded, "Oh, don't worry Penny. I'm harmless. My heart hurt some over her sudden disappearance. She's a good listener and treated me like I had a brain." Elmo's expression turned from amiable to sad over the realization what he had said was true. The pretty librarian patted his hand. They spent the next two hours together talking about Professor Gloria Dobbins and her bird Pete.

THREE

Gloria stopped at Clyde's Gas and Convenience Store a few miles north of *Lost in Sunshine*. She rarely gave food much thought but was struck by the word convenient. It had an interesting etymology differing from its current use, derived from the Latin word convenire meaning to convene. It evolved in *Late Middle English* and was often used to mean befitting or becoming. Actually, Gloria liked the idea of all mundane tasks being convenient, allowing her brain to be occupied with studious mental pursuits. She busied herself inside Aaron's book fascinated by the importance he places on understanding the proliferation of corporate assholes and how they came to be so abundant, and why they are dangerous while also useful on occasion.

When in line, a man holding a quart of milk and a nutrition bar began to annoy the customers in front of him. "Can't you people have your money out ready to pay?" A nicely dressed older lady pulled a small change purse from her larger purse and began counting change. This annoyed the man even more. "We're going to be here all day." Others in line glared at him but were afraid to say anything. Gloria, however, took the opportunity to pull out a notebook and ask the man a few questions.

"Sir, why does it bother you to wait in line?"

Startled by the question, the man answered without hesitation, "Because they're wasting my time. I shouldn't have to stand behind a buncha rednecks who don't have the brains to be prepared to pay for their goods." The people in line were relieved to have him distracted.

Gloria jotted down a few notes and continued her line of questioning. "It follows then you feel superior to the people in front of you, who arrived before you. Is this so?"

"Well of course I'm superior as the Almighty created me. Lookee here, I got my money in my hand, enough to cover both items." He waved a ten-dollar bill in her face.

"Just to clarify. Have you ever been called an asshole? I mean has your behavior ever been questioned in one of these exchanges like the one you're having now?" Gloria posed her pen to make an entry in her notebook.

The man grabbed Gloria's notebook and tossed it in a nearby trash can. "Does that answer your question?" The man leaned toward Gloria with an expression of menace on his face.

This motion was followed by a collective gasp from the onlookers. Fortunately, an officer of the law had been peering over the cereal boxes watching the entire display.

"Thank you, sir. I think we've established you're an asshole and worthy of further study." Gloria smiled sweetly and retrieved her notebook from the trash can at the same moment the man reached to grab her by the hair.

Suddenly, the long and skinny officer made an appearance. "This here redneck causing you a mite bit o' trouble little lady?"

Gloria laughed out loud when hearing herself being referred to as a little lady. She wondered if she had stumbled onto another asshole or was it common to call a woman little lady in this part of the country. "Not a bit, Officer." She smiled and moved in front of both men to the head of the line.

"Now lookee here!"

"Let the little lady pay for her groceries and no never mind coming from you, or I'll lock you up for grins. Yer got yerself a foot in my jurisdiction."

Gloria eavesdropped on the conversation, jotting down more notes on the way to her car. The first man flew out the door and yelled, "Lady, you should burn in hell for riling a man's temper." She found this statement of particular interest when noting he blamed her for losing control, which was typical asshole behavior. She felt satisfied and drove the rest of the way with a smile on her face and the company of Pete sitting on her shoulder.

Pete gawked out the window chirping at all the other birds and a dog called Manuel followed by a little Beagle who smiled when she saw the ornate bird leaning out the car window repeating the word "hello". Even Maisie heard his voice from inside and opened the screen door to wave the newcomers over to park in front of her small cottage now used as an office and bakery.

Pete studied his surroundings surprised to discover paradise does exist on the earth plane. He wondered how all these beings knew to come here where their souls could catch a respite from the chaotic invention of man's collective unconscious. He also wondered if the cat sitting in front of Maisie's cottage like a trained Doberman guard dog would grab a few feathers when he flew just above her airspace in an effort to glide through the open door and enjoy the refreshments waiting inside.

"Light shimmers off the tree bark and lifts the flowers to glory in the Divine· The heavenly spheres bring their beauty to a place not known by many people but crowded by

animals of all kinds· They're smiling at me now· I can see the earth worms turning all eyes in my direction and laughing because they know I am one with them· The bumble-bees speak softly and stick their noses in the nectar inside the flowers growing abundantly in the village of mostly happy people and a few who haven't quite got the hang of giving up control to the mighty force that runs their lives with a loving hand and a tendency toward leniency· Otherwise, they would find themselves without daisies in Bosnia or some-place where the gold dust blew away a long time ago and people walk around with sad faces and smiles that got lost in the strife of poverty·"

"Domesticated animals play happily together unaware of a primal need to roam freely among their own kind· Fortunately, their souls have a mystical bent so natu-rally all things merge together pleasing them with good fortune while they frolic in the sunshine·"

"I'm a bird who takes pride in his appear-ance fanning out my feathers whenever happiness overcomes me· I hear a melody that sets my feet to keeping the beat inside the sound so sweet my beak lets go of a good chortle that makes others laugh louder *than a prairie dog when he's being chased by a gopher· Fortunately, I got a human person who watches my back, feeds me, gives me plenty of water, and laughs at her own words when I send them flying back to her· I got a good thing going and never forget to thank the Almighty for smiling on me each and every day, even though I suffer some from the weakness of vanity, but I can easily rationalize my shortcomings by sharing my good looks for all to see· Your humble servant, Pete·"*

Esther stared at the stylish bird appreciating its beauty but concerned about its large feet and a beak rivaling that of a Harpy Eagle. Her disposition improved somewhat after Maisie became a permanent fixture in Cat-Dad's life and by default in her life as well. Esther had agreed with Maisie she did benefit by their living arrangements when noticing she received twice as much attention and was lavished with endless praise and affection. This helped calm her hackles and afforded her an easy life where she rested comfortably in the knowledge she would never be left alone. Her mind often dwelled on the lonely periods when Cat-Dad had worked in other parts of the world and was gone for weeks at a time. She languished in the *Feline*

Spa & Sanctuary owned by two over-indulgent cat lovers who spend twelve-hour days catering to the needs of their clientele. The two ladies recognized Esther as being special so gave her a living area designed for the discerning cat. They placed it near a window with a view of a coy pond surrounded by low hanging trees where squirrels scampered on the branches stopping occasionally to stare at her through the picture window. Now, though, she was faced with something that had wings and flew. She viewed this as a threat to her current position on the top rung of the social ladder.

Pete knew it behooved him to make friends with the large feline sitting at the door. Unfortunately, he lost interest in an extended conversation when hearing the music coming from Maisie's living room. Pete stepped on the car roof, spread his wings, turned sideways clearing Esther's head by a good three inches, and then careened to the right coming to rest on a drop-leaf table with plenty of room to glide. His toes began tapping to the funky sound of soft rock sung by Austin Brown, voice like an angel. Pete thought he was in heaven and decided to shine a little for Maisie. He swayed to the rhythm of two four time with a slow tempo and strutted when the bass picked up the beat, throwing back his head as the music swelled to a crescendo, and then bowed the second the music ended on the down beat with a flourish.

Maisie clapped her hands delighted over Pete's natural tendency to rock to the beat of a good song. Arabella barked and Esther frowned from the showy display of an inferior being she thought belonged on a tree limb. Gloria appeared and motioned for Pete to rest comfortably on her shoulder pad she wore not to enhance her figure but to give Pete a soft spot to rest.

"Please have a seat. Thank you so much, Pete. That was lovely."

"Thank you! Thank you so much!" Pete repeated.

Maisie laughed harder and Arabella jumped on the couch to inspect his beak while Esther considered the possibility she may have just slipped a rung on the social ladder.

FOUR

Gloria and Pete became excited when seeing their new house prettily situated on a sizeable piece of land. Sweet pea vines with pink flowers grew up a trellis covering the rear wheel. A wooden patio extended twelve feet from French doors with a railing along the right side and across the front. As per Gloria's request, Maisie had hired a local contractor to build the custom railing for Pete, allowing him to dance outside to the music softly playing from a radio placed on the windowsill. Large tubs of flowers intermingled with blonde rattan furniture giving it a cozy look and a comfortable place for Gloria to idle in her lofty thoughts on the morality of assholes. She had decided the subject may be too narrow for her sizeable brain and maybe she should turn her attention to the downward spiral of contemporary morality with emphasis on man's inhumanity to everyone else.

Gloria had grown up in a quiet house under the care of her soft-spoken academic parents. Their evenings were spent reading books with occasional excited outbursts over a particularly dazzling amusement like the tiny tardigrades resembling cartoon characters with the constitution of an extraterrestrial dating back five-hundred million years. Her first glimpse at the mini water bear remains with her as a fond memory. Both parents were killed in an automobile accident on Gloria's twentieth birthday. She carried her sadness with her, quietly though, without the need for psychiatric intervention.

As a result of the sudden loss, Gloria found it difficult to form lasting relationships with men. She often wondered if they were born clueless or society allowed them enormous entitlement when it came to the practicality of life. They all tended to tell Gloria what she already knew and some even asked her for help choosing paint colors to enliven their naked walls. Many dates ended in disappointment. And then one day, Gloria stopped spending time in their company. She found life easier without expectation. Shortly after this realization, Pete flew in her kitchen window and filled the void left by her parents.

When looking at her new house, she saw her and Pete happy in the perfection of smallness. However, the compost toilet left her baffled when noticing it didn't flush in the traditional sense. She wondered if it could be converted to the local water supply. Afterall, water flowed freely into the sinks and down the shower drain. Why not the toilet?

Gloria had never owned a house before acquiring the deed to this delightful looking twenty-foot purple and green rectangular box with high ceilings and a sky light. After college, she had rented a New England carriage house behind a mansion, eventually teaching at that same college so felt no need to move. On rainy days in the heat of the summer, she could smell the horses previously occupying her residence. The odorous mixture of horse sweat and dung made her feel connected to the earth in an exquisite sense of existing in Oneness written about in her Eastern philosophy books. She marveled over the phenomenon of not fitting in where she belonged. Your most adept psychotherapist could not solve this mystery even if they were aware of its existence in the first place, especially if they hadn't studied it in a textbook written by someone else.

Pete jumped on the railing, twirled a couple of times, and flew inside to land on a perch bought by Maisie from *Dave's Aviary Store*. A litter box had been placed at the bottom for Pete's dainty droppings. He was a housebroken bird with a fastidious bath routine and a habit of squirting himself from Gloria's expensive eau de cologne bottles. Maisie watched the pair coo over their new home. She loved being a bystander to other people's happiness.

Gloria climbed the stairs to the loft and Pete flew from his perch to land on the ledge behind the large mattress occupying most of the room. Small windows flanked the bed with an equally inviting ledge for Pete to practice his moves while Gloria propped herself against several decorator pillows and settled into read. A crosswalk had been built connecting the bedroom to the far wall allowing her to access the bookshelves cleverly situated with enough room for her to sit on a small stool with wheels. Maisie smiled at Pete and Gloria as they exclaimed over every detail of their new home. Watching Pete fly in the enormous air space over the living area gave Gloria confidence she had made the right decision.

"Wow, the whole place is an architectural masterpiece like a dollhouse you can live in." Gloria eased herself down the wooden steps while thinking she would ask the carpet store to install a runner to keep her from sliding off the edges. She envisioned a Persian design, vintage, the kind you see in New England houses laying modestly on hardwood floors bought from Sotheby's and worth a tidy sum of money.

"A husband and wife had it especially designed for their needs but unfortunately the husband died days before they were to move in. Which is why everything is so new."

"That's the saddest story I ever heard. What happened to the wife?" Gloria asked, making herself comfortable on the small sectional in the corner. Fold down tables were screwed against the wall to maximize space. Maisie lowered one which doubled as a desk where Gloria sat delighted over the possibility of having a comfortable place where she could put her feet up and rest in her thoughts of turning the question of morality into something your average person could grasp for reference. Not an easy task, considering today's descension and the tendency of a few ignoramuses to trounce on the Constitution's 1st amendment.

Maisie sat across from her. "She found a lovely cottage in town and opened a small antique store. A nice woman from Up North like yourself." Maisie looked sad over the memory for a moment and then smiled sweetly.

"Up North?"

"Pretty much anything north of Kentucky is Up North down here." Maisie laughed.

"Makes it sound like a foreign country. Although, we Northerners do use the term Down South but without bearing any ill will. Except, some Northerners pride themselves on being superior to anyone with an accent and are dumb enough to consider Southerners less intelligent. A ploy I've always thought." Gloria appeared vacant when stepping inside her thoughts to expand a good thread.

"Oh yes, I agree. There is that tendency of really smart Southerners to let Northerners underestimate them."

"Toward what purpose?" Gloria asked, cocking her head to the side waiting to take in an explanation.

"Underestimating a genius gives them the advantage to catch their opponent unawares and verbally flogged them to death with the truth as they see it." Maisie laughed again.

Both women laughed and Pete chimed in, "Let It Be Me. Let It Be Me!"

"Pete's favorite Everly Brothers' song. I play it for him at night before bed. He used to have a little girlfriend but she moved away. He often sang it to her." Gloria turned sad.

"Oh, I play lullabies on the violin. Usually in the early evening. I'll play it for him tonight."

"Oh, would you? How kind. We would enjoy hearing you." Gloria glanced at Maisie with appreciation. She wondered if they could be friends. She reminded her of Penelope and felt a wave of nostalgia for the happy hours spent chatting in the campus library.

"Of course. Now, though, I should get back to baking scones. Tomorrow's the Ladies' Tea. You'll have to come when you get settled." Maisie smiled and waved goodbye to Pete.

"Ladies' Tea?" Gloria stood on the wooden porch and called after her.

"Later!" Maisie glanced back over her shoulder, smiling at her new neighbor's perplexity. Gloria's heavy intellect and unwavering curiosity had not been lost on her.

FIVE

Elmo Bond, despite having a father with questionable morals, grew into a nice young man. He kept his promise to Penelope and read *Pride and Prejudice* all the way to the end. Elmo guffawed when reading the part where Mr. Darcy confesses to Elizabeth that he's a virgin, implied in the sentence about saving himself for her. This after being an arrogant jerk who insults her family's social standing. Elmo thought the book must have been written for women to enjoy the flirtatious antics in the faltering courtships of couples stuck in a class system that belied understanding.

Elmo gave little thought to a person's background either as an excuse for their bad behavior or something that should be pitied for its lack of refinement. His thoughts lit upon his father's rough edges and his mother's sweetness. He wondered from time to time how they ever got together and why. He had noticed his father's habit of knocking him and his brother senseless in the barn and then quickly changing moods to nuzzle their mother in the kitchen while she was cooking supper. This made her giggle and nauseated young Elmo. It put him off marriage and caused him to turn his attention toward a career in agricultural science combined with botany.

Elmo found *Lost in Sunshine* on Google Maps, a tiny dot on the landscape. He studied the surrounding farmland and noticed the large cultivated areas. He searched the want ads for jobs in his field but only found one at a non-profit group called *Farm Rite*. Elmo distrusted intentional misspellings of important words, especially shortening 'right to rite' and 'night to nite'. He wondered about the creditability of their organization if they couldn't give it a proper name, something serious like *Farming Science and Ecology*. He decided to apply and sent off his resume listing his degrees in botany and agriculture science with a minor in business management. He also listed the twelve years doing back breaking field work for his father or what he referred to in his cover letter as hands-on. The following day he received a phone call from an eager young voice asking, "When can you start?" He gave himself a week to grab his diploma, say goodbye to Penelope, and pack his few belongings in his Chevy truck before hitting the road, excited over soon seeing his favorite professor. Penelope promised to visit him but he held little expectation he would see her again. This caused his spirits to lag some when staring into the uncertainty of his future. Elmo, for some strange reason, felt Miss Professor Dobbins held all the answers to the mystery of living life lightly while stepping into a tenuous future.

~

The following morning, Pete stood on his railing and took a long look at his surroundings. He listened to the other birds, watched Hugo and his puppies, plus the irascible cat he had encountered the previous day. They were praying at a bush, mumbling something about Mother Mary having been generous to them, especially Hugo, who had been recently reunited with his parents. They chattered on about learning English and being grateful to work in Senor Benny's flower garden. Mostly, Hugo stressed the importance of feeling like he had a real home.

Pete understood exactly how the little boy felt. His early years had been spent locked in an ancient woman's bird cage and told daily to shut his beak, otherwise she would toss him out the window and let him fend for himself. At some point, Pete thought the threat of being homeless sounded like the better alternative than being stifled by the unhappy soul who felt the need to lock him in a cage. The confinement hampered his natural tendency to be a happy bird with the voice of a young Pavarotti. He knew how to unlock his cage and waited patiently for her to open a window. Finally, an opportunity presented itself. He zipped past her knotted grey hair and found freedom on the other side of the window. It smelled like sweet air wafting from a lilac bush.

Pete spent several days flying freely, eating berries, and sitting on people's windowsills to sing his early morning arias to their delighted faces. One day he sat on the windowsill of a bookish type named Gloria Dobbins. She didn't look up from the book she was reading at the kitchen table when he first began singing. But being a tenacious little bird, he kept singing. The moment a perfect rendition of 'Let It Be Me' eased from his beak emphasized by melodic breaks of whistling, she glanced at him and smiled. When she opened the window, Pete flew inside and never left. He understood exactly how the small boy felt and admired the tenacity of prayer, although thinking it often alternated between gratitude and begging.

Pete being a mystical bird always lived in a state of gratitude. His travels to the higher realms of consciousness allowed for quick respites in the lap of the Divine where living was easy and time was endless. The saints called him Dadhu, which he knew wasn't exactly a compliment but a tribute to his good looks and charm in the worldly world having no place in the ethereal company of the pure of heart. Mostly, he suffered from bouts of vanity when peacocking in the regions beyond the trees. On the earth plane, your average bird lived at the mercy of the elements under the constant threat of being knocked off his perch and left to linger on the ground prey to all things walking on legs. It was a harsh life for a bird, especially a proud cockatoo who believed he was a sight for sore eyes and placed here to love all beings.

Suddenly, he heard guitar music coming from his neighbor's log house accompanied by a gruff voice singing in the groove of funk music, heavy on the bass scales with the note-wise sound of James Brown. Pete began to tap his feet and slide up and down his railing but when glancing over to the singer's house, he noticed a long black thing lying motionless in the front yard. Feeling the need to get closer, Pete flew over and landed on the black surface hopping to the beat, a happy bird unaware of having awakened Charlie Walker. He glided up and down Charlie's smooth back for a full five minutes before noticing his surface was moving toward the middle eventually winding itself into a circle where Pete kept on grooving, coming down hard on the funky beat. Meanwhile, Charlie Walker hollered for Esther to hurry over and have a swat at the bothersome bird before he squeezed the last peep from his warbling beak.

Esther and her entourage rushed over to check out the commotion but upon arriving in Bo's front yard, they found a funny scene that sent them all into fits of laughter. Esther told Charlie to pull himself together and look for common ground when living next door to a harmless bird oblivious to his wicked ways. Charlie only took in the compliment of being considered wicked by Esther, who disliked sniveling creatures and half-baked stories about coming from the swamp ghetto. She was a hard cat to please.

"The saints call me Dadhu, my Bird-Mom calls me handsome, and the ancient lady called me a nuisance. While I may be many things, I'm a bird groovin' on the beat of a good song and one who was born to love. I slide around people's moods and smile at their eccentricities while moving to a funky motion. I can hear the melodies coming from the trees sung by birds with big hearts enchanted by sound."

"A saint named Baba Das says, "Dadhu,

why you don't sit still and listen to the sound of the flute coming from the heavenly spheres? It will purify your soul and take you back Home where you yearn to go."

"Naturally, I give this some serious thought and sit next to the radiant being, but notice we aren't exactly working it out on the highest plane. So, I say, "Baba Das, I do little harm on the Earth plane and meditate on my perch in the afternoons but am flawed by my tendency to show off my plumage and spread my wings when overcome by the Funkadelic. My feet start tapping to the birds singing their righteous song. What chance do I have to follow the flute back Home where I will be embraced by heavenly love? Where I will no longer be I but thou?"

"Dadhu, you have a bird's chance. Last time you came into this world, you were an insect searching for crumbs. What say you spend more time in meditation and less time toe-tapping so you can enjoy the perks of a human birth next life time?"

"But Baba Boss, what will a human birth give me, I don't already have? They're not God's best from my vantage point. A dog has better manners, wouldn't torture her babies, destroy the ground she walks on, and live in the delusion of self-importance."

"Dadhu, I was sent down to this realm to have a talk with you. You got to work a little harder, be still a little longer, and catch a ride on the sound of the flute. Next time I see you, I'll be whistling the same tune." Imagine my confusion when hearing these words. Here I think I've got it going on and then suddenly discover this is not all there is. I figure it's probably best to follow a saint's advice and spend more time on my perch listening to the inner music."

Your humble servant, Pete

SIX

Gloria stood at the kitchen sink peeling an apple to share with Pete. Lately, he had been spending an inordinate amount of time meditating on his perch. They repeated the same dialogue when he finally opened his eyes.

"Watcha doin'?" Gloria would ask.

"Meditatin'. Watcha doin'?" This made Gloria laugh and she would always answer with whatever activity she was doing at the time.

Today though a scrawny figure crossed her line of vision from the kitchen window. It reminded her of the second man in the convenience store. When putting on her glasses for a closer look, she was convinced he had followed her down the road to her new home and was now lurking at the edge of her backyard like a man stalking his prey. She deliberated over calling the police or Maisie. Finally, deciding to take matters into her own hands when the man turned to stare directly at her with a menacing expression on his face.

She ran out the back door picking up a broom

on her way in case she needed to defend herself. She considered going back for her notebook but decided time was of the essence. Earl recognized the crazy woman from the convenience store and wondered for a second what to do about her if she hit him with the broom.

"Hold on, little lady. Not bothering you none. Jus' walkin' the periphery."

"Why?"

"I'm Earl Hubbard, the police chief of the local jurisdiction," he responded with a note of self-importance. "My job to kep you all safe and sound."

"*Lost in Sunshine* is an unincorporated area, so your jurisdiction would stop short of the boundary line. This means you're trespassing."

"Well now, ain't you an uppity thing. Some Up North piece o' know it all come down har to change our ways. You best be gittin' on back home whar yer come from."

"You better watch the way you speak to me, or I'll call the county sheriff and have you charged for being a peeping Tom."

Earl's temper caused the vein to bulge at his temple and his jaw to tighten like a mason jar. "Don't truck with me none, or I might lose control of my shootin' finger." He pulled his rifle up and rested it on his free arm in a threatening manner.

Gloria's brain went into overdrive when witnessing the idiocy of the town law enforcement. She wondered, in fact, if the man was an idiot or an asshole and upon further reflection decided a man could be both. She then entertained such a man would be irrational and possibly bordering on dangerous. In one fell swoop, she bashed the side of his head with the broom and then had a go at his legs causing his rifle to go off the second he lost his balance and keeled over.

Bo and Charlie Walker heard the shot and hurried out the back door to find the source. They figured it might be a hunter or possibly Earl shooting at the animal population. Bo looked around for his reptile and saw him slithering safely up a tree. He turned back to see his new neighbor throttling a prone figure on the ground with a broom. When realizing it must be Earl, he began to laugh so loud, Gloria stopped a second to see where the noise was coming from. Bo stood behind her, grinning. He gently removed the broom from Gloria's hands and told Earl to pick himself up off the ground. It wasn't dignified.

"I've been neglectin' my manners. I'm Bo Walker and my reptile Charlie Walker is hanging in the tree behind us." He extended his hand. "Welcome to the neighborhood. This here is the local chief of police. He's harmless 'nough but can irritate a person with his constant presence and false sense of authority. Best to ignore him." Bo walked his neighbor to her backdoor while offering to be of service whenever she came upon a problem like a leaky faucet or an intrusive field mouse. Gloria smiled and invited him to the front porch where she would join him shortly with her notebook and a pitcher of black iced tea. She told him Pete had learned Charlie Walker's name so don't be surprised to hear it come sailing out the front window. Bo laughed happy anyone would pay a bit of attention to his sidekick. He then wondered about the notebook.

SEVEN

Elmo Bond drove an easy pace toward his destination, a country rooming house called *Sam's Place*. He pulled into the dirt parking lot and took in the charming farmhouse with an addition on the back where a sign hung by the door reading Sam's Office. The white clapboard house possessed a homey charm accentuated by two ducks and a chicken pecking at the grass. A hog stood nearby enjoying a soft warm breeze coming from the south. The hog smiled with a cheery obliviousness often seen on parish priests supported by their parishioners. Elmo wondered if the large pink animal had been put there for decoration or had she decided to take a stroll among the lush foliage. Just then, he was startled by three piglets squealing under the bushes calling to their mother. Having grown up on a farm, Elmo knew this was odd behavior for a new mother. Usually, animals pulled their young close after birth and never let them go until it was time to wean.

Elmo bent over and picked up one of the

piglets only to find himself lying on the ground looking up at a pretty sky full of fluffy clouds and the brightness of the summer sun. Then he heard someone laughing in the background.

"I agree, the little ones are irresistible, but you should mind their mama is a big 'un." A tall sapphic woman stood outside the office door. She appeared to be about fifty-years old, someone who would be called handsome due to her tanned leathery skin, and eyes as green as emeralds and twice as bright. "You must be Elmo Bond. Welcome to Sam's." She pulled him swiftly to his feet.

"Pleased to meet you, ma'am." Elmo shook her hand and bowed slightly as a courtesy to her formidable demeanor. He found himself level with her breasts, enormous cushions where a man-boy could rest his head and sigh from years of torment. He resisted the urge and tried not to stare at the way her waist tapered only to expand into hips that could draw a body to lie down and feel safe. He straightened himself up and made an effort to look manly.

"Call me Sam. Your room is ready for you. Since we don't get many guests this time of year, I gave you the large ensuite with an alcove overlooking the pond." She flashed Elmo a dazzling smile filled with bright white teeth and downhome sincerity. He relaxed in her presence and looked forward to settling into his new home.

Elmo's nerves began to tremble on the way down due to being so young and giving too much thought over a decision that could be undone. His chest tightened from thinking too much. He stopped and said goodbye to his mother when driving through Kentucky. His father hollered in his truck window, "Don't do anythin' stupid to embarrass the family!" Elmo considered his father to be the only embarrassment in their family. Still though, hearing his old man hurl these spiteful words caused his mind to revisit childhood, which had always been a dangerous place to be. On the days it rained, he felt the aches and pains of all the broken bones given to him by a man with a violent temper and no inclination to evolve into kindness. The man seemed to enjoy a cathartic experience every time he slammed one of his sons against the side of the barn. Childhood had left him feeling depleted, but now he looked forward to a future of new beginnings. His professor came to mind as someone who could help sort through his father's morality. A hard task for a boy to decipher, but now he was a man and ready to go to the darker regions of his father's mind.

~

Gloria sat across from Bo on her front porch, notebook in hand, and Pete settled on the railing. Pete beckoned for Charlie Walker to join him. It took some convincing Esther wasn't going to appear suddenly and sink her claws into his delicate body. After a few minutes, Charlie made himself comfortable on the railing next to Pete and began to tell his story about coming from a swamp ghetto, clearly forgetting he had once told Esther it was paradise in the Everglades. Now though, he could see Pete was a sympathetic listener and began filling his ears with a vagabond, hard-luck story of being tossed hither and yon until he finally landed in what he thought was nearly paradise. He paused for a moment and added the man at the petting zoo was a cruel boss and pulled all his teeth out so he couldn't bite the children.

Pete listened intently and sympathized in the appropriate places and then told him all of God's creatures had value. He borrowed a few words from Baba Das when encouraging him to meditate on the heavenly realms. Charlie had no idea what the little bird was talking about but liked the melodic sound of his whistling and the comfort it gave him to find a friend. He smiled a toothless grin.

"Well, I'll be damned, aren't they a pair?" Bo said, marveling over Pete giving his reptile a kiss and saying "pretty boy" causing Charlie to smile like a silly fool hungering for approval.

"Do you mind if I turn on Pete's radio? He loves to dance. I'll keep the volume down." Gloria was pleased the python hadn't swallowed her bird whole and spit him out when a feather stuck in his throat.

"No, of course not. The little guy does love to dance. He's got better moves than the patrons at *Duke's Rye Bar* where my band plays ever' weekend. Come some time. I'd be happy to buy you a drink." Bo beamed at Gloria while thinking she would be a beauty with some sun on her face, take the white out of her skin, and let her dark hair fall down from the knot clamped to the back of her head. He noticed she was a skinny sort, not much bigger than your average eleven-year-old boy. He saw a lovely lady underneath the rigid pretense. He wondered what caused all the constriction but let it go when stumbling across the thought everybody has their own burden to carry. Maybe he ought to take a good hard look in the mirror at his own appearance and clean it up a bit.

"Oh, I shouldn't think so. Probably too many assholes sitting on barstools for me to sift through," Gloria said, uneasy at the thought of being overwhelmed.

"Whoa there, the patrons come to unwind and take a load off." Bo seemed offended by her words.

"Oh, I'm so sorry. I should explain myself." She sat back in her chair when hearing Pete's favorite song playing on the radio.

"No, I'm sorry. Forgettin' my manners. Ever'body judges people different."

"Let me expound upon that last sentence. Put it in context. I'm examining the possibility of redeeming assholes by introducing them to Eastern philosophy's concept of Oneness." She smiled brightly as though any downhome boy would have a clue as to what she was talking about. Bo liked her despite himself.

"That's a tall order, Gloria. There are so many of them. Where would you begin?" Bo found himself enjoying the professor's company, mostly because her unaffected manner was refreshing. His women companions tended to be stylized with an abundance of makeup and low cut, short dresses with long tan legs, and usually slightly drunk on alcohol causing them to slur their words.

"Police Chief Earl comes to mind."

Bo laughed so hard, he choked on an ice cube. "Yes, he's prime asshole material. The best we got 'round here."

"Oh, I'm pleased you're not offended I chose one of your locals." Gloria jotted down a few words in her notebook."

Again, Bo laughed. "Well now, none of

us here take responsibility for Earl's actions. He's a rare breed. Doesn't take no never mind at where he points that rifle of his. The man's a hazard on his good days." Bo shook his head and smiled. "'Xactly how would you categorize him among the others, or do they all have the same leanings?"

"That's an excellent question. One of the more prevalent types doesn't like to wait in line, shows little empathy for those in front of him, and can't help question why they left the house that day if they can't manage to have their money in hand when putting their items on the counter." Gloria wrote an entire sentence in her notebook and glanced appreciatively at Bo.

"Definitely describing Earl. I saw him once at *Jack's Groceries* nudging the lady in front him with his rifle nearly scaring her to death before he had time to shoot her for loitering. He's a sorry sort in some ways. Doesn't seem to be able to hep himself. I spoke to him on that occasion and he threatened to shoot Charlie Walker next time he was out my way. Frightened me a little. The man must be half-baked. You think maybe his problems might be a bit more serious than your common ever'day asshole?" Bo began to make himself comfortable in their conversation. He couldn't remember the last time somebody grabbed his attention long enough to listen.

"Yes, you're onto something there. He may be a low-level psychopath, one who doesn't actually kill people but does enjoy tormenting them and watching for signs of fear. Makes him feel powerful. No empathy there, either. Hard to tell."

"I 'spect so."

"Does beg an answer. I wonder if he would let me follow him around for a day to observe his behavior." Gloria glanced at Bo who busied himself giving it some thought.

"Don't think it'd be safe. But if it heps, he begins the day eating breakfast at *Maggie's Diner*. Mostly botherin' the customers and grabbin' at the waitresses. The man's never heard of the 'Me Too' movement and appears unable to keep a respectable distance behind a boundary. Don't know if it's his natural tendency or part of being a psychopath you were talkin' about."

"Psychopaths have no awareness of others and don't suffer remorse. You can get an asshole to apologize if he's smart enough to see your perspective. Do you know if he's ever been evaluated in the psych ward at the hospital?"

"Earl! Good Lord, woman, I don't think anyone within a fair distance from here has been evaluated for possessin' a loose screw." Bo rumbled with laughter. "Not sure we even have a psych ward. Usually, people go to Maisie for help with their troubles. Somehow, she even managed to get Esther to have patience with Charlie Walker and prove to ever' body he could behave himself in civilized company. A miracle if you ask me. Yep, Maisie can hep you fill your notebook. Wouldn't hurt to go to one of her Ladies' Teas and listen to the women talk about their husbands. 'Nough to raise the hair on a man's neck and make him doubt hisself."

"That's a brilliant idea. Thank you for being patient." Gloria thought he might be good looking if he changed his T-shirt and used Clorox on the tobacco stain at the corners of his mouth.

They sat awhile and watched Pete dance along the railing occasionally hopping on Charlie's smooth back to slide easily into his funk groove.

EIGHT

Maisie opened her window when seeing Pete land on the sill. He began to sing 'I'm goin' off the grid' repeating the line several times before singing 'take a breath' several more times. Maisie picked up her violin and played the harmony, prompting Pete to continue with even more gusto. They worked on the song together for half an hour with Maisie singing along with him. She taught Pete a few more stanzas. He flapped his wings with joy and now sang 'I'm goin' off the grid, take a breath, talk to God, I'm goin' off the grid' repeating this refrain, pleased with himself. Maisie thought the little bird must be a cockatoo music prodigy.

Esther sat in the background nauseated over the *Austin City Limits* display of what she perceived as nonsensical chirping. Her mood took a downward turn causing her to cling to Benny for comfort. He always ministered to her needs but since inviting Maisie into his house, he felt the need to share himself. Actually, Benny was besotted with the love-of-his-life, which also annoyed Esther. She had decided to leave home for a while, move in with Manuel and enjoy being the center of attention. This lasted until Esther discovered a bowl had been set for her next to Manuel's bowl filled with black beans and Cheetos. She turned up her nose and scampered back to her own bowel filled with her special blend of cat food for pampered pets. After giving it some thought, she decided her life wasn't so bad after all. This happened previous to Pete's arrival.

Maisie spent most of the day perfecting recipes for the Ladies' Tea and scouring the countryside with Benny where they searched for antiques to complement the new addition to his Spanish adobe style house. Maisie found a brass bed and a small painting from the interior of Mexico reminding her of Frida Kahlo, her favorite artist. She put these in their new bedroom. Benny had also thought to add an adjacent sunroom where Maisie could grow an indoor garden and escape with a good book or whatever a woman does when in need of privacy. He made his house their home.

Benny spent his days working in the gardens next to Hugo's parents, who were adding to their basic plant knowledge by taking classes in herbalism. Benny had incorporated their backlot into his allowing them extra room to grow their herbs. So far, they had learned to cultivate ginseng, echinacea, turmeric, ginkgo biloba, and elderberry. Later, they would learn the art of turning them into medicinal concoctions to advertise on the underground newsletter *Mountaineers' Grapevine* in hopes of alleviating discomfort at a small price and profit. Altogether, everyone lived in harmony enjoying each other's company and loving their working lives.

Occasionally, Benny retrieved his mother's letter, cried a little when reading it, feeling the pangs of nostalgia. This made him appreciate his present life and allowed him an understanding that nothing's permanent. He cherished the moment. His former life as an explosives expert receded into the background along with Elena. A postcard had arrived one day from the old General with the words 'No worries, Benny Boy. Success on the frontlines'. Benny interpreted this to mean Elena had been put to good use, allowing him to rest easy. Nothing could ruffle his feathers. Even Gloria and Bo made him smile, especially when seeing them strolling on the lanes together. He wondered what they had in common and made a mental note to invite them to a barbecue.

~

The following morning, Gloria once again glanced out the kitchen window to see a man in her backyard, only this time it was someone with a beautiful, serene face sitting in a meditative pose, waiting. She recognized her student Elmo Bond and wondered why he suddenly appeared in her backyard. Possibly he levitated there, she thought, or maybe he bilocated his mystical form to go where his heart took him. Either way, his sudden appearance gave her spirits a lift. She hurried out the backdoor and sat down next to him.

Elmo opened his eyes. "Took a while to find you. Shocked when the Dean showed up in class those last few days." He looked hard at her as though expecting an explanation for abandoning him.

"I do apologize for the disruption but our illustrious Dean felt the need to send me on a sabbatical, so I could write my opinions down on paper instead of sharing them in the classroom. I'm trying to prove my theories and wondering if assholes are worth the effort of being understood." She jumped up.

Elmo fell in stride with her, walking back to the kitchen where she invited him inside. "You still working out the morality question?" He sat at the kitchen table. Pete flew from his perch and landed on the chair across from him.

"Hello, pretty boy! Hello, pretty boy."

"Well, hello yourself, pretty boy." Elmo

laughed gently and his eyes brightened for the first time in years.

"I'm living off the grid, take a breath, talk to God, I'm living off the grid." Pete sang with gusto.

"Well now, you made my day. Heck, you made my year, and put a smile on my face. What's your name, pretty boy?"

"Pete Pretty Boy. What's your name? What's your name?"

"Elmo. Elmo Bond." Elmo laughed and shook his head. Pete flew back to his perch and left a stranger feeling better for having met him. Elmo was convinced the little bird sang with the angels and sat on God's shoulders, words spoken by his mother when meeting a kindly soul who took the time to ask how she was doing today.

Gloria placed the iced tea pitcher, along with two glasses, and a plate of lemon cookies on the table and sat down. "Yes, the morality question. It does pique a person's interest in finding answers. At the moment, I'm thinking morality concerning assholes has to do with their perspective of themselves through social conditioning. If they've been raised in a society that glorifies a man's bad-boy behavior, then of course, they will feel entitled to bulldoze their way into any situation, such as cutting in line, honking at the pedestrians for stepping off the curb, or speaking harshly to people they consider inferior to themselves, which seems to be about everyone but themselves. So, from their limited viewpoint, they are morally justified in behaving badly. They don't understand other people have the right to stand peacefully in line and wait their turn, or not be yelled at by a random stranger, and expect others to abide by the morals put in place for everyone to honor. The entitled asshole simply doesn't get it."

"Are you saying they shouldn't be held accountable because of their upbringing?" Elmo leaned forward to hear her answer. He was thinking about his father, wondering if he was raised in a household that failed to punish his reprehensible behavior and gave a nod to his kick-ass ways.

"Not at all. Professor James brings up the concept of free will, and I agree with him." Gloria munched on a cookie, deep in thought, hardly aware of the sweet tang of lemon and sugar. "It just occurred to me you might want to join me tomorrow at a place called *Maggie's Diner*. The town asshole I'm observing right now is Police Chief Earl Hubbard. I'm told he's there most mornings at nine bothering the customers and often creating a scene that makes the nerves of everyone in the vicinity stand on edge. What do you think?"

"Sure. I don't start my first day at work until afternoon." Elmo beamed at the idea of being invited to help one of the most controversial yet endearing professors at the university.

"You have a job already?"

"Oh, I was hired before arriving here. At a non-profit called Farm Rite. Helping farmers switch to organic farming, not an easy process. Farm Rite also goes into the Hills and teaches the farmers how to irrigate, avoid certain viruses that proliferate in this area, and grow marketable crops on the hillsides, replace the topsoil, and cultivate gardens to feed the family during the winter months. And much more. They also gave me a greenhouse to perfect my botany experiments. All fascinating work, but I'm going to have to keep my side job as a consultant to a chemical company for real money. Man can't make much these days doing the right thing." Elmo frowned and drank his iced tea.

"That's wonderful. Where are you living?"

"At a nice rooming house called *Sam's Place*. It's really a farmhouse converted to a bed and breakfast. Sam lets the livestock meander to create atmosphere for the city guests. They're treated like pets, really, even the hog named Daisy who's a real hoot. Likes to be scratched behind the ears and often forgets she gave birth to the three piglets running behind her. Poor things have to remind her she's their mother and only source of food. All very funny in a sweet way."

"You're a beautiful soul, Elmo Bond. Speaking of beautiful souls, how's Penelope? She's the only person who knows my whereabouts." Gloria stared at Elmo waiting for him to answer, curious as to whether he was smitten by the pretty librarian.

"Causes my heart to sigh just thinkin' about her. What a lovely sad thing, hidin' downstairs in the labyrinth of learnin'. That girl belongs in the sunshine with me walking woodland paths and smelling the wild roses draped over a fence post." Elmo's thoughts drifted to their last meeting, a sad moment, both thinking of the possibility they may never see each other again.

"Oh no, you are smitten with her. She is as lovely as a rose. You two would be happy together. Maybe, I'll give her a call." Gloria studied Elmo's face for a reaction but he had already gone blank from nearing the emotion of loss.

"Did you know there's a rose called Steve?"

Gloria laughed. "I had no idea. What does Steve look like?"

"A pretty orange and apricot ruffled beauty with dark pink edges," Elmo replied. "Well, I've taken up enough of yours and Pete's time. I'll see you tomorrow, Professor, and we'll go videotape ourselves an asshole." He stood and proffered a hand. Instead, Gloria gave him a hug and called for Pete to say goodbye.

"Goodbye Elmo Bond. Goodbye." Pete flew around the corner and landed on Gloria's shoulder craning his neck to look into her eyes. "Peekaboo. Peekaboo. Wanna kiss? Wanna kiss?"

"He's a charmin' fella." Elmo smiled and walked out the backdoor turning to wave at Gloria and her bird.

Thirty minutes later, he sat in his truck talking to his mother on the phone. 'Tell me, Mama, what was the old man's upbringing like. What made him so mean? No disrespect, Mama. But I would like to have some understandin' before he up and dies from anger."

Mrs. Bond heard the pleading in her son's voice. She felt bad for not making a better home for him. Her husband was her only visible means of support, which forced her to please his every whim in hopes it would calm his temper and cause him to be kinder to his sons. It never did. She told Elmo as much as she knew about his father's upbringing as a rodeo child who was first put in a saddle at age of four and made to ride a steer at the age of ten before being placed on a bull by the time he was fourteen and told if he got tossed from the bull, he could expect a beating when he came home. He quickly turned into a crackerjack rider and won monies for his courage. Naturally, he was praised by the enthralled spectators, his own father, and the other bull riders. He made a name for himself and sent money home, all causing him to become a prideful man. Sometimes, though, his nerves shook so hard, he felt the need to calm them with a drink that led to a night of brawling in the bars and waking up in the local jail. But being a rodeo circuit hero, the sheriff always let him go without charges and asked for his autograph when returning his personal effects.

Then one day, he saw his future wife looking pretty as a picture, a tiny thing with a big smile and breasts the size of small honeydew melons and a behind shaped like a pear. His limited exposure to female anatomy left him only with fruit analogies and an awkward grin that captivated his future wife. They settled on a farm and not five years later, he had turned into a restless man with a temper as fierce as the bulls he used to ride. He couldn't acclimate his nature to farm work and children. Not to mention, he noticed his wife had lost her pear-shaped behind and her breasts began to sag from feeding their children.

Mr. Bond had no way of measuring his manhood resulting in his fury being thrown at his family. Unfortunately, even the town doctor couldn't settle him down. The sheriff was too afraid of him to press assault charges so let him spend the night in a jail cell, offering the sorrowful prisoner a respite from his troubles.

The rodeo hero fell into the asshole category. He couldn't see the wrong in his behavior and remained bent on beating his sons until they developed a backbone, something he told them repeatedly. He sometimes tossed them on the neighbor's bull and watched them fly through the air causing him to bend double in spasms of laughter after yelling, "Yer never goin' be real men like yer daddy."

Elmo's mother apologized for not telling her son the childhood story of Mr. Bond sooner in hopes of alleviating the inadequacy he may feel when using his father's spiteful words as a yardstick to measure his own manhood. She reminded him a man is a gentle soul with the ability to see God in all living beings and by this definition she went on to say, "Yer the man yourn daddy will never be."

Elmo let go of a few tears when hearing these words. He thanked his mother for sharing what he knew to be a painful memory and said someday he would build her a pretty house. She thanked him politely and said she had made a vow to God and the preacher, "Till death us do part." Elmo hoped God would take pity on his mama and shorten his father's life span. Meanwhile, he looked forward to drawing similarities between the town asshole and his father.

NINE

Pete remembered the words of Baba Das telling him to sit in stillness. The little bird took offense when the saint alluded to his flighty nature, but after all he was a bird with wings. He decided to take a spin to the higher realms and ask a few questions for Bird-Mom.

"Every time I find myself in the light, I feel as weightless as an autumn leaf catching a ride on a soft breeze. I look down and see my feet dancing atop a tree branch held up by the divine hand that keeps me afloat in the heavenly spheres where time is an illusion and even my presence may be a question-able figment. I glance around and see all the souls shining like three-hundred-watt bulbs, each doing their own thing hardly noticing my hollow-boned body."

"I keep an eye out for Baba Das while pretending I'm meditating on the tree branch just in case he catches sight of me first, tossing a look of disappointment at his lackluster devotee. The only time I shine is in my own mind where I'm getting down to the rhyme tapping my feet and feeling the beat of the music. Just then, I see the saint himself calling for me to perch on his knee and tell him exactly what I've been up to, like he doesn't already know this sorry bird is not exactly killing it in the celestial regions meditating on a passing cloud."

"What brings you here, Dadhu Pete? He calls me by my earthly name, which means I'm nowhere near to being invited as a permanent resident in the divine sanctuary."

"I got some questions Baba Boss. Want to know when the sense of Oneness settles on an earthly soul and alleviates his loneliness and the fear that drives him to drink and generally become a nuisance to others only wanting to live in peace and harmony."

"Are you talking about Earl Hubbard?"

"One and the same. My Bird-Mom believes the man can be redeemed to enjoy the Oneness of all things. I suffer from doubts but love her for her optimism and the beauty of her intention."

"There's hope for you yet, Dadhu Pete." He smiles a saintly smile giving me a blissful feeling I am in his good grace again. He must have noticed I have been putting regular hours to my meditations, enjoying the divine sound current that will someday take me back to my original Home.

"You mean, you got an answer to my question?"

"Oneness occurs when we love all others. Then there is no separation. Only love."

"That's a tall order for most humans, who spend their time watching Netflix, drinking beer, and talking bad about their fellow man."

"Yes, Dadhu Pete. It is a tall order. Meditation is the answer." He smiles at me and then disappears into the nether regions where the saints go. I ponder the meaning of his words and wonder how to tell Gloria she's climbing uphill dragging an unconscious man behind her. Next thing I know, my feet are tapping along the porch railing picking up the beat to funk with a few angels dancing along with me." Your humble servant, Pete

TEN

The following morning Gloria and Elmo sat in the corner booth at *Maggie's Diner*. They sat together on one side of the booth making them appear to be lovers, but fortunately the second Earl stepped inside carrying his rifle, all heads turned in his direction. The jovial atmosphere went silent and three of the waitresses disappeared behind the swivel door to the kitchen. Gloria had ordered two man-sized breakfasts complete with pancake stacks and a side of bacon for show. Elmo didn't eat meat but in order to keep up the pretense was forced to act interested in chomping on the animal parts that nauseated him on a hungry day.

A video camera covered with cloth was propped on the napkin dispenser pointed in the direction of Earl seating himself at the bar and demanding to be fed. "Hey thar Brenda, I knowed yer back thar. Best be rustlin' up my over-easy eggs and a quarter pound o' ham. Git a move on. I feel like arrestin' somebody today." Earl glanced around the room, eyes pausing a few seconds on Gloria and the stranger sitting next to her. Just then, Brenda appeared from the kitchen and set his order in front of him. She poured three cups of coffee and left the pot. "You knowed Brenda I like my coffee hot. Aggravates me some when you ain't standin' thar waitin' to pour my next cup." He hollered so loud, a small boy began to cry from fright.

Gloria took notes, mostly on his sense of entitlement and general obliviousness to the feelings of those around him. Gloria remembered Bo's words and now agreed with him. Earl was definitely the town asshole no one would want to take responsibility for. He was a textbook case but worth a closer look for signs of psychopathy. The opportunity presented itself when the much-loved nursery owner Bob stopped by for his take-out order. Bob tipped his hat to the diners and smiled in Gloria's direction. She gave a little wave and then waited to see what would happen next.

"Laverne's been wanting daisies planted in the tractor tire layin' in the front yard. Called me useless fer not draggin' the thing to the dump. Says she's gonna plant daisies in it." Gloria snorted from reflex. Elmo put his hand on her arm, but Earl's attention had already turned in her direction. "Hey Missy, yer disrespectin' me?"

"No sir, I would never dream of disrespecting anyone, not even the town law officer," Gloria said matter-of-factly.

Bob felt obliged to intervene before Earl went on his usual morning rant. "Laverne hasn't contacted me about those daisies but am happy to spruce up the yard for her." Bob spoke softly in an effort to calm Earl's nerves before they took on a life of their own.

"You callin' the little woman a liar?" Earl's jaw went tense. He picked up his rifle leaning against the counter.

Again, Gloria snorted. She had never heard a wife being referred to as 'the little woman'. You could hear a collective gasp.

"Yer beginnin' to tire my butt." Earl flung off Bob's hand and went straight to Gloria's table where he threw her breakfast on the floor and dropped his cigarette in her coffee. She didn't appear stunned but stood up in order to avert any attention from Elmo who was busy filming the entire scene. Suddenly, a waitress came running with a mop and dustpan, scooped up the mess and hurried back to the kitchen. "Now thar, watcha gonna do about yer breakfast?" Earl jutted out his chin like a school yard bully causing Gloria to laugh out loud.

"I wasn't really hungry any way. I do apologize Brenda for the gentleman's bad behavior. I expect I'm going to be the person he arrests today." Gloria stepped closer and stared into the eyes of mad Earl Hubbard. Bob pulled him back, calming him down by telling him he was too much of a man to arrest a naive Northerner. Earl wasn't sure what naïve meant but decided it wasn't a compliment, which eased his mood some and allowed him to return to his own breakfast, manhood intact.

"Ya know, Bob, yer a right nice feller. Sit down and et yer breakfast next to me?" Before Bob could respond, Brenda shoved his to-go order at him and said they would settle up later. Bob turned on his heel and left.

'Well now, pertty lady. How about we go fer a walk in the back woods and have ourselves a picnic?"

"I'm a married woman, Earl." Brenda waved to her husband through the diner window. He had agreed to walk by every morning on his way to work at the newspaper office to make sure Earl wasn't bothering her. He saw her waving frantically so stepped inside the diner. Brenda's husband was six-foot four inches tall with a black belt in karate and a PI license for investigative work on the side. His dark hair and beard gave him a formidable demeanor that was both movie star handsome and slightly menacing when riled by Earl Hubbard.

He leaned on the counter next to Earl and asked if he was treating his wife with kindness or had he asked her out on a date again. The police chief often times missed the inuendo of a person's words and would plow through the conversation like a wild boar with blinders.

"Well, so what if'n I was? No blame in tryin'. 'Sides somebody that pertty oughta be shared." Several of the diners tucked money under their plates and hurried out the door. Among other things, Earl was bad for business.

Brenda's husband picked up Earl's hand and squeezed his fingers till they crumpled together into a mess of pain. "Tomorrow on your way here, I'll be waiting for you, pull you into an alley and bend your bones, so you'll be walking sideways. Ya hear, Earl?" Brenda's husband whispered through clinched teeth. No one heard the threat and if they did, knew enough to pretend otherwise. Fortunately, Elmo put a gizmo on his video recorder to pick up soft sounds.

Brenda's husband turned to walk out the door but not before discovering how impervious to sincerity Earl could be. The police chief pressed his rifle to the back of the tall man and said, "Reckon my rifle trumps yer fists either ways." Before Earl could finish feeling smug about his artillery, he found himself bent double with the butt of his own rifle stuck between his legs pressing heavy on his manly parts. He screamed like a banshee and slumped to the floor, lacking in dignity and mad enough to shoot somebody. The second Brenda's husband let go, Earl grabbed his rifle and took aim at Gloria leaving a bullet hole three inches above her head. Gloria scribbled one word in her notebook and lowered her head in case another bullet flew by. *Psychopath.*

Brenda's husband grabbed him by the scruff of the neck and threw him outside, calling over his shoulder to his wife. "Love ya, babe." She blew him a kiss and wiped off the counter with her dish rag.

The other waitresses scurried around Gloria's and Elmo's table clearing off their breakfasts and bringing a fresh plate of today's special along with a pot of coffee and reassurances today's meal would be on the house.

"Does this happen often?" Gloria asked, not wanting to miss the opportunity of interviewing people who dealt with Earl's antics on a daily basis.

"Most mornings the chief doesn't shoot at our diners, but he does enjoy scaring the ones who are new in town. Almost like he's got a need to show off."

"But why hasn't something been done about

him? He should be behind bars," Gloria persisted, staring at the young woman in disbelief. "You deserve a better work environment. Where's the chef?"

"Oh, Bernie? He's hiding in the kitchen. Normally, he would come out and greet newcomers, make them feel welcome to his establishment, but he's afraid o' Chief Earl. Most of us have been shot at one time or 'nother." The perky waitress smiled at Gloria and Elmo, told them to have a nice day, and 'y'al come back now'.

When left alone with their breakfast plates, Gloria moved to the other side of the table and continued taking notes. Elmo packed his video recorder in its case and turned his attention to pouring maple syrup on his pancakes. He shook some but then coming from Eastern Kentucky a person does on occasion encounter a stray bullet. Still though, he was surprised when seeing the bite of pancake on the end of his fork flapping around before landing in the sticky syrup. Gloria handed him a tin of Rescue Remedy lozenges and kept writing. He popped a few in his mouth and let his mind wander while waiting for them to work.

"Professor, you giving any thought to his being a psychopath instead of an asshole?"

"That's in my notes. I think he might be a homegrown asshole who was allowed to run amuck, resulting in psychopathic tendencies. I've not had a sane conversation with him yet and the town seems to hobble along without professionals to analyze his behavior." Gloria finished writing and smiled at Elmo. "Thank you for being here. Who knows what would have happened without a male presence?" Gloria visibly shuddered and then busied herself cutting her pancakes in tiny squares, which she smothered in maple syrup and proceeded to enjoy every last bite.

"What about your theory assholes can be redeemed by practicing the philosophy of Oneness?" Naturally, Elmo's thoughts traveled to his father, a man he considered lacking in human kindness. He had taken to heart his mother's sad description of his father's childhood constantly being challenged by a demanding father. Elmo didn't consider bull riding a heroic sport but instead thought it fell into the category of animal abuse. He had no use for people who tormented animals, no matter what their rationale.

"I have been poring through all the sacred texts and haven't found any instructions on how this can occur by a person's free will. From what I've gleaned so far, a person has to be touched by divinity itself." Gloria sighed over Earl's plight. "I've almost come to the conclusion not just Earl but all of us haven't a clue how this miracle can be achieved without a mystic. The only one who may fit that description would be Pete. The little bird has been charmed by God Himself and sits on his perch enjoying a place I can only imagine."

"Pete?"

"Yes, I've noticed over the years he goes to where somebody needs a soft- shoe dance and a pretty song. I figure he gets his instructions from a higher place than this one."

The two finished their breakfasts deep in thought, left a sizeable tip and waved at the hired help on their way out the door, but not before noticing Bernie's frazzled, sweet face smiling at them from the round window in the kitchen swivel door.

ELEVEN

Gloria watched Pete dance on the porch railing where she sat nearby drinking lemonade. Since the morning's falderal, her thoughts ran amuck trying to downplay the incident and at times shoving it aside as though she had not been shot at by a gun-crazed police chief. The enormity of this experience had yet to settle into her conscious awareness for its lack of ethics, not to mention, the law arrested your every-day citizen for shooting at people willy nilly and without thought given to consequences. She then tumbled onto the realization the town's police chief indulged in criminal behavior without giving credence to people's feelings. And does this make him an asshole, a narcissist or a psychopath? Or possibly all three? She wished Professor James was available to mull over the inner workings of Earl's mind. On the outside, it appeared to be a treacherous quagmire of compulsive actions rather than possessing any rationale for his random misdeeds and general aggravation over the mere presence of others in his comfort zone. The term comfort zone implied he might possess a few feelings, but even these could be classified as self-absorption.

Just then, Bo hollered over and asked if she would like some company. Naturally, she waved for him and Charlie Walker to join her and Pete on the porch. She ran inside and threw some lemon cookies and another glass on the tray. She wondered for a moment if snakes drank water and if so, do they drink it out of a bowl? Just in case, she put a small bowl of water on the tray and hurried outside to serve her guests.

"I didn't know whether or not Charlie would like some water. It is a warm day and well, frankly, I'm not sure how heat affects reptiles or any cold-blooded animal for that matter." Gloria caught a hold of her tongue when noticing she was rambling about nothing. She still felt shaky from the morning's ordeal.

"Not in the traditional sense like dogs lapping water from a bowl. Reptiles absorb water. Sometimes, I put Charlie Walker's rubber swimmin' pool out front and let him go for a swim. I figure he gets 'nough water for a small snake." They both glanced at Charlie stretched out on the railing content to let Pete practice his slide moves atop his smooth body. It felt like a Japanese foot massage, once again, leaving the reptile with a silly grin on his face.

Bo turned to Gloria with an expression of seriousness. "How did you make out at the *Diner* this morning?"

"If I were three inches taller, there would be a hole in the middle of my forehead. The man's a lunatic. Not sure how that plays into the asshole theory. I mean your average asshole doesn't shoot at you." Gloria sighed.

"Oh, I'm so sorry. If it helps, Earl's a crack shot and wouldna hurt you intentional. I git yer drift, though. People been sayin' that fer years but nobody's been able to do a thing about it. I 'spect he's gonna haveta hit rock bottom before changin' his nasty ways." Bo reached over and patted her hand. Since the last time they met, he had gone to the barber who not only cut his hair, gave him a shave, but also bleached the tobacco stains from the corners of his mouth. Gloria noticed he looked almost handsome. She studied his face for a second, long enough for him to give her a lovely smile that lit up his blue eyes expressing the pleasure he felt at being in her company.

Gloria's lackluster love life didn't leave her many memories to comfort the long sleepless nights or offer a blueprint on how to get a man to love her for the brainy nerd she presented to the world of academia. She had rarely traipsed further than the hallowed halls of university life and her parents left little in the way of encouragement to love. Her life had been gleaned from books, even the concept of Oneness remained elusive and something that only piqued her curiosity instead of compelling her to take a good look at what her soul got up to while her nose was stuck in a book. In some respects, Gloria limped along in a haze of confusion with only concrete facts to guide her from one day to the next. Occasionally, she felt something was lacking in her life.

The warmth of Bo's hand calmed her down, but unfortunately she felt the need to run this phenomenon through her mental grist mill to sort through its meaning. Maybe, she liked the man. Or maybe his body was warmer than hers creating the sensation of well-being. Gloria often considered passion a wasted emotion but sometimes wondered if she would benefit from having enough to draw her to a man's heat. These thoughts made her anxious, made her mind wander in a direction she had never been, which she considered a hazy place lacking in familiarity and possibly treacherous. Suddenly, her brain hit upon the idea of throwing herself at Bo for further study on whether or not humans needed to rub against each other for anything more than survival in the winter months. She shelved this notion for further processing and refilled their lemonade glasses.

"Maybe I'm wasting my time with Earl. I don't know what rock bottom would be for him. And besides, how can a man, who I suspect has never been raised with consideration for others, be expected to accept everyone as his equal, or in the words of the sacred texts '*We're all drops from the same ocean*'? Even my mind balks when trying to wrap my thoughts around the notion Earl and I are exactly the same, genetically speaking." Gloria shuddered and again Bo put his hand on her hand. She nearly leaped from her chair and threw herself in his lap, compelled to press her tiny breasts against his manly chest. Instead, she remained seated waiting for the yearning to pass.

They both watched Pete and Charlie Walker enjoying each other's company. Occasionally, a villager would wave when passing by. Life was easy on Gloria's front porch.

~

Charlie Walker flourished in the presence of Pete and lit up every time he saw the little bird fly by his window. Lying on Gloria's front porch railing offered him the opportunity to elicit Pete's opinion on anything that happened to be bothering him that day. Charlie had a lot on his mind and worried incessantly over the state of the environment. Yesterday, he noticed something amiss in the ecological balance of nature. The mosquitoes had decreased in numbers and the chipmunks appeared to be missing altogether. Charlie's concern also possessed existential ramifications when considering man failed to ask the animals how they felt about the planes dropping several tons of insecticide over the land. He considered land something to be shared rather than owned. He let his mind ponder the concept of ownership and sometimes considered himself an indentured servant although well-treated and lacking for nothing in the way of housing. Occasionally, his thoughts meandered over to the possible loss of freedom in exchange for security. And was it a false sense of security or was he overthinking the annihilation of the animal kingdom and sounding like a conspiracy theorist?

Pete stopped dancing for a moment to address his friend's concerns. "The world is but an illusion, a collection of molecules that take form while we're alive and then dissipate into the permanent existence that is our soul. Humans are on a path of destruction that only the saints can avert. And since neither one of us is a saint, it's best to keep smiling, Charlie Walker, and enjoy the show." Pete pressed his tiny head against Charlie's with affection.

"Peekaboo pretty boy. I love you."

At times like these, Charlie wished he could talk out loud instead of letting his thoughts travel through the air in hopes his words remained intact creating discernable sentences for Pete to contemplate. He couldn't even tell the little bird how much he appreciated him and what a gift to have him grace his small reptile world. Pete, of course, knew and loved him all the more. Just then Esther appeared, jumped on the railing, and proceeded to sniff Charlie like he was an object of curiosity. Soon a verbal clash broke out over who was the superior species. Pete turned up the volume on his speaker and danced till his legs grew tired and his mind empty of all thoughts, leaving him in peace.

Eventually, Esther hurried back home with the vague sense a member of her entourage had gone to the dark side. She yawned and fell asleep against Manuel underneath the weeping willow tree.

TWELVE

Elmo spent the afternoon editing the video footage of the diner incident. He created a story line and plot structure worthy of a small short film up for an academy award. Earl's character again leaned toward an extra from a Quentin Tarantino film, wearing his customary black ensemble, slinking into the diner, rifle in hand, and a grim, demanding expression on his face. Earl gave his mother fits at birth when he arrived with a frown and a fussy disposition that couldn't be quieted with milk or sugar water. Finally, the doctor not being able to stand the racket, put a drop of whiskey in his formula without telling his mother, who was too weak to nurse and had enough to handle from a contrary husband refusing to claim Earl as his own. The doctor knew Mrs. Hubbard was a good Christian woman and never once considered stepping out with another man, although no one would blame the poor woman for seeking comfort wherever she could find it.

Of course, Elmo didn't have the back story, but he could imagine Earl was born an aggravation to everybody around him. He experienced a moment of awe when the bullet flew over his professor while she continued writing before lowering her head. Not even a scream. He had felt a sudden lurch in his stomach and nearly screamed like a hen caught in a fox's mouth, but instead took her hand for comfort. He noticed it was a tiny, delicate hand, soft from never working in the fields but instead living in her mind where all the big notions came and the wonderment over people's unethical behaviors hung on a clothesline for her to inspect and eventually draw the conclusion morality suffered a downward trend and lying was now dismissed as bullshit coming from an inventive mind. Elmo had read all her books and especially enjoyed the one entitled, *Lying, the Common Language of Politics*.

A knock on the door interrupted his thoughts. "Come in." Sam entered the room and laid a stack of clean towels and bed sheets on his dresser, smiled sweetly and sat down a minute to chat. The surprise visit caught Elmo off guard. Usually, she left his linens on the little table in the hallway.

"Sorry to intrude."

"No intrusion. I'm happy for your company."

Elmo meant these words. He hadn't come across any new friends yet and Sam's company possessed an easy manner that made him feel at home in her presence. "Something bothering you? Need to raise my rent? Am happy to pay six months in advance if you want or add extra for the utilities. I've been told most men don't bathe every day." They both laughed.

"No, you're fine. I was hoping you could help me sort through a romance problem." She spoke matter-of-factly while staring at the floor, a soft pine usually found on second story farm houses.

"I'm happy to try although can't brag about being an expert in the romance department being as how I've had little experience and have suffered mostly from too much longing." He grinned, a shy grin but sincere. "The world at times appears full of pretty women always walking in the other direction." They both laughed.

"I've invited someone for dinner but now that I reflect upon the situation, I am not sure she feels the same way or even has the same romantic inclinations that I do. I mean what if she likes men, and I misunderstood the signals she appeared to be sending when we both picked up the same eggplant at the produce stand. She smiled like an enamored woman, and then suddenly I offered to bake the eggplant for dinner and the next thing I know she's coming to my house, and I haven't a clue what it all means." Sam became overwrought from too many words and was about to hyperventilate when Elmo reached over and patted her gently on the back and told her to breathe slower.

"It means two lovely women are getting together to extend a happy moment over an eggplant."

"You think it's just about the eggplant?" Sam's disappointed expression touched Elmo, having once been similarly confused when mistakenly asking out a lesbian who said she didn't 'do men'. He found her response offensive and somewhat presumptuous. He would have been happy with lively conversation and a good meal.

"These days it's hard tellin'. But one thing's for sure if you stay in the moment, don't suffer from too many expectations, and laugh a lot, you're both bound to have a good time."

"You're right. I'm making too much out of a meal, and I'm not exactly sure how to cook an eggplant."

"My mama always cubed the eggplant and soaked it in milk for a half an hour before frying in a saucepan with other vegetables. If that helps."

"Sure does. Thank you, Elmo. I'm so grateful

you're here. It's like having a real man around the house without all the testosterone mingling with my own."

"Well, thank you!"

They both laughed and parted ways. Elmo made a mental note to spend the evening in a coffee shop reading a book.

THIRTEEN

Gloria idled the better part of a week sitting on her porch studying her notes when coming upon the common thread: assholes, as a whole, disrespected women. They chased after young women, objectified their bodies, and maligned them when uncooperative by calling them lesbians, a term they considered an insult to all women. Assholes were so caught up in their own self-absorption, they had no idea being called a lesbian was preferable to being called man hungry. Most women considered the latter a weakness.

The assholes general disregard for women over forty brought their intelligence into question. Did the likes of Earl Hubbard really believe a young woman slobbered over the prospect of his affection? Did he believe she overlooked the youthful beauty of her own age group to follow a grizzled half-wit into a withered autumn romance? Gloria then mused over the possibility assholes may be singularly responsible for ageism. They put women over forty into the undesirable category and tossed the exquisite grayheads in the trash bin to be discarded when past childbearing age. They made fun of the pendulous breasts that fed their children and laughed at the women using a cane to support legs weak from a life spent carrying the weight of menial jobs and housework.

Gloria, when noticing the connection between a woman's poor self-image and the constant oppressiveness coming from all the assholes, felt a slow burn to anger. She wondered if it were passion of a different sort. Could she be passionate about crushing the collective hold assholes have on the flourishing of women? Yes, she thought she could be, and then suddenly her mouth opened and let out a scream so despairing Bo and Charlie Walker hurried over to check on her well-being. Maisie also appeared to find the musician holding an angry woman almost broken from too much emotion.

"Oh, for fuck sakes! I can't believe I've been so stupid. Why didn't I see it? See the harm to all our girl children, our beautiful ancients who walk in wisdom, the child bearers, and the tender-hearted poetesses. ALL diminished by an asshole's hateful words aimed like arrows in a quiver, too impotent to love. For fuck sakes! How could I be so stupid?" Gloria bowed her head to her lap and wept from years of grief.

She understood why she never felt passion for a man. The real ones, the nice ones, were hidden behind the assholes of the world. She cried even louder when remembering the Dean grabbing at her many years ago and telling her if she wouldn't play nice with him than not to expect tenure.

"Darlin' girl, what's the matter?" Bo stroked her shaking body. Pete sat on her shoulder and Charlie Walker stayed close enough not to be a bother but available if needed.

Maisie kneeled in front of the weeping professor and took her hands. "It's Maisie. Let us help you."

"That man nearly killed me!" Gloria laid her head on Maisie's shoulder.

"Who, sweetheart?"

Bo piped up. "Earl, of course, shot at her while she was eatin' breakfast at the *Diner*. Only missed by three inches. They're talkin' about it all over town. People are beside themselves with what to do. They figure a book-smart lady like the professor shouldn't haveta put up with Earl's gun happy ways."

"Pretty girl, pretty girl. I love you," Pete chimed in.

Gloria straightened and dried her eyes on the large red bandana Bo handed her. She began to laugh. "I'm so sorry. But I had a revelation."

"Yes, sweetheart." Maisie pulled up a chair and sat down to listen while Gloria with an eerie calmness told her she thought her studies were going in the wrong direction. She went into minute detail describing centuries of man's inhumanity to women and how assholes have been roaming the earth since the beginning of time as a malevolent force to keep women enslaved to do their bidding. She even described the tools women had invented, the first fire, and the berries they had gathered, which contributed eighty-percent to the collective food source while men's contribution was a scant twenty-percent of dead animals brought back for the women to skin.

Bo hurried to his house for a bottle of vodka to pour in Gloria's lemonade in hopes of calming her nerves, allowing Maisie to put her to bed with ease. At times like this, he thought, maybe they needed a professional to help clean up the mess Earl left behind. No one should have that much power. His heart melted when seeing Gloria reduced to tears by a man undeserving of her smile.

Pete began to sing, "I bless the day I found you. Let it be me."

Gloria turned and kissed the little bird. "It will always be you."

Everyone smiled and pulled Gloria to her feet,

moving her inside to rest on the couch where Maisie sat by her side while she slept off the ill-effects of Earl and a quarter bottle of vodka.

"You thinkin' she'll be all right, Maisie?" Bo whispered.

"Yes, in time. She seems to have gotten her mind busy elaborating on her revelation. But let's keep an eye on her."

"Of course. She looks a frail little thing." Bo and Maisie glanced at the tiny form, hardly a lump under the coverlet. Suddenly, they became sad. Pete sat hunkered down in the warm spot between the blanket and his Bird-Mom's neck.

"Pretty girl."

"For sure, Pete," Bo agreed. "I should be leavin' you both to your privacy. If you need a break, I'm next door for the rest of the day."

"Thanks, Bo. Wanted to ask if'n you think inviting her to the Ladies' Tea a good idea? Get her mind off things."

"Sure. Might help being around other women." Bo slipped outside followed by Charlie Walker, both returning home heavy-hearted over the ordeal of their new neighbor. They sighed from the prospect of being in love. Each unaware of the other's feelings and Charlie Walker not having a clue he might be gay. He only knew he was happy in his heart.

~

Benny and Esther joined Maisie on the porch while Gloria continued to sleep inside. Benny thought Earl a disgrace to law enforcement and for a moment considered reporting him to his higher-ups or possibly bringing a class action suit against him for being a threat to his jurisdiction, except he didn't live in Earl's jurisdiction so had little power.

Mostly, he had been distracted by helping Hugo's parents become acclimated to their new home. He was pleased they had thrown themselves into learning English and were now enjoying their herbal medicine studies. Life began to flow easily for the family. Benny felt confident they would eventually become citizens of their chosen country and support themselves with their herbal medicine company.

Maisie held his hand. Esther sat nearby raging from jealousy although without cause. Benny spent at least two hours a day fussing over her and continuing to take her on walks around the garden and sometimes Bob's Nursery when she became bored with her surroundings. He noticed Manuel arrived every morning at exactly five minutes after eight to pick up Esther for a stroll along the lake. Benny considered the little dog a blessing and was grateful he continued to believe the sun rose and set on his cat. Manuel was like a metronome that kept their life in harmony. Fortunately, he possessed an easy disposition and a steady rhythm.

Benny let go of his thoughts and stared at his beloved Maisie. Sometimes, he couldn't believe his good fortune and wondered what he had done to deserve such sweetness in his life. They rarely argued except over Esther during the times she was mean to Arabella, which happened mostly when the little dog sniffed her food. Benny tried to explain to Esther that Beagles sniff everything and in fact were employed by pest companies to sniff out bed bugs. Esther had walked away in disgust.

Lost in Sunshine maintained its delightful community atmosphere and grew even more cheerful with the arrival of Pete. Benny noticed the little bird often sat in their kitchen window and sang Everly Brothers' songs while Maisie accompanied him on the violin. At moments like these, his life took on a surreal aspect set against a background of exploding hillsides and warring countries where he had spent a great deal of his working life. Now though, he felt nurtured by abundance and wanted to help the newcomer adapt to the likes of Earl without having to give away her dignity.

Just then, Gloria stepped outside wrapped in a blanket and stared at the interlopers on her front porch. She couldn't remember having invited anyone to tea and why did her head hurt. Maisie wrapped an arm around her and began to explain the situation in a gentle voice emphasizing the revelation Gloria would be expounding upon in her writings.

"Don't you remember, sweetheart?"

"Yes, now that you mention it. I was making notes and had connected the pieces with alarming results. I remember swearing. I'm so sorry. No one swore in my house. It was considered uncouth and beneath those with intellectual capabilities. Although, new scientific studies show intelligent people swear more than your average blue-collar worker." Gloria yawned throughout her recollections, went off track, but was soon brought back by the presence of Benny.

"Who are you?" she asked.

"Who are you?" Pete repeated.

"Maisie's friend. Don't mean to intrude." Benny slipped on home and left Maisie to tidy up Gloria's thought processes.

"Let me fix you some toast and jam. Make you feel better. And we'll look in your cupboard for herbal tea." Gloria was surprisingly pliable and allowed her new friend to steer her in the direction of the couch. "If you feel up to it, I'd like you to come as my guest to the Ladies' Tea this Friday. Do you good to meet some of the gentle folk here."

"That's for sure. I could interview them. Get more material. My thesis is coming back to me. Thanks, Maisie. I hope I didn't make a fool of myself last night. Where's Bo?"

"I sent him home. Thought you would want some privacy while you slept." Maisie stifled her concerns over Gloria questioning the local women. They tended to keep themselves private and rarely warmed up to strangers.

"He has been very kind to me." Gloria remained huddled underneath the cover until Maisie handed her a tray. "Thank you, Maisie. You are also very kind."

"It's the least we can do after what you've been through, and we also like having you and Pete here. I'll leave you to yourself. If you need anything, give a holler."

"Thank you." The two women waved good-bye.

Gloria set the tray on the coffee table and fell back to sleep. Pete decided to spend the rest of the night in meditation where Baba Das waited for him. Maybe his Guru could lift the energy in their small house and give his Bird-Mom the love she needed for herself.

FOURTEEN

Gloria looked forward to Friday. She had never been to a Ladies' Tea so didn't know what to expect. The University served alcohol and soda with a twist of lime for teetotalers. This allowed everyone to stand for a long period of time and talk to their fellow academics, catching up on their current publications and expressing excitement over their next brilliant idea. Most conversations would put a toad to sleep, but they kept each other entertained by criticizing the papers of their peer group when recollecting the last conference in their field. Gloria rarely attended, mostly due to her shyness and inability to criticize others. Her parents had told her gossip led to mischief and was beneath anyone with a working brain.

Duke greeted her out front despite having been discouraged from being overly friendly with his downhome charm and ability to make a woman feel special. He continued to worry the ladies were talking about him and fretted over the possibility his own behavior was being scrutinized with the use of a magnifying glass strong enough to lay his weaknesses to bare. When he saw the petite professor, he nearly slipped into his usual patter complimenting her delicate beauty and using the pickup line, "Where have you been hidin'?" Fortunately, he caught himself and gave her a benign smile while walking her to the backroom. She smiled and thanked him politely. Duke considered her abruptness a denial of his obvious good looks and charm, which prompted a moment of self-reflection. Had he lost his edge? Was he no longer attractive to women and worse did they dismiss him as a lonely guy in need of shoring up by a good woman? The bartender noticed the pained expression on his boss's face. He handed him a whiskey neat to soften his worries. Duke thanked him and disappeared on the other side of his office door.

Gloria hadn't given the owner of *Duke's Rye Bar* a thought but instead concentrated on the sounds of happy women coming from the back. She had never heard grown women giggle and was delighted with the tinkling sound expressing happiness over being together. She wondered if she would fit in and could she actually giggle. Her parents had discouraged girlish displays, including pampering Barbie dolls and excessive bouncing. She watched the other girls playing from the schoolhouse window where she stood swooning with envy but was confined to her desk, under her parents' instructions, to improve her Latin and Greek vocabulary during recess. Even the teachers felt sorry for her, although they admired her brilliant mind and inherent sweetness.

Maisie saw Gloria enter the crowded room, hurried over to welcome her, and cast about for someone she might enjoy meeting. Her eyes lit upon the Library Book Club members sitting together. She steered her in their direction.

"Hi ladies, I want you to meet Professor Gloria Dobbins who is a newcomer to the village. She's here on sabbatical writing a book on well, let's just say the downside of living with a contrary man." Everyone laughed and asked Gloria to join them.

'Welcome, please enlighten us," Margie the Club's leader said with a cheery smile and twinkling eyes that immediately put Gloria at ease.

"What would you like to drink? Our barista can fix anything hot or cold," Maisie asked.

"A double espresso, please," Gloria responded and smiled at Maisie.

The women stared at her with large smiles and a great deal of blonde hair set off with artfully made-up eyes. Their faces resembled the pretty dolls she was never allowed to play with. She found their eagerness intimidating and hurried through her mind for an answer to Margie's question. How do you tell these genteel, stylized women you spent your days studying assholes? "Well, I don't wish to offend anyone, but initially my topic was the proliferation of assholes in this country and how to live with them. I don't know if you've heard of Aaron James, but he wrote an informative contemporary philosophy book entitled *Assholes a theory.*"

"Oh, honey, we read that in our book club. We all got one of those at home. We wanted to learn how to handle living with one. But the section entitled Asshole Management didn't seem to apply to the live-in variety." A fluffy woman wearing all linen and big jewelry sighed when telling Gloria of their collective disappointment. "Oh, I'm forgetting my manners. I'm Dandelion and this is Margie, Izzie, Mary Sue, and Fred our treasurer."

Gloria nodded and then asked, "Were you able to find a way to live harmoniously with your husbands?"

"We tried different approaches. Ignoring them, leaving their dinner on the table and then getting a prearranged call for an emergency, and finally pointing out their insensitivity to our feelings." Everyone broke out into laughter and even Gloria found that amusing when remembering her exchange with Earl. "We also tried kindness to the point of nausea, but they still trampled our feelings and just had to have the last word."

"That's sure ever-lovin' true. 'Nuff to make you want to grab 'em by the throat jus' to git 'em to stop talkin'," Izzie chimed in. She was a small woman, wearing a cloche hat and silk tunic with a string of Viennese crystal hanging from her neck.

"For sure, Izzie. So sorry you had to go through that. Did George recover from his accident?" Mary Sue glanced at the small woman with sympathy.

"Yes, but he pressed charges, and now I have a felony conviction on my record, which the insensitive brute didn't find a contradiction when released from the hospital and moving back into what he calls the family home. Still expects my services. That's what we mean, Gloria, when we say there's no winning with an asshole in the house." Everyone nodded in agreement.

"Am I understanding correctly your husband met with an accident and you were blamed for it?" Gloria's curiosity got the better of her. She had been raised never to ask personal questions. Again, the other women laughed.

"Yes, Gloria honey. Poor Izzie here has been living with the mother of all assholes for twenty years and there's been no improvement. One day when noticing Izzie hadn't emptied his ashtray, her husband George threw it on the floor scattering ashes everywhere and then told her to clean it up. So naturally, in a fit of temper and his walking past her naked while she was getting ready to vacuum the carpet, she brushed the hose against him and sucked up his penis."

"Neat as you please. We were hoping it would send a message to all our husbands to stop trucking with us, but it didn't. They all flew to George's bedside in the hospital and encouraged him to throw the book at poor Izzie here," Margie said with solemnity.

Gloria's shock over the incident kept her from laughing. "I'm so sorry that happened to you. Do you think the basis of all your misery might be the asshole's inability to feel empathy and the need to be right all the time?"

"Oh definitely, not an ounce of compassion. It's always about them."

"We been comparin' notes for years now. No room for someone else's opinion 'cept theirs."

"We thought about getting a group divorce, but Margie's married to the town judge and property division wouldn't favor us. No ma'am."

"The worst is the insults. Mine told me if I

gained any more weight, he'd put me in the barn with the cows," Dandelion said.

"It don't matter Dandelion. George told me I didn't have enough meat on my bones to make me desirable as a woman. Said I looked like a boy," Izzie added.

"I'm so sorry. I can't imagine how painful it must be. I've never been married but there are plenty of them stalking the university halls for signs of prey."

"We heard what happened with Earl at the *Diner*. The whole town's embarrassed by it, you being new and all."

"That's Earl's wife over there, Laverne. She has a hard row to hoe living with him." Dandelion pointed to a tall pretty woman wearing jeans, a colorful blouse and a turquoise belt buckle. She looked like a picture from Vogue for the mature woman.

"Maybe you could interview her?" Everyone beamed from Fred's brilliant idea. "Unless of course you gotta gripe for her living with the maniac who coulda kilt you on an off day. Nobody'd blame you for sure."

"Oh no. I wouldn't want to impose. Talking about him might be painful."

"Laverne loves to talk about Earl. That's what keeps her sane. We have a support group. We could introduce you to her." Dandelion handed

Gloria a business card with her phone number and a dandelion on it. "Call me and I'll give you the address."

"Thank you. That's very kind." Gloria felt touched by the women's generosity in sharing their stories. The afternoon continued on in a more lighthearted manner, sharing their reading lists and analyzing character and plot development. She couldn't remember the last time she enjoyed herself surrounded by people. Possibly never.

Maisie waved when seeing Gloria make her way to the door. Once outside she ran into Duke looking dejected beside a wooden sculpture of himself. She stifled her laughter and told him to enjoy his evening and going on to say how much she appreciated his lovely establishment. She then promptly worried the use of 'lovely' when describing a bar might be too feminine. Her worries dissipated when seeing him brighten from the compliment.

~

Gloria let her mind sift through the events at the Ladies' Tea. She found it hard to believe such kind souls could put up with the likes of their husbands. The falderal with Izzie's George appeared as a vivid image she would rather not have cluttering up her mind while at the same time causing her to admire the woman's small act of rebellion. Gloria was delighted to discover she enjoyed the company of women, usually not in such large batches, but still she found charm in their gaiety filling the room with a lightheartedness she had hitherto only enjoyed from Pete. When reviewing her notes, she noticed the women suffered enormously from husbands who criticized their bodies, leaving them fretful over the physical deterioration that is the human condition.

Gloria's imagination took charge and caused an explosion of wild ideas that might help women set themselves free. Maybe stage a demonstration, ride a horse naked through the town square, or possibly recite slam poetry on a street corner to raise the consciousness of others and stamp out assholery. She wanted to send a message to embrace our bodies with an understanding a body's only purpose is to house our souls.

Pete scampered back and forth on the railing chirping 'let there be light, God of mercy, God Almighty, let there be light'. Just then Maisie strolled by with her violin and began playing the music to Pete's halleluiah song. He had tuned into his Bird-Mom's musings and found them too grim to bear. Baba Das always reminded Pete 'we are not the body but the soul'. If only his Bird-Mom could communicate with him the same way Maisie sent her thoughts on the lightest breeze. Perhaps, Maisie could be his messenger and convey his Guru's pearls of mystic wisdom. He continued singing, 'let there be light, God of mercy, God Almighty, let there be light'.

When seeing Charlie Walker slide out his front door, Pete flew over and gave him a peck on the cheek, calling him 'pretty boy'. Maisie smiled at the duo and laid her violin on a lounge chair. Gloria poured her a glass of lemonade and thanked her for introducing her to the Library Book Club.

"Did you find it useful?" Maisie asked. The two women had become comfortable in each other's company, recognizing the value of their differences.

"Oh yes, their experiences supported my revelations. Assholes single-handedly championed the concept of ageism. Possibly because of getting older themselves or feeling relief when diminishing others by pointing out their obvious decrepitude. You only have to study the women's magazines to know they're the creation of men. All airbrushed and photoshopped. Real women cannot compete with stylized versions of themselves." Gloria shook her head in disdain.

"It keeps plastic surgeons in business and sells billions of dollars in beauty products. My vanity is covered with jars and bottles. Is there a solution?"

"Convince women they have inherent value and to accept the fading of beauty while at the same time cultivating their talents so they have something that gives them pleasure as they age."

"That's a brilliant idea but maybe we should have classes on how to find a nice man. Embracing nice men's characteristics and also how to spot and avoid a narcissist. When listening to you talk about assholes it seems to me they're also narcissists. Maybe I'm just grasping here." Maisie drifted away from her thoughts and gave thanks to God for putting a nice man in her path to stumble over.

"That's both clever and practical. I was thinking along the lines of demonstrations, but the possibilities appear to be endless."

"Did Izzie tell you about George?"

"Yes, and I found it to be a darkly comic story. They also mentioned having a support group and introducing me to Earl's wife Laverne for more material. It might be awkward."

"Oh no, it would be fruitful and in a perverse way make you laugh until your sides hurt. That woman can spin a yarn that will leave you in stitches."

Both women collapsed into laughter bringing Pete and Charlie Walker over to check out the commotion. They hovered on the railing and stared at the humans. Suddenly, Maisie stopped and turned to Pete, listening.

"Pete says to tell you the only way to evolve is to love everyone. Loving everyone allows for Oneness. He says this is the guidance he receives from his trips to the inner realms. He also says hawkish man may have to come back in another lifetime to change his ways. He says to try and love him. He's really a lama in a human body." Pete then jumped on Charlie Walker's back and began practicing his slide move.

"Oh, I knew my little bird possesses mystical powers that are beyond me. And now he's talking to me through you. Are you one of those communicators?"

"Only in an amateurish way. I must confess Pete and I have been communicating since before you arrived. And just now when he was singing his gospel number, he called over and asked me to bring my fiddle. He uses the word fiddle. Obviously, he wanted musical accompaniment." Maisie smiled with chagrin.

"Do you think Earl is irredeemable?"

"Yes, actually I do. Known him since childhood. Unless of course, God forgives a man who is born mean and can't help sliding sideways with his morals."

"This is going to require some effort for me

to wrap my mind around."

"I'll leave you to it. I need to get back home and make dinner with Benny." Maisie picked up her violin and hurried home feeling grateful.

Gloria wrote everything Pete had said in her notebook and thanked her companion for helping her see the light.

"See the light, Pretty Girl. See the light. Pete loves you."

"As I you."

Charlie Walker turned into a mush of feelings upon watching love swirl around him. He thought he'd died and gone to heaven when in Pete's presence. He wondered if they could have a sleepover.

FIFTEEN

"Why does Chief Hubbard carry a gun when love works just as well? Some men infiltrate, annihilate, and downright navigate a woman's life until she's tired from too much calibratin'. 'Causes women to turn sour, even dour, and sometimes downright done when living with a man who does not see her light and no longer finds her fun but criticizes, demoralizes, and gives her grief that sends her looking for some relief."

A small crowd gathered where Gloria stood repeating her refrain adding more lyrics as she went along. The women cheered and the men stared at her like she was a bug on the sidewalk about to crawl under their pant leg.

"You go girl!" The women in the crowd cheered her on despite standing next to disapproving husbands guilty of her taunts.

"Yeah, you go girl!"

"Speakin' for all of us here."

"We got yer back!"

Gloria continued only louder while the crowd repeated 'Gloria speaks for all of us' followed by the women on the side chanting "yes, she does'. Their support moved her to encourage the women to rise up and say no. This was followed by 'say no' from several women prompting Gloria to counter with her own refrain *'say no to infiltratin', annihilatin' and calibratin' men'*.

Maisie stood in the back smiling and waving along with Elmo who was videotaping Gloria's diatribe while also scanning the crowd, which continued to grow requiring him to move around to capture their response from all angles. He was joined by Sam asking questions and yelling 'Gloria be badass'. Soon the women began chanting 'Gloria be badass' so loud, it carried across the town square straight into the ears of Earl Hubbard having his morning coffee at *Maggie's Diner*.

"What the tarnation is all that racket. Man can't even enjoy a cuppa coffee without bein' disturbed." He glanced around noticing everyone else was leaving to join the others across the street. Even Brenda took off her apron and left Bernie in the kitchen frying up five to-go orders. "What's so important yer got to leave yer vittles?" He finished his pancakes in three bites and picked up his rifle. No one was left to care.

Earl drove his police car across the town square and arrived in time to hear the first refrain beginning with, *'Why does Chief Hubbard carry a gun when love works just as well?'*

"This ain't no gun Missy. It's a assault rifle. You best beware!"

Everyone gasped. Even the men were unhappy with Earl's stupidity in not realizing the ramifications of being recorded. Earl had little use for his government-issue laptop and rarely opened it except to file reports and send them off to the mayor. He didn't have a Facebook account, Twitter or Instagram. If he had paid attention to the current social media trends, he would know police brutality and gun violence were the hot topics right now. His browsing history consisted of various online stores selling fly fishing gear along with camouflage wear for deer hunting season. Not that Earl paid too much attention to the government hunting seasons tacked to the fence posts when deciding to pick up his 12-gauge shotgun to kill a deer. His sense of morality was a tenuous occurrence and rarely prickled his conscience with the concept of ethics. Earl's bankrupt soul came under the dominance of a casual mind and languished in a moral wasteland, separated from the Divine from whence it came.

He made his way through the crowd, grabbed

Gloria by the arm, and escorted her to his police car and drove her to the other side of the street to the police station. The crowd jeered and even the nice men shrunk from his violent actions and were once again embarrassed by their gender. They receded to the back, too afraid to join the women in trampling Earl's minions standing nearby captivated by the extreme behavior of their chief. They hesitated to report him for fear the mayor would fire the whole lot and restore order in the ranks with replacement officers. Besides most of their wives were among the women calling for all assholes to be stoned in the town square. Their sphincter muscles tightened into a collective grip. They eased themselves into their cars and left the wives to fight their own battles. Little did they know, nice men championing their cause to be treated with respect and given equal pay would go a long way to restoring familial harmony.

Elmo and Sam hurried to the front of Earl's car and moved in for a closeup, especially excited over the dialogue being recorded.

"You Missy are a thorn in my side. I will see to it life in my jurisdiction becomes yer worst nightmare. So go ahead and make my day!" Earl's red angry face and tightened jaw with throbbing vein running up the side of his forehead made for a dramatic closeup combined with the Clint Eastwood quote. Earl idolized Clint and failed to separate the actor from his *Dirty Harry* character. Not to mention, Earl's complete lack of self-reflection enabled him to believe he himself was a handsome renegade, a tough steely man who got the job done. Most people just groaned over this overblown image he carried with him to the job, but now things are not looking good for the law officer.

Laverne stood at the front of the crowd screaming through a megaphone she had taken earlier from her husband's car, "Just wait till yer git home tonight, Earl Hubbard! Yer gonna feel the backside of my tongue lashing at yer manly parts. I'm gonna reduce you, Earl Hubbard! A woman can only take so much and when she's done, she's done. Yer better believe it." The crowd became quiet, letting her words travel through the air to the police chief, who by now was beginning to have doubts. However, the need to save face by throwing Gloria in a cell was stronger than the prudence it would take to listen to his wife.

Earl locked the door to the police station, removed Gloria's wrist band and shoved her into a vacant cell. He scrambled around the empty space of his brain for a charge he could use to hold her for seventy-two hours. The best he could come up with was demonstrating without a permit.

Laverne used her key to let the tea ladies and herself into Earl's sacred space. He became disgruntled over the intrusion and threatened to lock up the entire bunch for trespassing until Dandelion reminded him it was a public building and not his private property.

"You can't just lock a person up for speaking her mind, especially on the sidewalk in a public place. It's our First Amendment Right," Izzie said.

"You broke the law Chief Earl when you grabbed her by the arm. You could be facing an assault charge," Dandelion added.

Earl listened to the facts while leaning back in his chair with one foot on his desk and his rifle laying across his lap. He never read the Constitution, not being much of a reader, but thought he might want to give it a perusal when he had some time to spare. Earl's tendency to play fast and loose with the law he is supposed to uphold left a sizeable dent in his thinking process.

~

Gloria surprised herself when expressing feelings tucked inside her heart where she rarely looked for guidance. Her parents pressed her to use her brain. They told her to put more stock in what her brain had to say, use logic in analyzing a situation, and save emotions for a rainy day when the clouds hovered and occasionally dropped rain on her parade. She had no idea what they were talking about at the time. Mostly her confusion lingered on her emotions being tied to a rainy day often causing her to wonder if that's why rainy days always made her sad.

Her parents taught her how to create a pro and con list when she began first grade and needed to make a decision on choosing a best friend. Little Gloria really liked Becky, a budding blonde girl without the aptitude for writing her name at the top of her yellow tablet paper. Her parents put this on the con side of her list. Gloria put 'she makes me laugh' on the pro side of the list. Her parents discussed at length whether or not this was a valid point finally deciding to let it sit there while the con side filled up with negative attributes they thought might be a deterrent to Gloria's social development. They glanced around the playground for a more suitable prospect, eyes lighting upon a little girl with glasses reading a book. Ruthie Willinger became her new best friend.

Gloria learned a lot from Ruthie. Ruthie when not reading enjoyed regaling Gloria with stories of her homelife. Both parents bought brown bottles and spent their time drinking and laughing until falling into bed at night.

Once they accidently flushed Ruthie's cat down the toilet just before her uncle grabbed the poor tabby and rescued it from certain death. She also told Gloria how her older cousins liked to touch her girl parts and tug at her panties to look inside. One day Ruthie came to school wearing her mom's T-shirt with the words *Nice Pussy* written above a picture of a pretty cat. The T-shirt also featured an arrow pointing downwards.

The teacher became enraged and began yelling at Gloria's best friend. Naturally, Ruthie did not have a clue as to why the teacher was so upset. Neither did any of the other children in the classroom. They all looked frightened but absorbed the word 'pussy' into their vocabulary using it freely for the remainder of the school year. Finally, Gloria raised her hand.

"Yes, Miss Dobbins. You have something to add?"

"I think you're behaving badly and owe Ruthie an apology for raising your voice. Polite people do not raise their voices." Gloria's stern little face shocked the teacher prompting her to send both girls to Principal Decker's office. This proved to be a mistake for the misguided teacher. Principal Decker prided himself on his social grace. He did, however, ponder on what to do about Ruthie's T-shirt, an obvious hand-me-down from her besotted mother, he thought. He knew the Willingers patronized the local sports bar where he often retrieved his teenage son from drinking with his buddies using a false driver's license for easy entrance. Both little girls sat in his office wondering why grown-ups made no sense. They wondered why their expectations contradicted each other's, bringing them at a crossroads on what's appropriate behavior for their children. This contrasted thinking triggered the mess in which Ruthie and Gloria now found themselves.

The principal glanced at his charges with sympathy. He also knew Gloria's parents leaned toward hovering over their only child with the meticulousness of lab technicians studying clinical trials of mice in a maze. He felt sorry for both of them, but knew he had to address the problem at hand, Ruthie's T-shirt. He picked up the phone and called Ms. Hardy, the girls' peewee soccer coach, and asked her to bring one of the school's sports T-shirts into his office. He apologized for the inconvenience. Minutes later, Ruthie left outfitted in her new T-shirt with the school's colors and a picture of the peewee mascot, a small badger holding a soccer ball looking slightly puzzled. Ruthie and Gloria admired her new ensemble and returned to their classroom smiling.

Altogether, first grade was an interesting experience for Gloria. She threw out her parents' pro and con list and kept Ruthie as her best friend throughout school until Ruthie married the football team's captain and enjoyed being a housewife with three children. Eventually, Gloria came to believe her parents relied on a compilation of facts to give them a semblance of control in an illusionary world. Now, she wondered about herself.

~

Laverne unlocked Gloria's jail cell, took her by the hand, and helped her into Maisie's car waiting at the curb. The crowd had dispersed allowing them room to navigate their way through town to home. People waved and gave her a thumbs up. Earl stood frowning in front of the police station wondering how his authority had been left in tatters by a group of women. He considered the idea Laverne must be having female troubles. Never once did it enter his mind that he may be the problem, that Laverne may actually be done with him. He only saw value in himself and thought Laverne should be grateful her husband was a man of stature. Mostly, Earl walked in a bent fashion, head slunk forward giving him a rabbity appearance about the face and causing some concern over whether or not he suffered from early onset osteoporosis. At this point, Laverne really didn't care about her husband or his stature. She felt buoyed over the day's events and made mental notes on the support group's next topic. Naturally, a united front crossed her mind.

Maisie chattered excitedly in the car on the way back to the village. She thanked Gloria for bringing the inequity to the attention of the townspeople, laughing over the part Earl played in driving her point home. "Gloria, honey, you're a wonder girl. Didn't know you had it in you."

"Neither did I. Something snapped, and I found myself writing what I was feeling on paper and then suddenly it turned into a swirl of words I don't normally express. Not very academic of me. I lost all objectivity, but I have to confess it gave me some satisfaction to express myself. Better than before when I sat on my feelings for long periods of time wondering if I even had any." Gloria's thoughts drifted to Earl's mean and angry face. "Do you think I would be arrested again if I were to enlist some other ladies to help with a sidewalk demonstration?"

"I think that's a great idea. We've scheduled an emergency meeting of our support group tonight. Usually, I don't go because of being with a nice man, but I want to support women being freed from tyranny. Naturally, the ladies are hoping you'll come and give them ideas."

"Thank you. I'd love that." Gloria reached for the door handle but was surprised when Maisie gave her an old-fashioned hug before she stepped out of the car.

"Pick you up at 7:30. Oh, and don't worry about that other thing. We're within our rights if we stay on the sidewalk and don't obstruct the flow of foot traffic." She grinned at Gloria and waved good-bye.

Bo called after her while crossing their lawn. "I looked in on Pete earlier. I heard him squawking up a storm. Seems a big ol' horse fly got inside and was driving him crazy from the sound and flitting all over your tiny house. Hope you don't mind." He grinned and handed her a glass of elderberry juice.

"Thank you. I'm grateful. Would you like to join me on the porch?" Gloria opened the door and let Pete outside. He flew to the railing and began to survey his surroundings.

"Duke called about an outdoor gig. Brought me up to speed on today's events. Sorry you were at the mercy of our demented poleece chief. He's a nail in the bottom of everybody's shoe."

Gloria began to laugh. Bo always had a way of lifting her spirits. Her jail house experience left her feeling depleted of her last ounce of energy after rhyming words lamenting over academia being a man's domain and apparently all significant environments belonged to men. Even the actual environment had become depleted due to rich men's greed. She looked at her neighbor with new interest, wondering if she could ever rest easy with a man in her bed. Immediately, she shoved this thought aside and asked Bo if he would mind her taking a nap.

"Of course not, you want me to hustle Pete on home to visit Charlie Walker? I'll bring him back in an hour and stick him inside your door." Pete began to jump up and down, causing them both to laugh. Her little bird flew onto Bo's shoulder. Gloria heard Bo singing to him 'when the red red robin comes bob-bob-bobbin along'. Minutes later, she eased herself into bed and fell asleep immediately.

SIXTEEN

Everyone applauded when Gloria entered the church basement for her first support group meeting. She had heard support groups were helpful, but thought they were for alcoholics, soldiers with PTSD, and people wanting to lose weight or others who had been abused by family members. She often wondered if 'over instructed' fell into the category of parental abuse. Her brain had nearly drowned in a myriad of facts crammed into her head by parents who lacked affection.

She nodded at the women staring at her with expectant faces, as though she had the answers on how to handle their problematic husbands. Personally, she would run away from home if the Library Book Club represented your typical day in the marital domicile. Laverne stood at the podium welcoming Gloria. In her wildest dreams, she never thought she would enjoy the day Earl's wife would become her ally. She followed Maisie to the front row and settled into listen.

"To help things stay on track, I've gone over all our dirty laundry we've aired in this room and come up with a list of complaints needing to be addressed. I've tried to keep it short to give Gloria an idea of life at the hands of a difficult husband. And on that note, I know you're all wonderin' if Earl was madder than a wet hen when he got home today. Aside from callin' me a skinny-assed bitch, he also said I was lucky to have such a man as himself bein' as how I'm headin' toward fifty and no other man would want me. Said I should be lickin' his boots. You catch my drift here?" Laverne looked around the room at the sympathetic women nodding their heads.

"We hear ya, honey. We see ya and now we gots to do somethin' 'bout our good fer nothins' at home insultin' us cus we're growin' older."

"You got that right!"

Several Amens later, Laverne resumed talking. "All rightie then, I think that will substantiate what I put on our list. The two main concerns are body shaming and ageism. Does everyone agree?"

"Yes, my Albert told me I had an ass the size of a hippo about to give birth."

"Yes, this is what I'm talkin' about. I'm sorry that happened to you Dandelion. No woman should be treated with such disrespect." Laverne sympathized.

A hand went up in the back and Laverne called on a well-dressed older woman no one had ever seen before. "I'm new in town so don't want to seem forward but was at today's demonstration and now listening to everyone here, has all y'al considered divorcing the bastards you're married to? I'm a retired divorce attorney and saw stuff like this happenin' every day. Broke my heart."

"Yes, thank you. That topic has been discussed and temporarily discarded, but if you would be kind enough to stay after our meeting, I'm sure there are some ladies here who would like to talk to you. This may require another private meeting. Maybe a group rate if you decide to come out of retirement. What's yer name, honey?"

"Laura Hanigan. I bought the old Gibbs house. Yes, I'm happy to listen and help where I can be of use. Like I say I'm retired so am not looking for compensation." A comfortable sigh settled over the group and even Laverne smiled with appreciation.

"Moving right along. I think it's time to hand the podium over to our heroine Professor Gloria Dobbins of *Lost in Sunshine*." Everyone applauded and Gloria graciously stood before them with several suggestions she thought might further the cause.

"May I suggest beginning with a nude tableau that would cover both ageism and body shaming?"

"Darlin', what's a nude tableau? I mean I understand you to say nude but tableau is beyond my comprehension. Is it like them Brits do on their comedy bits where ever'body is jus standin' there wearing a costume of sorts like well-dressed statues. But sounds like you mean fer us to be buck nekid." Most of the ladies appeared startled at the thought.

"Yes, exactly."

"Oh, that sounds fun. Can I come as Lady Godiva?" Laverne chimed in, excited by the prospect of throwing a lasso around her husband and dragging him through the town square. She subdued the image and returned her attention to Gloria.

"Yes, of course, Lady Godiva was a freedom rider against taxation."

"I wonder why they named a chocolate after her," Dandelion said.

Gloria answered Dandelion's question with the hopes they could move on to the subject at hand, although she was pleased at the lively response. "The Draps family in Brussels opened their first shop in the Grand Place and called it Lady Godiva in honor of the freedom rider.

She, too, protested her husband's behavior and wanted him, Leofric the Dane, to lower taxes."

"Yes, in answer to Laverne's question, I think that's a great idea and most appropriate. Shall we bandy about several scenarios that would drive home our point and perhaps give the recalcitrant husbands something to think about?" Gloria continued.

Everyone began talking at once. The night ended late and when Gloria arrived home, she found Bo asleep on her porch with Pete and Charlie Walker inside also asleep, Pete on his perch and Charlie Walker wrapped around the base as though protecting his beloved friend from a fly he ate hours ago.

SEVENTEEN

Pete felt the need to expand his horizons by flying over to the weeping willow tree where Esther, Manuel, and Arabella lay together in relative calm. Except for Esther, who seemed to be peevish about her lot in life. Pete followed her memories back to the days when she and Cat-Dad spent their evenings alone and strolled along the streets listening to the birds chirp in the trees where they belonged. Pete knew this last bit referred to his tendency to walk in the grass at times when needing to feel close to the earth. He now stood in front of Esther calling her 'brat cat', which riled her temper and in response she hissed at him, but undeterred by Esther's spittle, Pete repeated 'brat cat', 'brat cat'. Her tail waved from agitation as she prepared to take a swipe at the small bird when suddenly Charlie Walker dropped from the tree sending all three fleeing in different directions.

Charlie and Pete glanced at each other perplexed over why the other village animals couldn't bring themselves to stay and talk through their differences. At times like these, Charlie continued to feel like an outsider among his neighbors but was grateful to Pete for his friendship. The little bird jumped on his back and together they hurried to Gloria's porch when catching the sounds coming from the tiny radio playing MJ's *Thriller*, Pete's favorite dance number. They climbed on top of the railing where he began some toe tapping moves, temporarily forgetting Esther's fiery temper and her tendency to be unhappy wherever she found herself.

Charlie Walker fell asleep on the railing. After MJ brought *Thriller* to a climactic end, Pete slipped into the higher realms to calm his ruffled feathers. Esther had become a worrisome thing again, and he needed his Guru to help him clear out the negativity and get him back on the fast track to spiritual refinement. Pete's thoughts took on a lofty air at times. He enjoyed twirling words around inside his tiny head and watching them float through the air and dissipate in the morning dew. He just knew he possessed the heart of a poet if only he weren't hampered by the need to be in constant motion, which kept the words from settling on the beat of a perfect mot-bon.

He felt comfort in knowing if he waited long enough, his Baba Das would appear and calm his agitation, and let the halleluiah-sun shine on his ethereal self. The air was so light in the higher realms, he felt the words glide over him until coming to the feet of his beloved Guru.

"Dadhu Pete!"

"Yes, Baba Boss. I was missing you and know you know what I'm about to say."

"Yes, Dadhu, but it wasn't nice to call the kitty a brat cat. Like you, she's one of God's creatures, all drops from the same ocean, as the saints say."

"I'm weak, Baba." Pete hung his head before his beloved Guru.

"Yes, Dadhu, but weakness is no excuse for hurting someone's feelings. You can do better."

"Yes, Baba." Pete found himself lost in his Guru's eyes seeing only bright blue circles staring at him with love he could not find on the earth plane. He felt his body floating through the white light and then just as suddenly he was plunked down on the railing next to Charlie Walker snoring like a truck driver. As much as the little guy loved Charlie, he would rather have stayed in the higher realms where the living was easier and the cats didn't eat small birds.

~

Elmo sat at his desk in the alcove and went over yesterday's videotaped events trying to decide which parts to edit. The large crowd scenes could be shortened, but every frame of the chief needed to be left for its dramatic effect in portraying him as the villain. Elmo had asked Sam to stop by and take a look at what he had spliced together, omitted, and where music might heighten the viewer's emotions.

"This is too delicious, Elmo. Got yerself a real award winner here. Down home with Chief Earl Hubbard, the blight of law enforcement and the bully to the locals." Sam laughed as she studied in minute detail the chief's movements from *Maggie's Diner* to the mob scene where Gloria stood trying to unite her own gender against the assholes inhabiting their houses and dampening their work-place. "That woman has got a future in politics. She's a real dynamo for such an itty-bitty thing."

"Professor Dobbins taught me everything worth knowin'. She's the cream of her university, mistreated and underestimated by the powers-that-be. She's a dynamo all right. That day at the *Diner*, she didn't flinch when the chief's bullet soared not three inches above her head. How come he hasn't been locked up, strung up, or tied to a bull to let run loose for the folks he ever wronged to see?" Elmo stared at Sam like she had an answer.

"I reckon people's afraid of him. I know the mayor quakes whenever a complaint is registered. You should read the daily police report in the Gazette. Set yer nerves on edge." Sam patted Elmo on the shoulder. "Don't worry Professor Dobbins will come out of this all right. Besides, Laverne's got her back. She's Earl's wife. The one with the megaphone."

"You don't say. We need voiceover." Elmo's mind spun around on this idea for a while. Sam excused herself after telling him the bits she liked best and reassuring him social media would come alive to support the woman with a poem, a regular folk heroine. Gotta love her."

Elmo revered Gloria too much to love her. Besides, previous to Penelope's last letter he thought she was waiting for him to return to Boston. He had told her several times how much he enjoyed his job and the down-home people working together to create a better way of farming and probably wouldn't be returning. He found a small niche for himself and treasured the idea of being near Gloria. She recently said living life in the sunshine had a natural feeling to it and was considering staying put after her sabbatical ended. She mentioned teaching online courses with the occasional guest appearance at the university. Her books had been published by Oxford University Press and were earning her a tidy sum. The idea Gloria would be nearby enhanced his experience of doing some good for the local farmers and after all, he also enjoyed the greenhouse at his disposal to create hybrids and on the side grow some pretty flowers in hopes of cross pollinating them to create the loveliest flower he would someday call a 'Gloria'.

Penelope's last letter sounded disheartened but ended with a sentence informing him she met another archival librarian who shared her interest and would probably be considering him in a permanent way. The last sentence slapped Elmo upside the head with its abruptness, especially when recalling she never liked being a librarian much less spending her daily life in a basement surrounded by mildew on yellowing paper.

Maybe it was too much to ask a city girl to move to the country where the spiders roamed freely and the field mice lived in the walls and talked all night. He had held onto the dream of owning a farmhouse together similar to Sam's bed and breakfast complete with happy barnyard animals and a silly blood hound too old to run after his nose when it picked up a good scent. Elmo had been living off his dreams but now put them away after reading Penelope's last letter. He appreciated the time she took in writing him an old-fashioned missive on pink paper with a water mark of a swan, the elegant kind often found floating on city ponds. The

South teemed with pretty women, but he liked the way Penelope's brain wrapped itself around a subject and never let go until it got a thorough going over, and she found something funny to enliven her mind and amuse him with the power of language. She reminded him of a mini-Gloria, which caused him to suffer from longing.

He returned to studying Earl Hubbard's movements. His driving the three hundred feet to the scene of what he perceived as a crime would make Penelope laugh, especially when seeing him shove Gloria in the back of his cruiser all trussed up in handcuffs. He knew she would be rollicking over watching him drive the same three hundred feet to the police station next to the *Diner*. He could hear her laughing beside him in a make-believe world of wishes that didn't have a hell's chance of coming true.

Gloria had no idea he intended to post the finished video on all social media platforms and send the current footage to the news media with an invitation to the women's nude tableau taking place on Saturday.

She was considering what to wear if anything at all. She saw some of the costumes of the other ladies and laughed when describing the breadth of their imagination in hiding their lady parts behind the flimsiest material where there might as well be nothing at all. She had seen Izzie pluck a rose from a bush and hold it up to herself and ask the other ladies if they thought it would make a nice statement. No one wanted to hurt her feelings until Dandelion piped up and said, "Izzie girl, you would look like you were gettin' ready to dance the flamenco but dropped yer rose." Everyone laughed causing Izzie to discard the idea and visit the fabric store to peruse the bolts of material for a yard of gauzy muslin.

So far, the reporters had not responded but Elmo remained hopeful and dwelled a few minutes on whether or not he should tell Gloria. He wanted Saturday's events to unfold without her feeling the anticipation the press might come. He knew underneath her courageous stance was a shy woman who liked nothing better than to slip between the pages of a good book. He also considered the nude tableau to be a fitting end to Gloria's position, the world would be a better place without the assholes cluttering up the landscape. This last thought caused a smile to brighten his face.

EIGHTEEN

Gloria sat on her small porch with Bo. They fell into the habit of ending their day with a glass of lemonade and some of Maisie's tea biscuits he had picked up at Duke's. Conversations often lapsed into periods of comfortable silence where they both spent the time enjoying the easiness of their friendship. They both wondered if there were more and would they want more than having the day end in each other's company. Neither one had ever married but on occasion thought it a natural turn of events if only they had found someone who accepted their foibles and the animal who was part of the package. At that very moment, Pete leaned against Charlie Walker with his eyes closed going in and out of meditation where the radiant form of Baba Das hovered to help him reach mystical heights above the fray of his often-tattered ego.

Charlie Walker began to stir. A voice prickled his slumber, a disturbing voice telling him he was God's lowliest creature, slithering on the ground without legs to run and jump like cats of superior breeding. Naturally, the voice wafting through the air into his tired ears belonged to Esther. He took her words to heart and began to weep. His whimpering brought Pete out of his contemplative state.

"What's the matter friend?" Pete asked while nuzzling Charlie's puckered face.

"Esther told me I was the lowliest of God's creatures." Charlie slipped off the railing and hurried home to hide in his aquarium. Pete squawked rousing the humans who glanced about to locate the source of the commotion.

Just then Maisie came running across the grounds waving at them. "I'm so sorry." She appeared panicky.

"What is it, Maisie?"

"It's Esther. She's got her tail tied in a knot over Charlie Walker, and I'm afraid she put a bug in his ear about being one of God's lowliest creatures. Charlie's feelings have been hurt terrible and his spirits have sunk so low, he may be having a crisis of faith." Maisie's words spread themselves all over Bo and Gloria's quiet time. Pete squawked even louder and was relentless in expressing concern for his friend.

"What should we do?" Gloria asked. She marveled at Maisie's ability to communicate with animals and often thought of asking her if Pete was happy living with her or would he rather be set free in a jungle somewhere. Pete overheard her concerns and thought they were silly and wondered how she could possibly have doubts. Afterall, wasn't it obvious he chose to be with her the day he landed on her windowsill?

"Comfort Charlie I suppose. An animal's spiritual trajectory is out of my area of expertise. To tell you the truth Esther's a handful. I spend a great deal of time cleaning up after her messes of hurt feelings and misunderstandings. But attacking Charlie's standing with divinity is beyond hurtful." Everyone looked at Pete.

"What about Pete? Could you tell him how to help his friend?" Gloria asked. Bo seemed confused over the whole event and decided it was probably best to let the others sort it out until he got home to take a look at his reptile.

"Yes, of course, Pete's Guru could help."

"He has a Guru?" Bo and Gloria responded in unison.

"Oh, yes, he does. Someone he calls Baba Das. He appears to be in constant touch with him from what I can tell."

Pete flew over to Bo's house and flapped at the window. He saw Charlie hiding in his aquarium sunk low in self-pity and stuck in a permanent silence. Not even Pete's telling him how much he loved his friend brought Charlie out of his malaise.

The humans hurried inside and stood looking down at Charlie's inert body. Finally, Bo spoke. "I think it's best if I spend the night sitting with him. Maybe he'll pull out of this by morning." He turned to Gloria. "I know you got a lot on yer mind, so don't want you worryin' none about Charlie Walker." Pete began squawking and jumping up and down on the edge of Charlie's glass hidey hole.

"He wants to spend the night with him, too," Maisie said, matter-of-factly. This put Gloria in a quandary, wondering what was best for her little bird. He squawked louder.

"Yes, of course. But would you mind Bo if I sat up with you?"

Bo put his arm around Gloria and kissed the top of her head. Never had he been so touched by a woman than he was that night. Even the generosity of the town pump held little appeal when compared to Gloria's kindness.

"Well, that's a good idea. I'll leave you to it. And check back tomorrow. Meanwhile, I'll have another talk with Esther and maybe get her to smooth things over. Maybe she could tell Charlie she didn't know what she was talking about." Everyone looked doubtful.

Bo fixed a pot of coffee and moved his best comfy chair near Charlie so Pete could use the back as his perch and settle in for the night.

Gloria found her own comfort wrapped in Bo's arms.

~

The following morning, Benny Swan knocked on Bo's door. Maisie had told him about the situation and even went so far as to criticize his cat for treating others without regard for their feelings. Benny had often taken her animal communication abilities for granted but now wished to know less about the shadowy side of Esther's disposition. He supposed her having to adjust to a society of other animals caused her to flex her social muscles or maybe she didn't have any and was too blunt for her own good. Either way, he needed to help fix the problem. First, he had talked to Esther with Maisie sitting nearby to translate.

"Esther, it's not nice to hurt the feelings of others. It's the first time I've ever been disappointed in you." Esther picked up on Benny's anguish. She always knew exactly what she was doing and had intended to take Charlie Walker down a peg or two. She resented his hanging out with the new resident bird. "Do you hear me, Esther?" She purred and rubbed up against her Cat-Dad, causing his heart to melt.

Maisie piped up, "She's playing you. Isn't suffering a tinge of guilt." She shook her head in disgust.

"What should I do?" Benny was at a loss. It hurt him to know Esther was the cause of anyone's unhappiness, even Charlie Walker had feelings.

"Make it right!"

"What if I throw a barbecue and invite everyone including all our animals, so we can have one of those circles where you hand a talking stick around?" Benny had seen several women in a circle passing around something that looked like a shepherd's staff on a British sit com. When he thought more about it, he remembered it ended badly with the women having a go at each other with the talking stick.

He appeared forlorn. Maisie began to feel sorry for him. "The barbecue is a good idea, but I'm not sure about the talking stick. Maybe if we made an effort to include Charlie, he would feel better about himself." Maisie glanced at Esther. She was putting her paws on Benny's face in a tender fashion as though butter wouldn't melt in her mouth.

Ten minutes later, Benny stood on the front porch of Bo's cabin knocking on the door. Bo invited him inside for a cup of coffee and some of Maisie's biscuits.

"Thank you. That's very nice of you." He nodded at Gloria. She appeared disheveled and need of a nap. The small bird had jumped in

Charlie's aquarium and fallen asleep on his back. Benny had never seen anything like it. He felt morose over the turn of events caused by his cat. "I'm so sorry. Maisie told me what happened." Benny's spirits wilted some by the tragic scene taking place in Bo's living room. "I would like to invite everyone to a backyard barbecue in the hopes we can all help our animals resolve their issues. After having said that, I realize Esther is the source of the problem and again I'm sorry for that. Will you please come and bring Charlie and Pete with you?" All eyes turned toward the aquarium.

Gloria burst out laughing followed by Bo who knew his reptile wasn't going anywhere without help. "That's very kind of you, but as you can see, we'd have to rig up transport for Charlie. Maybe leave him in his aquarium. Been like that all night."

Just then there was a scratch at the screen door. Esther stood on the other side looking contrite. She didn't like the idea her Cat-Dad was apologizing for her but had decided to appear remorseful so he didn't look like a fool. Bo let Esther inside. She jumped on the back of Pete's chair and peered into the tank. Pete opened his eyes and upon seeing Esther squawked like a rooster. Charlie, on the other hand, remained motionless. Esther was doing her best to apologize but he was too far down in his abyss to hear. She gave up, turned, and shoved the screen door open with one paw and left. Her tail was held high with the same haughty attitude she used to face life's absurdities. Once again, Benny apologized for his cat.

"It's a lovely idea," Gloria said in a quiet voice. "May I invite my friend Elmo Bond. He's good in these kinds of situations and maybe Bob from the nursery would be a comfort to Charlie."

Benny was delighted with Gloria's suggestions. "Thank you so much." He shook Bo's hand and nodded to Gloria in appreciation. Esther waited for him on the sidewalk. She caught enough of the conversation to know her nemesis would be the main attraction at a party tonight. Together she and Benny strolled through the gardens like years' past, bringing back memories of the good old days for Esther. Benny had never been happier living in the present moment. His thoughts drifted to the Eckhart Tolle's CDs Maisie often played in her sunroom. He realized he had spent years living in the past with his parents and the joy his mother had brought to their family. He never thought it would be possible to experience such happiness in his own life. He couldn't wait to tell Maisie.

Meanwhile, Gloria called Elmo and explained

the situation to him. Not that he could fully understand the seriousness of it. Down home where he came from snakes were considered low-life creatures next to white trash. The latter you couldn't kill but everybody dispensed with a snake if one crossed their path. Even Elmo recollected snapping a few necks just for grins. He tried to take her seriously by holding his breath to keep from laughing, especially when Gloria described Charlie Walker's desolation and possible crises of faith after being insulted by Esther. People who didn't know animals could communicate with each other were at a disadvantage. He did however agree to work with Bob on a solution for transporting Charlie to the party. This alone sent him into fits of laughter the second he hung up the phone. Eventually, he pulled himself together and hurried over to Bob's nursery.

"Just the man I need right now," Bob called over when seeing Elmo jump from his truck.

"About a snake named Charlie Walker?" Elmo lifted a wagon from the back of his truck.

"The one and only. You get used to it in these parts after a while. What you got there?"

"This here's a Radio Flyer I found in Sam's barn. Reckon it to be at least fifty years old."

They both admired the wagon and the nice lacquered panels. It looked as good as new. They set about gussying up the wagon for Charlie's comfort, pleased with the results an hour later. Elmo agreed to meet him at Bo's house where they would try their best to make Charlie comfortable for his ride to Benny's backyard on the other side of the street beyond the trees.

NINETEEN

Pete spent the afternoon perched on a tree limb in the higher realms. His meditations improved allowing him quick access to a place filled with gold dust and butterflies. Pete watched the mingling of plants and animals from his perch and noticed the unnecessary need to eat something. The animals smiled at each other and softened the atmosphere with an abundance of love that flowed like water from a spring on the side of a mountain. He saw tiny houses on God's land, looking somewhat similar to the ones in *Lost in Sunshine*. He could idle away his time staring at beauty and enjoying the lightness of being but shoved his observations aside when remembering he went there to talk to Baba Das about the plight of Charlie Walker's soul.

Suddenly, his beloved Guru appeared kicking the heady atmosphere up a notch with his beatific smile and endless fount of love for all. "Dadhu, you've come about your friend?"

"Yes, Baba Boss. Charlie Walker's in a bad way. The humans are talking about his having a crisis of faith. Esther the nasty cat we chatted about the last time I was yanked from the earth plane to have a jawbone session with the One who-knows-all called him God's lowliest creature."

"Yes, I remember. I also remember asking you to temper your attitude toward your feline neighbor. Everyone has their own boat to row."

Pete puzzled over his words for a second when visualizing Esther sitting in a rowboat trying to move the large oars through the water. He knew of course his Guru was speaking metaphorically, but Esther having to do anything requiring work made him gleeful, another sorry flaw in his mental makeup. He worried over softening his own rough edges and thought the task too mighty for a small bird who liked nothing better than to dance on a wood plank and hang out with his best friend. The only thing that could make his life perfect was having Charlie next to him in the higher realms.

The second that last thought flitted through his head, Charlie suddenly appeared wrapped around the tree limb grinning like one of God's angels. "Whoa, Charlie mah man, what you got to say for yaself. This here's the One who can cure what ails ya." Pete spoke like a bird bro with the beat of a rapper. Baba Das found Pete to be a funny being with a penchant for amusing others, making them laugh, and creating sunshine when it rained all day.

"Charlie and I go way back. He's on his last animal lifetime and will be returning as a human someday soon to uplift humanity in an important role. His past lives have been full of noble deeds, but now he has to burn his karma in the body of a reptile suffering the ignominy that is his fate. It's a temporary condition that will disappear when he transmigrates. Everyone has a time for their ending and a set place to end after all their karmas are done and there's nothing left but the eternity of our soul. So, take heart Charlie Walker, you will soon be free of your current predicament. Come to this understanding and life will flow smoothly for you."

"Did you hear, Charlie Walker?" Pete studied his friend's crumpled face. Charlie nodded satisfying both Guru and devotee he would be fine. Later, Pete would have to reassure Charlie when a saint said 'soon' that meant in God's time, which could be eons from now or could be tomorrow.

"Also, Dadhu Pete, I'm going to give Charlie meditation instructions. It would do you both good to meditate together at least a couple of hours a day, more if you can spare the time." Baba Das appeared amused in knowing the two had little to do that pressed upon their time.

Shortly after his flight into the invisible realms, Pete stood on the back of Bo's chair staring at his friend's inert body, who by all appearances hadn't moved since yesterday. He heard a commotion at the door and turned around to see Elmo and Bob carrying a red wagon into the house. They set it down next to the aquarium. Both men stared at Charlie, slightly intimidated over the thought of picking up his shiny body and placing it in the wagon. Bo admired the sod of grass they had placed on the bottom decorated with pretty pink flowers and a few ivy vines hanging over the edges. They had also strewn rose petals to add a touch of elegance and a sweet smell, even though neither one knew whether a snake would appreciate the heady scent, or would he consider it an affrontery to his pride. Actually, they were clueless on the care of cold-blooded animals and looked at Bo for guidance.

"Charlie will love this, fellas. I mean, yer know, when he comes out of his stupor." Everyone peered over the edge of the aquarium. Pete on such occasions would normally be filled with doubts if it weren't for their brief sojourn to visit his Guru, who set Charlie's mind right and took his soul to the promise land allowing him to peek at his future home. But for now, they had to deal with earth's reality of often being a cruel place to live, except for a few good people trying to turn it into something beautiful.

"No worries, fellas, I got this." Fortunately, Charlie had wrapped himself into a tight circle making it easy for Bo to slip his hands underneath and settle him in the wagon on a bed of grass surrounded by flowers. Pete flew through the open door over to Maisie's house where his Bird-Mom sat waiting for him on a fancy lounge chair.

"Here comes pretty boy. Pretty boy." Pete chirped until the men appeared around the corner pulling the Radio Flyer surprising Benny and his party guests, Hugo and his parents, Manuel, Arabella, and Esther. The latter silently groaned at the inevitable and hoped she wouldn't be asked to make a public apology of some sort. She considered Pete the cause of all the troubles what with his annoying sunny disposition and tendency to show off by talking out loud instead of keeping his thoughts to himself. "Time to pray. Time to pray."

"He wants us to pray for the Lord to help Charlie in his time of need." Maisie glanced at the startled faces. "I'm not making this stuff up. He really wants us to pray. Keeps talking about his Guru standing nearby waiting for us to show compassion. Waiting for us to step up and love all of God's creatures. He says it's the only way to live in Oneness. Otherwise, we're nothing but alienated beings just getting through the days of our own isolation."

Hugo kneeled next to the Radio Flyer with his hands folded, followed by his parents, Benny, and the others. Manuel, Arabella, and Pete bowed their heads. Hugo thanked everyone for coming together to help their beloved Charlie Walker loved by Mother Mary and now waiting for the upliftment of his spirits by his neighbors. Hugo went on in this vein despite Esther yawning halfway through the prayer circle. She felt nauseous over the evangelical display and couldn't wait until it ended so she could chomp down on a hot dog before it burned on the grill. She glanced about for a field mouse to snack on while waiting for her overdue dinner. "And finally let us give thanks to our Divine Mother for bringing us together." Everyone said amen. When they opened their eyes, Charlie hung over the edge of the paneled wagon sharing a toothless grin.

"Pretty boy. Pretty boy!" Pete flew to Charlie and sat with him watching their neighbors celebrate the resurrection of his best friend. Pete glanced into the distance and saw the radiant form of his beloved Guru disappear into the evening mist. Later, Maisie would take out her violin and serenade the guest of honor while Pete sang, "Let it be me."

TWENTY

Gloria mused over the previous night's events as being eccentric in a loving way and for a moment wondered what her parents would think of her new life. She smiled to herself when considering Bo and his affection for a quirky pet that belied the average woman's imagination. When her thoughts lit on Bo, the word fancy came to mind. Yes, she had to admit to herself she fancied a man who was rough around the edges, possessed a gravelly voice, but was kinder than any preacher she had ever heard pontificating in the Lord's pulpit.

The word marriage had never entered her mind even in an idle moment at the beauty salon when noticing the copies of *Modern Bride Magazine* arranged neatly on a table next to her. But now she found herself wondering what life would be like permanently attached to a man. Would it be suffocating? Or would all the togetherness alleviate fears of loneliness in an uncertain world? Her mind went so far as to consider the saner option of remaining in their respective houses, continuing to enjoy their evenings together on her small porch. At this point, her mind moved into the bedroom where she saw herself in the throes of passion with a musician who had a natural-born sense of rhythm. What could be better? Again, she smiled to herself, and then shoved her lusty notions aside, and got down to the business of envisioning the nude tableau, which was to take place tomorrow in the town square.

Friday afternoon teatime at *Duke's Rye Bar* was employed as a dress rehearsal for their demonstration. Gloria had drawn a map of the town square and placed a cluster of circles where they would be standing on all four street corners. She was overwhelmed by the ladies' response and instead of only having one tableau, she redesigned the whole affair, so no matter where the passersby went about their business, they would be bumping up against a bevy of nude bodies making a statement about the plight of the American woman.

Large theatrical signs resembling 1940's playbills would be standing nearby tastefully listing the offenses suffered by women over centuries of oppression. The worst now being the lack of the *Equal Rights Amendment* that has yet to be permanently placed in our *U. S. Constitution*. In fact, on one playbill it plainly states it's time to put the word 'woman' in our Constitution. This omission had always been Gloria's pet peeve and when telling the support group at the last meeting, they all appeared shocked as though ignorant of just how deeply rooted inequality was in this country called the *'land of the free and the home of the brave'*. Was there anyone braver than Harriet Tubman or Susan B. Anthony?

The ladies suffered some embarrassment over trying on their flimsy costumes in front of each other, but Izzie stood nearby with a basket of stick-on flowers to help drape a bolt of gauzy material and pasties for those who preferred to have their nipples covered but their breasts on full display. Dandelion, due to her size, had given the matter a great deal of thought. She decided to wear nothing but a pair of red high-heeled shoes and a smile. Her group went through their rehearsal first and everyone was shocked at seeing such a voluptuous display of flesh that looked like it belonged in a Botticelli painting.

"Yer husband must be a latent homosexual man if he doesn't see yer naked beauty my dear Dandelion." Laverne shouted from across the room at the same time Duke was passing by the door to the back room on the way to his office. He wondered what they were getting up to and when one of the waitresses mentioned the nude tableau, Duke became put out he was not invited to demonstrate with them. He loved women and would be happy to take off his clothes for 'the cause'. Fortunately, he hurried on before hearing Izzie remonstrate over one of her husband's peccadillos.

"Well, maybe that accounts for why my husband is always flipping my scrawny body over so he can use the back door."

Everyone laughed except Izzie who felt demoralized at the thought of being married to a man with a penchant for boys. What would happen when she let her hair turn grey? At least now she had an understanding as to why the man wouldn't leave home after the penis incident. Very few women had the body of a barn plank, so he had to make do with what was on hand. The thought annoyed her, agitated her nerves, which began to turn into violent things ending with her running over him with their John Deere lawnmower.

She glanced down at her body and decided it might look best to tape on a tiny bouquet of daisies to her lady parts and run some bamboo grasses up the middle of her backside and use matching daisy pasties for her nipples no bigger than a penny. The other ladies admired her artistry inspiring her to stick a flower in her over-permed auburn hair. Once finished, the most startling aspect of Izzie's appearance were her large brown eyes set off by flawless white skin and a button nose. She was a beautiful woman and now when taking a peek in the full-length mirror, she decided to treat herself to modest breast implants and a divorce.

Gloria grouped the ladies according to their size but decided to use Dandelion as the main attraction surrounded by the others in a way that gave the most dramatic effect. Everyone stood in awe of the outcome and thanked Gloria for her artistic gifts. Actually, Gloria had been discouraged from picking up a paint brush so was surprised to hear herself described as artistic. She loved beauty and possessed the aesthetic sense of a wood nymph, which now came in handy to arrange all the floral designs into a pleasing bouquet of beautiful women.

Laverne piped up at the same time Duke left his office, once again passing the door to the backroom. "I got myself a pretty stallion for my Lady Godiva debut and a blonde wig that covers my breasts and drapes my ass but leaves me in a pickle over what to do about my lady parts."

"What color is your stallion?"

"Black as midnight. One of Ned Smith's champions. I ride him once in a while when Ned's on his fishing trips."

"Here, try this red rose with a stem." Izzie handed Laverne a rose that would fit nicely between her legs.

"Does Earl know?" Dandelion asked. At this point, Duke's ear was pressed to the keyhole.

"Man's not gotta clue. Lives in his own world. He's a frustrated warrior with no war to fight and an inclination to hold himself higher than the stallion I will be riding come tomorrow. So don't all y'al worry none."

Duke hurried behind the bar and fixed himself a drink. "What time is all this happening?" He asked the waitress.

"Around eleven o'clock. You thinkin' 'bout goin'?"

"Wouldn't miss it," Duke grinned and then took a gulp of his own rye whiskey.

"Me neither."

The ladies vacated the tearoom at their usual time as though nothing spectacular was about to happen. Duke nodded as they passed the bar, nearly drooling in anticipation.

TWENTY-ONE

That afternoon, Elmo had sat at his computer trying to decide whether to release a few scenes on social media from his nearly finished video called *The Travails of an Intelligent Woman*. Finally, he spliced together Gloria reciting her poetry on the street corner only to be arrested seconds later by a police chief carrying an assault rifle. The same evening, he went back to his computer and noticed his Twitter feed had received over 200,000 views and nearly ten thousand comments, mostly wanting to know what happened to the pretty poetess, her name, the town, and the name of the crazy officer handcuffing a tiny woman. The numerous responses frightened Elmo. He had no idea they would be so indignant. Suddenly, he remembered having felt the same way at the time of Gloria's arrest.

The local reporters had not replied to his emails entreating them to cover tomorrow's events. When scrolling through his Twitter feed, he noticed a video of a large face from CNN with a microphone stuck against his lips. He stood in the local town square inviting people to come to Police Chief Earl Hubbard's jurisdiction and show their solidarity for Professor Gloria Dobbins, a well-known contemporary philosopher, who has suffered at the hands of the over-zealous officer. He called her a female Walt Whitman, which in Elmo's mind was an insult for a woman demonstrating against male oppression to have her gender swept out from under her by being compared to a man. For a moment, he felt embarrassed by his own gender.

While Elmo ruminated over the business of being male, Sam burst into his room without knocking. "You won't believe this. I got a call from Burt down at the local college NPR and he says the place is buzzing with tomorrow's events. When I asked where he got his information, he said he has a cousin of a cousin demonstrating with a buncha nekid ladies. Says a crew will be on sight with cameras and reporters. I shit you not, Elmo. Better not tell yer friend Gloria."

"Oh, right. She might git the jitters. Jus' saw an idiot on CNN comparin' her to Walt Whitman."

"Yeah, like we don't have female poets?" This put Sam in a fit of temper. "I have half a mind to gather up my lady lesbians who would be all too happy to take off their clothes and throw in with Gloria." Sam pulled a red cell phone from her back pocket and encouraged all of her group chats to call in reinforcements. Elmo looked on in amazement. A wave of anxiety set his nerves on edge. He felt responsible for all the publicity and wasn't sure Gloria had a clue what she was signing onto. Elmo knew her original intention was to write a case study on the American asshole, but it had gone awry somewhere, probably with his help, and turned into a political affair that might put her in the middle of a gender war.

~

Friday night the ladies assembled at their respective corners and assumed their positions for the nude tableau, except they remained fully dressed for the run-through. They had decided to place Gloria standing next to the monument in the middle of the town square reading her poetry through Laverne's megaphone she had again borrowed from Earl's police car. Unfortunately, a World War II general with a gun tucked in his belt had been cast in bronze and towered over Gloria as she silently read through her poetry. A discussion ensued over what to do about having a military man distracting from Gloria's feminine presence.

"Well, we don't have time to take a sledgehammer to the thing so why don't we throw a blanket over it?" Laverne shouted. At this point, she glanced about and noticed not one female statue had been erected in her husband's jurisdiction. "Do you realize women have not been cast in bronze and put on display?"

"Now that you mention it, seems an oversight. But I remember the librarian years back bringing the matter up to the town council and she got laughed at for her trouble. Never mentioned it again," Dandelion responded, looking on edge and nearly ready to explode in a fit of anger. "Instead of a blanket, I've got a better idea but can't do it until right before the festivities."

"Okay, that's decided. Now, does everyone know their places with costumes ready?" Laverne shouted. She rarely talked in muffled sentences and never learned how to whisper. The other ladies had gotten used to her emphatic sentences and come to enjoy the enthusiasm behind everything Laverne said, which is why she was a much-loved member of their female society despite being married to the town bully. Actually, at that very moment, Laverne made up her mind to throw Earl out of the house and enjoy some peace and quiet for a change. She wasn't convinced divorce was the answer seeing as how Earl had his moments in the bedroom when he left his gun on the dresser.

Everybody seemed satisfied with the evening's run-through and decided to let

Dandelion take care of the bronze general. They agreed to meet in the church basement and wear raincoats until assuming their positions at exactly eleven the following morning. The only one missing was Maisie who out of respect for the gentle man in her life thought it best to keep a low profile. She would be on hand with small water bottles in case the sun spiked a fever causing the ladies to sweat. She also added sunscreen to her list to prevent sunburn. Gloria appreciated their organizational abilities and wondered why they weren't running the country. She dwelled some on this last thought before thanking everyone for their efforts. They agreed to return to the church basement when tomorrow's demonstration ran its course.

Gloria went to bed early but she wasn't ready to sleep. Her mind busied itself visualizing all the women in their respective places but wasn't sure about herself standing next to a towering male presence that could come alive any second and devour her with its hatred of all things feminine. She felt comfortable in her own costume, a diaphanous ivory shift circa 1930s, naked underneath, only decorated with a string of pearls around her neck on loan from Izzie. She had never been embarrassed by her own body, mostly because she considered it a vehicle for housing an enormous brain that sucked up the majority of her energy. She rarely ate due to living in a constant state of distraction. When her doctor questioned her about her dietary habits, she told him she didn't have any and rarely gave it much thought. It embarrassed her to confess she ate mostly nuts and berries same as Pete and was happy with this arrangement of using her bird's squawking for food as a meal-time reminder. Eventually, her mind grew tired of reliving the day and worrying about tomorrow so with nothing left to do, it turned silent and went to sleep.

TWENTY-TWO

The ladies decided to arrive early and linger on the sidewalk, pretend to window shop, and take turns checking on Earl's whereabouts. They observed him leaving the *Diner* and going into his office where they could see him reading the morning newspaper. He didn't notice a small throng of people creeping into town swelling into an enormous crowd by eleven. Gloria stood next to the general who was now dressed in Dandelion's black lacy night-gown and wearing a straw bonnet over his helmet. Gloria glanced around her to make sure everyone was in place and holding their positions for the nude tableau.

The passersby appeared awestruck but smiling with pleasure over the sight of so much force dressed in a swag of feminine beauty demanding to be taken seriously, demanding equal pay. She began her monologue:

Women will be taking back their power, setting their own standards for beauty, and no longer be aging by the number of years men have placed us on a shelf demanding we look pretty. Your machismo days are over. You're gonna find yourselves demoted, de-ranked and out flanked by women who are now faster at the starting gate, refusing to wait for a man to shake his head in approval. WE ARE THE POWER! WE ARE THE MAJORITY! WE GOT THE VOTE! AND WE'RE GONNA VOTE YOU OUT!

The women in the crowd began chanting: *We Are the Power! We are the Majority! We're Gonna Vote You Out!*

During all the shouting, a black stallion appeared out of nowhere, stood next to Gloria, reared up on its hind legs and snorted at the crowd. Laverne straddled the horse bare-back and naked. She had thrown out the wig and the long stem rose so everybody could behold her beauty and have a go at her audacity. Her wavy blonde hair barely covered her nipples and the only thing she wore was a lavalier microphone allowing her to speak to the people and holler at her husband if the need arose. "I don't care if all you men out there see my wilted flower. I'm done trying to look like the skinny Vogue model, no ass to grab, all hair extensions, and a spray-painted body that drips in the sunlight. I'm done with caring what y'al think of my sassy tongue 'cause so far as I'm concerned men are the blight on this here landscape when they don't know how to treat a woman with kindness, respect a woman, and remember we are the creators of every human walking this earth. So, you can kiss my dimpled ass and that goes for you too, Earl Hubbard!"

The police chief stepped out of his office the second he heard his name being called over the crowd. His eyes had trouble adjusting to the sight of his wife riding a horse naked through the streets, hair flying behind her at exactly the same time a pretty truck with the name *Sam's Place* written on the side drove around the square in circles carrying the lady lesbians standing in the back naked as jay birds joining the others in chanting "you better listen to your wife."

Gloria took in the magnitude of their demonstration and didn't know whether to be proud or nervous over the consequences. She saw several news crews lined up along the periphery and her former student Elmo videotaping the riotous scene. She looked down at her nipples and wondered for a second how they would look on camera and would they be featured in the evening news as daring to be seen. Suddenly, she broke into fits of laughter over the knowledge if her nearly naked body became the butt of controversary, it would be the first time anybody ever made a fuss over her without her clothes. And then she saw Bo in the distance waving and smiling at her. She waved back and at that very moment knew he was the man she wanted to stand by her side for the rest of her life.

Charlie Walker hung around his neck and Pete hunkered on his head, feet holding tight to his curly black hair. They were a sight for sore eyes and the love of her earth-bound life. Suddenly, Laverne rode up and told her to jump on the back of her horse. Gloria had never ridden a horse much less without a saddle and some confusion of having to hike up her dress without panties underneath.

"Grab my hand Gloria, and I'll swing ya 'round. Earl's sending his men to get us." Gloria tore a split up the side of her dress and grabbed Laverne's hand. She held on for dear life as they galloped in the direction of Sam's truck where Laverne shouted in the window for Sam to snatch the ladies off the street corners and bring them to the church basement. The lesbian ladies were dispatched to help them in the truck and even the crowd helped by moving against Earl's men keeping them from the demonstrators. Earl in a moment of pique fired his rifle in the air a few times but to his surprise Izzie discharged a small caliber pistol several times and then jumped in the truck along with Dandelion.

Bo and Duke moved to the periphery and watched the nude tableau come alive and then quickly disappear into the back of Sam's truck. Several masculine-looking women rode their motorcycles alongside the remaining tableaus, picked up the demonstrators and hustled them to the church basement.

"Where do you think they went?" Duke said to Bo.

"Haven't a clue but our illustrious police chief is bustin' his gasket trying to chase 'em on foot. Fer sure ain't goin' to have use of the police vehicles any time soon."

"Reckon we should do somethin'?" Bo asked.

"I feel what yer sayin' but don't know how to help."

Just then Benny appeared looking worried and sweating like he had never spent a day in the southern heat. "I can't find Maisie. She told me to meet her right here afterwards. I'm worried. Did you see all those reporters? These people don't look like locals. Not that I'm an expert." He mopped the sweat from his brow and stared at both men for answers.

"Church basement! Church basement!" Pete chirped, barely moving from the hot day. The naked shenanigans of humans ruffled his feathers and set him to discussing the situation with Charlie Walker. They agreed humans, for some confusing reason, put clothes on after they were born naked. Then finally Charlie settled on the notion humans were weaker than woodland creatures so needed to protect their outer covering with anything that made a fashion statement including the hide off a zebra. They both agreed humans were flawed and should be pitied instead of ridiculed. Pete could hear Baba Das whispering 'be kind' in his ear, so he decided to close his beak on the subject and let the three male humans work out what to do next.

"Thanks, Pete," Bo said.

"That's where their support group meets," Duke said. The other two looked at him wondering how he knew there even was a support group. "Well, working in a bar I hear things. Husbands talk. The second their wives are out of the house, they come ramrodding into my bar and order a double scotch neat as you please. Enough to put this poor man off marriage." Again, Bo and Benny looked at him as though the honest truth had no longer become relevant to Duke. The sad fact was every woman in town knew Duke to be an incorrigible flirt and dismissed him for anything more serious than a fling around the bedroom.

Just then a chubby man from CNN stuck a microphone in Duke's face and asked him if he agreed with the message the demonstrators were sending today.

"Holy shit, you ain't from 'round here. Of

course, anythin' our women say ought to be taken as gospel. 'Cause I'll tell ya one thing, we can't live without 'em and best be making them happy by givin' equal pay if'n that's what they want. Now, jus so ya know I practice what I preach. I am the proprietor of *Duke's Rye Bar*, and I pay my entire staff the exact same amount, male or female. We at *Duke's Rye Bar* are firm believers in 'equal pay for equal work'. So, mister you better be listening to what our women has to say all across America, otherwise you are in fer a helluva ride."

The newsman thanked Duke and said he would be sure to drop by his bar on the way out of town. He turned to interview Bo but noticed the sleepy snake draped around his shoulders, so he moved on down the line of men most of whom didn't know whether it was a good idea to go home tonight.

TWENTY-THREE

The ladies had locked themselves inside the church, a necessary action against the cloying reporters who followed them, insisting on an interview. They peeked in the windows, banged at the doors, and rang the church phone, but Dandelion told the caller she would need a three-course meal at the town's only four-star restaurant *Maggie's Diner* before giving him a tidbit of information. "Besides, didn't you see enough with yer own eyes to git the drift of what we were sayin'?" She sounded exasperated, but the reporter agreed to meet her at the Diner around two o'clock.

Unfortunately, in their hurry to escape, the ladies left their raincoats and other coverings on the street corners. Izzie came up with the bright idea of raiding the drama costumes hanging in the closet off the vestibule. Everyone found something from various periods and made do with ill-fitting ensembles causing them to appear like Hollywood extras on location. Gloria and Izzie could pass as hippies from the sixties in their nymphet white dresses with tie strings crisscrossing in front. Dandelion had shoved herself inside a long velvet dress with an outer bodice that when cinched tight, caused her large bosoms to bolt upwards revealing a lovely décolletage not six inches from her chin but enough to make a real man drool from want. Some of the ladies chose choir robes and others rummaged through the preacher's collection looking for something stylish.

Once covered, they sat on folding chairs and discussed their impressions and experiences of the day's events.

"That chubby man from CNN stuck a microphone in my face and kept asking me if I wanted a glass a water. He knew I couldn't talk, which leads me to believe the man has a sadistic sense of humor and ought to be stripped of his press credentials. It was unprofessional of him despite being kinda cute." Dandelion had briefly fantasized about dragging him into a side street where she could have a go at his credentials. She smiled silently while the other ladies sympathized with her discomfiture.

"Nobody gave me much notice, not like Dandelion here, but I did observe it was an orderly crowd with very few snickers coming from the men. Only one and his wife jammed her elbow against his windpipe, causing him to keel over backwards but was caught by a buncha other men before he hit the pavement," Izzie said.

"That's true. A pretty orderly crowd if you ast me."

"Sure was, but I think they was afeared of opening their mouths. Not being stupid, they probably figgered if we were willing to make our point buck-nekid, then we would be just as likely to bring them to their knees if need be."

"Sure as shit, Izzie."

"You better believe it."

"Gloria, what were your impressions?" Dandelion asked, wheezing slightly. She was beginning to heat up under her heavy costume.

"From where I was standing, the crowd itself was respectful, but Earl's men were laughing. They must chew tobacco, because I did notice all their teeth were brown." Bo had recently given up chewing tobacco and visited the dentist to have his teeth whitened. Now, every time he smiled, Gloria went weak in the knees. "I think we'll be judged in the evening news. Let's hope they're kind."

"But don't ya think the film footage will speak for itself?" Izzie asked.

"Yes, of course, that's a good point. Except, we don't know what the people said who were interviewed. Maybe there were some snickers,"

Gloria responded.

"And don't forget, it'll probably be broadcast on national news, too. Not just local." Everyone appeared horror-stricken at the thought.

Laverne responded, "I think it's in our best interest to git out o' here? What with all the hollerin' goin' on outside. They sound like they're tryin' to break a door down."

"Well, should we make a run for our cars? Don't seem likely we'll git there in one piece," Izzie added.

"Ya got that right." Just then the sound of Harley-Davidson motorcycles could be heard outside.

"The lady lesbians have come to rescue us," Izzie yelled. "Sam musta sent 'em."

"And I can see Benny Swan, Bo, and Duke come to quell the crowd," Dandelion said.

"Oh, I was supposed to meet Benny under the cherry tree but in all the commotion, I forgot and jumped in Sam's truck." Maisie felt touched by Benny's efforts to rescue her. She stood on a folding chair and peered out the tiny basement window. "They are battling back the press, so we can make a run for it. Y'al ready?"

The ladies ran out the side door and drove off in their cars and on the backs of several Harleys. Except for Laverne, who rode her horse to Ned's barn and decided to stay there until things blew over at home. Laverne often prayed Earl would be picked up by a windstorm and carried out to sea. Most people didn't know he couldn't swim and had never served in the military. She had promised to keep his lies secret on their wedding day twenty years earlier with nothing much to account for her time since agreeing to be Mrs. Earl Hubbard. When she had met him in Vegas, he was a dashing young man who could easily sweep an eighteen-year-old chorus girl off her feet. He talked big. She didn't realize what a small man he really was until seeing him in the light of other people's eyes. He was the town joke even back then. No one quite understood how he became police chief, except he kept talking about having the mayor's pecker in his pocket, a term Laverne found offensive even at age eighteen. She was raised in a genteel Alabama family and had quickly become a disappointment to her family.

Yes, she thought. It was time to remove Earl from the house her parents had bought to make their little girl happy. Right then and there while sitting on a bale of hay, she decided to contact Laura Hanigan and get that divorce she had been putting off for years.

Shortly after the women disappeared, Earl arrived at the church madder than a trapped badger looking to chew off a man's leg. Earl quickly discovered the demonstrators had eluded the police. It would be necessary to put out an APB if he wanted to apprehend them before they went underground. At this point, the tea ladies were all enjoying a nice cool bath to wash off the day's events along with the suntan oil Maisie had liberally sprayed on their delicate skin.

The press stuck several microphones in Earl's face and began to ask questions. "Looks like they got away, officer."

"It's Poleece Chief Earl Hubbard. They didn't git away. I knowed 'xactly where ever'one of those renegades lives." He adjusted his sunglasses pleased at sounding intelligent in front of all the cameras.

"Do you support their political positions?"

"No, siree, I don't agree a'tal. I'll be arrestin' the demonstrators for indecent exposure and disturbing the peace. Not to mention, I heard one of them thar ladies firing a pistol, scaring everybody to scatterin' fer the hills."

"We didn't see anyone scattering. Did you Nancy, Seymour, Bob?"

"No, not a one. The town square is full of people still milling around waiting to see what you're going to do Chief Hubbard." Most of the leftover people supported the ladies and were prepared to take Earl to task if he dared to haul one of their women to the police station. Earl had no idea husbands felt so strongly about their wives' political views. In fact, he thought they would be pleased he was going to teach them a lesson. Earl failed to see the gravity in a woman wanting men to recognize the immorality of treating them like second-class citizens, body shaming, and a list of other grievances they would be only too happy to share with the ignorant officer.

"Chief Hubbard, let me understand the thinking behind the charges. You're planning to arrest them for 'indecent exposure' when being judged for their appearance is part of what they are protesting in the first place?"

"Uhm, now that you put it that way, maybe I best be rethinkin' things. May haveta settle on disturbin' the peace and demonstratin' without a permit." Earl felt good about getting his mind right.

"It was a nude tableau. A tableau vivant, if you will. A group of ladies silently expressing the story of their oppression. They weren't disturbing anyone. In fact, from our point of view, it was a brilliant piece of political artistry," said the reporter from CNN. He had already fallen in love with Dandelion and couldn't wait to meet such a vivacious woman. She was everything his heart desired.

"I agree. You were the only one disturbing the peace when firing an assault rifle and scaring everyone. In fact, Chief Hubbard, you should be arrested. Not the women who in my belief are justified in getting their ratified amendment added to the U.S. Constitution," added another reporter

Everyone agreed causing Chief Hubbard to turn tail and run. Bo, Benny and Duke had remained on the sidelines waiting to see if Earl would add fuel to the flame. After listening to him babbling about his nonsensical point of view, they looked at each other in disbelief, but happy Earl had been gutted by the press and would likely be aired on the evening news.

TWENTY-FOUR

Gloria and Bo curled up on his couch together eating pizza while watching the evening news. Sure enough, a camera panned the large crowd and zoomed in on each of the tableaus behind a reporter talking about the demonstrators who dared to make their point in the nude. She saw herself holding up a megaphone, begging to be heard, her nipples pressing against the diaphanous material of a shift, hair down, looking feminine but at the same time as earnest as Joan of Arc when delivering her message to the public at large: women want to have a say in the decisions that affect the world, the environment, and the animals walking next to them. And they want equal pay for their expertise.

The two anchormen talked about the popular term 'body shaming' and discussed whether or not the women had a leg to stand on when they were willing to take off their clothes in full view of the country. The guest speaker, an expert in women's studies, laughed out loud over their ignorance. Both men took exception and made the mistake of asking for her opinion. Soon the discussion deteriorated into a battle of wills until finally the women's studies expert threw in the towel after telling the empty-headed anchormen they represented every woman's nightmare and the reason why women had been purposely left behind.

"Gentlemen, I want to make one last point here before going off the air. A pause for thought, if you will. It stands to reason since history shows us early women supplied eighty-percent of the food, stripped the hide off the game men brought back from their hunt to be repurposed for clothes, cleaned the meat from the bones to be eaten, and created tools from the leftover bones to work her magic, and I repeat doesn't it stand to reason women harnessed fire? Not men. Men spent three weeks out of every month resting for their next big hunt that only supplied twenty percent of the food. So now, gentlemen, tell me you really believe women are inferior to men or is the root cause of your reluctance to elect a female president, fear. Fear women will take over the world, rid it of war, cure pestilence, and level the income stream so everyone goes to bed at night on a full stomach, and the assurance of health care? Is that your fear, your reluctance, the reality of sharing your paycheck with others who have nothing, who work for pennies so corporations can run our country making a few greedy men wealthy enough to pay political idiots to vote for the agenda of big business? No need to answer, I'm done here. Goodnight gentlemen." The women's studies expert disappeared from the screen leaving the two anchormen dumbstruck without enough words to complete a sentence. The network broke for a commercial.

Bo flipped to another channel to hear Gloria being lauded as a folk heroine, bringing more women to the streets, not just in this country, but in major cities all over the world women were taking off their clothes in solidarity for the tiny professor who dared to be great, dared to live her dreams, and be a voice for other women. They loved her. Gloria wept from emotion. Bo wrapped her in his arms and kissed her gently, moving them to the bedroom followed by Pete and Charlie, who soon found themselves on the other side of the door. Gloria's phone began to ring but no one heard offers being sent to voice mail for her to come to their universities and speak, come to their public gatherings to raise awareness, and to be the calm voice for women in these turbulent times.

~

Three days later, Elmo's finished video of Gloria went viral on social media. He didn't know quite what to do about it or even how to answer people's questions. The comment boxes were filled with questions only Gloria could answer: Were you always so brave? Where can I find your books? Will you continue teaching at the university? I want to take your courses. And so, it went on until Elmo's brain shifted through all its gears and stalled out. He just knew, he wasn't brave enough to take off his clothes in public. He decided to pack up his computer and drive over to Gloria's house.

He all but leapt onto her front porch and hollered for help. She sat looking dazed on her lounge chair drinking an iced tea and talking to Pete about how life changes on you before you can get your mind steady enough to ease over the ramifications. Pete agreed while practicing some salsa moves. He had decided to expand his dance routines.

"Elmo, I'm so happy to see a familiar face. Bo is at the end of the drive trying to stop the hordes of people looking for me. It appears my life has become a circus since being on television."

"Well, I won't add to it but just wanted to say the video I posted of all the highlights has gone viral. Sorry, Professor. I only wanted to help you along a little. I mean we started out trying to understand the assholes inhabiting the country but ended up making a 'show and tell' of the damage they have done to women everywhere. Noble of you, if'n you ast me. But also, a might disturbin'."

"Yes, very disturbing."

"We did learn the meaning of Oneness from Pete. Remember at Charlie Walker's resurrection?"

"Yes, but I think the little guy was wanting to help me, also. Maybe the assholes will never manage to love all beings, but I could heed Pete's words and give it a try."

"That would mean you'd have to love the assholes, and I would have to give loving my dad a go. Uphill battle if'n you ast me." They both laughed, but their conversation was interrupted by a Mini Cooper S Countryman pulling up next to Pete's railing.

"Hello! Hello, pretty girl!" Pete repeated several times.

A familiar face popped up and smiled at both Elmo and Gloria. They nearly knocked each other over running to Penelope. "I quit my job and came to help you, Gloria. I figured you needed help managing your calendar and your life knowing you like I do."

"You're a savior. Yes, I feel paralyzed. My phone won't stop ringing. And my new boyfriend is out stopping traffic from coming in here." Gloria pulled Penelope to the front porch and poured her an iced tea. Elmo went inside to make her a cucumber and tomato sandwich with sliced fruit on the side.

"Yes, the handsome man named Bo is your new boyfriend?"

"I just like saying it. Haven't used that word since high school and then only briefly. Everything's changed Penelope except Elmo. He's been a Godsend. Pining for you, though. Hard to watch."

"I've been pining for him, too. I guess it took a Gloria miracle to give me the courage to leave the security of the library." The two women smiled at each other and held hands in the intimate fashion women do when acknowledging life would be too hard to cope without each other.

"Well, there's plenty of work here and judging by the fees people are offering me for speaking engagements, there will be no shortage of money to pay an assistant if you truly want the job."

"Oh, I do. Nothing would please me more."

"Nothin'?" Elmo asked and then laughed.

"Well, not quite. Oh, I met your landlady, Sam. She's gorgeous. Putting me up in a nice room on the first floor near her office where she said I'd be safe from the male boarders.

"I'm the only male boarder. She's teasing you. Listens patiently every night to my ramblings about the prettiest girl I ever seen named Penelope." They stared at each other with yearning.

"Pretty girl! Pretty boy!" Everyone laughed.

"Elmo, pack Penelope's lunch in the picnic basket on top of the fridge and run along while I write a job description and jot down some phone numbers for Penelope. Take your time. We can meet and go over what needs to be done in a couple of days. Meanwhile, I'll tell all the callers my assistant will be getting back to them." The women were gleeful over the prospect of working together.

A few minutes later, Gloria waved good-bye to the pretty young couple and breathed a sigh of relief over a beautiful ending to her troubles. She and Bo had talked all morning before coming to the decision it would be best if they occupied separate houses right now or at least until there was a semblance of orderliness to their lives together. It was also decided Pete would be staying with Bo and Charlie Walker when his Bird-Mom traveled to her speaking engagements and visited bookstores to sign autographs for all her books that had begun to fly off the shelves.

Gloria had never felt loved by another

human before Bo came along. She could hear her heart cry from the joy of it. Pete sang in the background of her thoughts. "Let it be me."

TWENTY-FIVE

Lieutenant Governor Anders held her cell phone up to Governor Hickam's face in dismay. He ogled the histrionic display of Police Chief Earl Hubbard shooting at a customer in *Maggie's Diner*. His eyeballs popped even more when he got to the part where the officer was hog tying a tiny woman and tossing her in his police car. The demonstration was too much for his sensibilities. The governor loved his wife and couldn't tolerate the mistreatment of women. He called the mayor in Earl Hubbard's jurisdiction and demanded the immediate relief of Earl's duties. He also necessitated the demented police chief be brought up on charges of assault with a deadly weapon, physical assault, false arrest, disorderly conduct, and behavior unbecoming an officer of the law. The mayor immediately agreed to tidy up the mess. He called the second in command and went to Earl's office with him to relieve the police chief of his duties.

Earl was arraigned the next day and let out on bail to wait for a trial date. No self-respecting local lawyer wanted anything to do with the case. Earl pleaded poverty and asked for a court-appointed lawyer. Meanwhile, being homeless since Laverne took away his keys to the house and had him served with divorce papers, he had been staying in a local motel. He begged Maisie to let him rent old man Hillard's tiny cabin set on the edge of *Lost in Sunshine*. Eventually, she relented with the understanding he left his neighbors alone and didn't bring any of his guns on the property. She pointed to the sign saying No Gun Zone. He agreed, which was easy since he had been stripped of his gun permits and couldn't afford to be charged with another offense. He would consider himself lucky if he only served two years and managed to get a job as a security guard. Although, he had his doubts anyone would hire him except his Cousin Elmer who owned a gas station on the other side of the holler. He considered the notion of applying for a job before news of his arrest traveled to Cousin Elmer's neck of the woods. There was also the matter of his side business in Canada, but he thought it might be a risk to cross the border being as how he was told not to leave his own jurisdiction. Then it occurred to him Cousin Elmer might like the idea of becoming a partner, expanding the business, and making the trips to Canada until he got his legal affairs in order.

Meanwhile, the mayor rummaged around inside his head for Earl's replacement. After some thought, his mind landed on Dandelion. Unlike Earl, she was career military and had spent twenty years as an artillery specialist. Fortunately, Dandelion, once dispensing with her husband, had time on her hands and was happy to accept the mayor's offer to be police chief.

Dandelion and the CNN reporter have been engaging in a torrid email affair, finally consummating their romance the day after she set the last of her husband's belongings, all neat and tidy in sturdy boxes, along the side of the road. Neither were disappointed and decided living together part-time suited them just fine. They cooed over each other, calling their love an eternal honeymoon. Izzie admired her friend Dandelion and so was naturally thrilled to be her assistant at the police station. The thought of being surrounded by all that masculinity set her nerves to twittering and her desire to burn like a chimney fire.

Earl kept a low-profile as promised and barely left his front porch lounge chair where a carton of beer set next to him chilling in a bucket of ice. His only visitors came from the animal kingdom, which eventually served to calm his anxiety over being dirt poor and disrespected. Charlie Walker had experienced ignominy before being baptized by Pete's heavenly Guru so considered the possibility the ignoble police officer could be redeemed. Pete agreed with Charlie and Manuel wagged his tail along with Arabella who didn't really have any thoughts on the subject of Earl Hubbard's downfall or the possibility of his redemption. Pete reminded all of them the power of Oneness began in a heart large enough to love all. Esther settled on the philosophical notion there is bound to be an asshole in every paradise.

Pete began to sing to the fallen police officer:

I'm goin' off the grid,
Take a breath,
Talk to God,
I'm goin' off the grid.

Everyone in the village stopped to listen to the tiny bird pour out his heart to a man so far down on his luck, it would take a crane to lift him. Fortunately, Pete and his Baba Das possessed the power of a thousand cranes, leaving open the possibility of Earl's spirit being lifted to linger in the light where a tiny bird waited to help him.

BIO

Bonnie Jae Dane, a native of Southern Appalachia, is the recipient of two National Endowment for the Humanities Awards. She is the author of many novels; her memoir entitled *The Book of Husbands*; a collection of short stories entitled *Women on Love;* script writer for film *SPEAKEASY women talkin' mostly 'bout men,* which won Most Creative Film, American Motion Picture Society; and the winner of many film awards, including finalist for the prestigious American Cable Excellence award. Ms. Dane is at present writing her next novel written in her trademark blend of wit and pathos style using a writing voice described by Yo-Yo Ma as being, 'Mellifluous'.

Praise for *Solitary Pussytoes*:

"Ironic wit is the tightrope that enables Bonnie Jae Dane to balance between anger and sentimentality as her language intoxicated young narrator—who is a real charmer—tells us about her struggle to survive the daily trauma of the inner city."

-Professor Allen Guttman, Amherst College

"*Solitary Pussytoes* is *True Grit* set in the inner city. Darlis, Bonnie Jae Dane's heroine, overdoses on the eloquence of the English language and seeks refuge from the violence and squalor of contemporary urban life."

-Roberta T. Manning, Historian, Boston College, Harvard Fellow